Southfalia

Copyright © 2007 Antonio Casella
All rights reserved.
ISBN: 1-4196-5820-4
ISBN-13: 978-1419658204

Visit www.booksurge.com to order additional copies.

Southfalia

Antonio Casella

2007

Southfalia

PROLOGUE

Atlantis, that fabled continent of immense wealth, was swallowed up by the ocean during one of its more voracious moods. It is not widely known that other civilizations have made their exit in a similar manner. Take Southfalia for instance. As late as the 15th century—so the story goes—Southfalia was the envy of the Southern Sea: an island paradise of sun, wealth and beauty, of gold-tanned men, smooth-limbed girls, white-fleeced sheep and high-twining vines, all thriving in harmony with one another in a unique way of life.

Food: they had so much of it. Every kitchen emitted delicious aromas of roasting pork or veal, lamb, turkey; the most tender, the juiciest, the best that mother nature could provide, and money could buy. The market stalls were piled high with peaches, pears, oranges, chestnuts, figs, grapes, berries...sweet gifts of a benevolent and bountiful nature. The island's vines vied with the best from Burgundy, and its golden ale was judged the best in the world by a large majority of the men, whose proof to this kind of connoisseurship hovered before them in the shape of a well-rounded belly.

The island was rich in minerals, including gold and precious stones, sent overseas to be worked by artisans into beautiful objects, for the islanders themselves were not very good with their hands. And really, who needs skills with all that wealth? Anything which required skill was simply imported, for all the world is only too happy to trade with one who spends big and can afford it.

Many a vessel sailed from Southfalia laden with minerals to bring back in return Venetian glass, Cretan pottery, silver lamps from Constantinople, Antioch leather, Arabian spices and perfumes, Florentine artefacts and other such precious delights. The great ladies of the land were richly attired in Tyrian purple, bejewelled in glittering gems and anointed in sweet-scented Syrian oils.

Yet Southfalians were loath to make vulgar show of all this. For one thing, it aroused the envy of their poor neighbours because, while Southfalia was truly the proverbial diamond isle, it lay embossed in a cluster of coals. It was a setting which gave it even greater splendour, yet made it more conspicuous and open to envy.

To appease these starving masses, and the conscience of a squeamish minority, Southfalians tried to help with a vessel or two of surplus grain, but the poor neighbours had nothing to give in return: no shining carriages, rich cloth or ornate candelabra; only hard-working serfs, as many as Southfalia needed, or was willing to accept.

In Southfalia there were no beggars in the streets, or hawkers at the market: the former were beaten up then sent to prison, the latter ran for the Senate. It won't come as a surprise, therefore, that Southfalians in general were quite happy with their lot. Certainly the knights, senators, merchants and judges were; the rest didn't count, for you always have a disgruntled majority whose function it is to satisfy the wants of the minority.

So you see, it was a contented society. Not perfect, mind you—which society ever was!—but given all that wealth and all those fine objects, new homes, fashionable clothes, plenty of food, plus the world's best beer as an added blessing, and you have what that celebrated philosopher, Monsieur Pangloss, calls 'the best of all possible worlds'.

In this best *of all possible worlds* lived an old man: an Egyptian by the name of Iscar, who kept a journal in which he wrote very little, just the occasional comment, or at most a brief sketch. From these it is possible—with help from the imagination—to reconstruct a picture of life in Southfalia as it was before its inexplicable decline and extinction. I lay no claim to complete veracity; my ill-furnished source has compelled me to fill in gaps ad-libitum. I should add that the journal itself is marked by acid humour and lack of reverence, suggesting some sort of deep-rooted resentment, if not bias, on the part of the author.

But, what about historical accuracy? You might well ask. Iscar, who was really no fool, despite admitting to some rather foolish behaviour, anticipated the very objection and provides us with a revealing comment in his journal,

> *'Can a story, which deals with human passions, be accurately told? The story I am about to recount is not history and I no historian. I subscribe to the credence that truth is no more than the affectation of the vain, the invention of the artful or, more often still, the illusion of the fool who claims to speak the truth. If there were some semblance of truth, it is to be found in the constant that joins events in a path of recurring patterns; playing the same stories all over again; or more precisely the same story, for there is but **one story**. And if the players do seem new, their physiognomy is but a mask that hides the age-old features of good and evil, love and hate, and their numberless progeny made of virtues and vices. . ...*
> *Far better then, to aim at the kind of story that is more authentic, if less factually accurate, than the historian's history which, too often, extends into the realm of myth.'*

So be it, then.

Southfalia was founded back in the days when Rome ruled the world and its proud centurions marched through far off lands and boasted—with a haughty toss of their feathered helmet, and a sniffle through their Roman noses—that any land Rome wanted, Rome had conquered.

Through the centuries the island grew from a small defence outpost to a great nation, yet people clung tenaciously to their Roman heritage; so that even a millennium after the fall of the Western Empire, Southfalians regarded themselves as the only inheritors of truly Roman culture left in the world.

'A nation of destitutes,' writes Iscar, *'cherishing the memory of an accomplished ancestor with pious reverence, whence they derive the self-respect which they do not possess of themselves.'*

Well, the age of the Caesars may have been dead, but in Southfalia, Caesar's memory was kept very much alive in the office of Governor. On official occasions you'd see him, emerging from some regal carriage with a nice smile, magnificently attired in a flowing gown, cape, ostrich feathers, ribbons and just about anything that floated and puffed with the wind. Whatever the momentous occasion: solemnizing a new investiture, opening a new session of the Senate or a new grooming centre for rare felines, presiding over the hunt or a beer-drinking competition, the Governor would be there. He would read out a speech, in the best classical Latin, followed by a few rousing bars of 'Hail to Thee Oh Mighty Caesar', then shake hands, smile regally and be off again with his attendants, in a flutter of silk and feathers, leaving behind a nostalgic feeling of old imperial magnificence.

In addition to the Governor there was a great number of Grandees, presiding over every town or hamlet in the island. These people compensated for their relative unimportance, by wearing even more lavish gowns than the Governor, and longer ostrich feathers, which were easier to come by in the country. Then there were the tribunes, the orators, the councillors and countless officials and aides; all of whom must have made the ordinary Southfalian feel quite inadequate.

> 'Southfalia has enough titled gentry to fill Europe's courts and governing houses to the brim. If the Empire should be reborn one day, Southfalians are well prepared to furnish it with officials from the Emperor down.'

Busy as they were with dressing-up and making speeches, the Governor and his friends had little time left for governance. Indeed, if we consider his sizeable entourage of over-dressed minions and under-dressed maids, it is unlikely that they had a great deal of muscle left for it either.

Officially, decisions were made by the Consul and ratified by the Senate, which *officially* elected him. In practice...well, Southfalians were pragmatic enough to know that the real power-wielders of the land were the great knights. Without their support no man could ever hope to climb up the Senate steps, let alone enter it. It follows that there was no prize more coveted than an investiture. It had everything going for it: status, power and wealth. It was the ultimate goal, the zenith of accomplishments, the realized dream for a few, the unattainable mirage for most.

Determination, ruthlessness and aristocratic connections were essential for success. To that end, schools trained the child to run, climb, swim, speak, write, do just about anything faster—though not necessarily better—than the next person. He was taught to endure pain without tears, to love without show of affection or not at all. All emotion, in fact, was dismissed as a sign of weakness. Spiritual or intellectual fulfilment, was not for the down-to-earth Southfalian character.

Of course, the path to knighthood was strewn with victims! Nothing could be more natural or inevitable. Southfalians did not need Darwin's theories to tell them about natural selection: they lived by it. If many broke down, fell under or dropped out, they knew it was the price of excellence, the collateral damage, the necessary dross to get to the refined product; or, to borrow again from that lucid genius of M. Pangloss, *'the necessary cause and effect in the best of all possible worlds'*.

The refined product of all that cause and effect was, as we have said, the knight. Investiture was awarded on merit.

'It is of great merit to speak Cicero's Latin and sport a Roman nose,' writes Iscar. It was highly desirable too, to be born into the right family and attend the right school; one blessed by the church and supported by the money of the rich. In such schools one met the right people, played the right games, acquired a taste for the right literature and for the arts, memorized the right quotations, and generally adopted the bearing of a knight.

No less important was the profession one chose. The most efficient carpenter could, at best, become the knights' coffin maker, yet with a judge, investiture was automatic; a senator worth his salt could call on the right people to pull the strings; as for the rich merchant, nothing was worthy of greater merit than sacks of gold, dangling from one's waist.

Let there be no misconceptions. Investitures could not be bought, as titles were in those days, from the Holy Father. Such practices were more in tune with the unashamed corruption of the Italian character. Southfalians always acted 'in good faith'; meaning that on that island it was regarded far less heinous to be branded stupid and incompetent, than cunning and corrupt.

The next step was to acquire a reputation for competence and efficiency, both measured in numerical terms, for the sake of objectivity. A Senator's worth was directly proportional to the number of votes he commanded in the Senate; that of the merchant to his millions; as for the General, the number of corpses he could produce after a battle.

How results were attained didn't really matter, but once on top, it was essential to reveal a selfless heart and generous purse: a virtue difficult to cultivate during the ruthless climb, but not impossible to acquire with a few well-chosen, well-timed acts of generosity. Wise old Iscar puts it well, 'Indiscriminate *generosity paves the way for ingratitude and resentment; properly directed it's a very wise investment.*' Best results were reaped by giving support, privately, to an influential Senator struggling to maintain a large family and refined tastes, and publicly to a respected charity or the arts. All charity to be performed without fanfare, though not anonymously, of course, that would be foolish as well as useless:

'*Southfalians much prefer modesty to vulgar ostentatiousness. Many a merchant has risen to the airy realm of knight riding the wings of public philanthropy in engaging style,*' comments Iscar.

PART ONE
THE ARTIST

I

The Making of a Knight

Although Bert Jones was born of plebeian stock, he was gifted with so much skill in wheeling and dealing that he was on the way to becoming the richest merchant on the island before middle age.

Equipped with such credentials, his candidacy for a knighthood was soon hinted at, then whispered in dark corridors of imposing old buildings, and finally debated in palatial halls.

'Bert Jones, Senator?' Sir Lucas Pompous Curse, Southfalia's Chief Justice raised his voice incredulously, as high as his exalted position allowed him, 'Bert Jones?' What kind of a name is that for a knight! Don't you know, my dear Senator, a knight's name is announced at the best gatherings?'

'Sir Lucas, he plans to add a middle name by deed poll. Something very Roman...we have considered Caligula.'

'Indeed, the name is vital. Let me see: Sir Bert Caligula Jones, hum! It has potential, undoubtedly. Tell me, Senator, what is the manner of his appearance?'

'Oh, distinguished, a very distinguished lemon-yellow colouring, very tall and elegant, and great pose...'

'Enough, enough, Senator! We don't want an effeminate actor in our midst. Height is immaterial—as you can see I am only five feet five myself...that is, without boots—does he have any chest, that's more to the point, and a middle. It's dignity and poise, not pose that makes a knight a knight. Dignity above all, Senator.'

'He certainly intends to work on that, Sir Lucas. He's had little time so far, but in future he intends to retire on one of his estates...'

'I hear he is a man of respectable means, Senator.'

'Oh, very respectable, Sir Lucas: one of the best homes in the city, right on the hilltop, several country estates and, of course, a castle surrounded by splendid hunting grounds, and stables with no less than one hundred thoroughbreds.'

'Indeed, horses has he?'

'And vineyards which produce excellent wines.'

'And wines! Indeed, Senator, your friend appears to have the means to attain a dignified aspect in a very short time. Such being the case, I envisage no major obstacle to his ambition. I am assuming, of course, that he has the Roman nose, the nose above all else, Senator!'

'Of course, Sir Lucas, as Roman as Constantine's arch.'

Before the final decision was taken his private conduct was investigated, for a knight had to show impeccable moral fibre and sober habits—in public anyway. Not that anyone expected a sound-bodied knight to be stuck with a dried-out old wife, or that he should drink only apple cider. Knights were men, after all; an exclusive breed, yes, but men; and to possess an eye for pretty girls, and a palate for rare wines, was regarded as manly then as it is today.

Hitherto Bert Jones had been too busy getting rich to worry about diversions, but he was an ambitious man; and determined to show that he was far from unsociable, he hosted a series of lavish hunts, after which the knights were entertained by pretty young dancers, and refreshed with excellent wines.

Soon after, the news broke that he was no longer Bert Jones, but Sir Bartholomew Caligula Jones: fully-fledged knight of the Order of Saint George and the Dragon. He would have the privilege of wearing the garter, suspenders, cape and feathers, and would move up into the best society, in a whirlwind of feasting, speeches and pleasant conversation.

Sir Bart, as he came to be known to his knightly friends, was looked upon with some curiosity at first, being not quite one of them. Soon, however, they grew accustomed to his unpolished ways and to-the-point manner of speaking. They even learned to admire it, along with his toughness and cunning. But more than any other virtue

SOUTHFALIA

they admired his wealth and good fortune, which Southfalians apparently could not distinguish.

'In Southfalia 'Fortuna' wears a golden blindfold and brandishes a knightly sword,' concludes Iscar.

II

Iscar's Loss

Sir Bart's investiture delighted many, but none more so than Iscar: the old philosopher, who had been employed, for some time, by the merchant as tutor to his son Andrew Gay Ganymede; a refined youth of cherubic beauty. Sir Bart, who had the appearance of a bulldog, could not understand how he had come to father a son of such ironic contrast to himself.

Iscar had landed on the island penniless, but he was a cultured man, with easy command of several languages, and well-schooled in all the major philosophies of the time. Above all, he was a man of the world, knowing not only what to say, but what to leave unsaid; well aware that there is no more effective way to boast than by omission. Add to this a quick wit and subtle *savoir faire* with the ladies, and it will come as no surprise that he became an instant success with the island's *bonne societé*.

The people of that island, as we have seen, could not have been more proud of their race, a pride which led them to disdain and mistrust their neighbours, along with most foreigners. Yet, hand in hand with this, went a pervasive sense of inadequacy, recognisable in the way that they admired anything foreign or exotic, except people, of course.

Anyway, Iscar wallowed in fame, as the ladies copied his cute accent and adored the lively twitch of his bristly moustache, whilst he declaimed the virtue of a new philosophy, or flattered a lady's ear lobe, with equal flair. And the men, noticing the facility with which he handled even the most capricious damsel, thought better of betraying any envy.

But most of all, he was loved by the young men of the island, who found his long philosophical orations, spoken through a pair of soft, fleshy pink lips, truly uplifting. In rows flocked the delicate youths eager to be tutored, while old Iscar attained great surges of ecstasy as he watched the effects of his words on the passionate eyes of his pupils. A few short sessions and the most indolent of youths was fired with idealism, fatalism, determinism, hedonism and all those wonderful 'isms' of philosophy.

Unfortunately for Iscar, life's course is patterned by cruel lines of unpredictability, and the good life cannot be relied upon to last indefinitely. It happened that one day, during a particularly engrossing in-put with wide-eyed Ganymede, he was caught raw-bottomed by a livid Sir Bart, who delivered Iscar into the hands of Sir Herod, chief of the feared *Law and Order* squad.

There never was on that island a man more feared than Sir Herodotus Moronus Nero, Grand Knight of the Order of the Cross and the Chain, pious ascetic, scourge of criminals and sinners, Black Knight. Calloused criminals trembled in terror at the sight of his black-robed figure riding in the street.

Sir Herod—as he preferred to be known—discharged his duties with the impeccable efficiency of a public servant. His means of enforcing the law were always simple and direct. A man who betrayed his wife for lust of another woman, would have his eyes plucked out, eliminating, thereby, all source of future temptation. If he dared sin again—a most unlikely occurrence—then, some other vital organ was put out of use, which solved the problem once and for all. Likewise the slanderous woman lost her tongue, the thief his hands, and so forth. In other words, he tackled the problem 'at grass-roots level' as a modern bureaucrat would say, making it such an effective form of deterrence that just about eradicated all crime from the island.

Anyway, having been wrenched away from his dear pupil, Iscar little suspected the worst. All too soon, alas, he was to suffer the cruel treatment accorded to offenders of his kind. Yes, one dark morning, following a visit from the monstrous Sir Herod, he found himself emasculated, deprived of his manhood, castrated like a steer or a gelding, and sobbing with terror. What a grim, tragic day that was! Not just for Iscar, but for Ganymede and all the other passionate young men, who pleaded, in vain, for their beloved mentor to be spared.

Iscar, thus mutilated, retired to the tiny hamlet of Belpied, converted to stoicism and embarked on a life of solitude.

III

Manuel

In that far-off village lived a young man so striking in appearance that he could not fail to attract Iscar's seasoned eye. He was tall, with powerful jaws, smooth forehead, wide shoulders and large hands. His complexion was olive brown and his eyes, very black, were transfixed with the astonishing stillness of the dreamer. Iscar's heart sank. Oh cursed me, thought he in his restless heart, if only that useless bum of Sir Herod had not cut short my career…how I should like to give that lovely youth some instruction!

It consoled him somewhat to see that this was no delicate, lost youth in need of instruction, but one in whom strength, gentleness and rustic nobility merged into a perfection that required nothing from others.

The young man's name was Manuel, son of old Joe the village carpenter. Joe, like a proper father, expected his son to clasp plane, hammer and saw, and earn a decent living in the respected trade that had belonged to the family for as many generations as anyone could recall.

Manuel however showed little enthusiasm for the trade. Not that he ever disobeyed his father—he loved him too much for that—but his constant absent-mindedness told plainly that his heart was elsewhere. Where, none knew. Not his father, who doted on him despite his recalcitrance. Not his companions, who watched him with a mixture of envy, admiration and resentment as he grew more distant. And certainly not Iscar, who watched him work in his father's shop, intrigued by the young man's serene, oblivious aspect.

He has no money and I no manhood, what good are we to each other? Iscar thought.

But even an old stoic can get bored in a dull, out-of-the-way village, so he decided to accost him.

'Who are you?' asked Manuel, in a tone that could have been haughty spoken by another youth.

'Why Squire, I am an Egyptian philosopher. I have groomed the restive spirit of youths from Alexandria to Smyrna with the balmy power of my philosophy. Now I am a rock, nay, a jagged old reef, watching with indifference the world sail by from tempest to storm. I am invincible because supremely adaptable like air. Finding myself too long in the tooth and too short in the…. of pennies; forsaken by patrons and pupils, derided by perverts and friends, I have followed in the footsteps of Zeno, Cato and Seneca, and learnt the art of doing without. In short, Squire, I am a stoic.'

'Does the stoic see the world all wrong?'

'Indeed he does.'

'And that men suffer unduly?'

'Men suffer because it is in their nature to suffer.'

'Oh, I don't believe that. I think they suffer because they don't believe in themselves or one another. I know I'm unhappy for that.'

'That they suffer?'

'And that no one believes any more.'

'What would you have them believe?'

'That they could be happy.'

'I see, Squire, that you are even younger than you look.'

'No, no old man. I will go to the city and show them.'

'Stay where you are, young man, if you value your manhood. I would still have mine, if it weren't for the city's trappings.'

Manuel's black eyes did not blink as Iscar told him about the Southfalia City and Sir Herod and the infamous *Law and Order*. Nothing, it seemed, surprised the young man; it was as if he had known it all along.

'Sit there, old man, I'll show you something.'

Then he proceeded to sketch Iscar a portrait, in swift, deliberate strokes, working with total absorption. The result astonished Iscar, for within the lights and shadows of its sure strokes transpired his life: intimate and triumphantly vibrant, encased within a hard shell of cynicism built over a lifetime's effort in self-preservation. Iscar felt like the fugitive being recognized in the street by an old acquaintance he wanted to avoid.

From that day their friendship grew, which gained him a regular meal, for Iscar, struggling as he was to make a living, needed all the friends he could muster.

Not long after, old Joe the carpenter died, and Manuel indicated that he would travel to the city as soon as he had given proper burial to his father. Iscar, fed up with his stoic life in the country, decided to join the young man, finding in the quiet strength of the latter the courage to face once again the terrible Sir Herod.

'Who knows,' thought he, 'maybe the lad is heading for a fast-rising career with the ladies of the city.'

He certainly had the looks and, he suspected, the attributes. Besides, there was his art. Now Iscar didn't know a great deal about art, even though he had lectured on it at one or two prestigious universities; but there was no doubting the young man's confidence and speed. Given a more refined, glossy finish, the portraits might prove very popular with the ladies and knights of the city, especially as they were done by one as young, handsome and exotic-looking as Manuel. All that was needed, thought Iscar, was good promotion, and as he felt confident of his own special ability to provide that, he decided to join his young friend and leave the sleepy world of Belpied for good.

IV

The City

Southfalia City was free of those aged structures referred to, euphemistically some think, as historical buildings. There were no such ugly vestiges of time, decay and death. No morbid relics of some past glory to upset the merry temperament of the people. As soon as a building became ingrained with the grime of age, down it came and up rose a new, very white, very clean, very practical one in all its brilliant glory. Thanks to this progressive policy of constant renewal, everything was thoroughly modern in that Romanesque city.

Iscar took his young master directly to the Midas Square, the vast throbbing heart of the city. Manuel was mute with wonder as he moved through the impersonal streets of the noisy, white giant. So heavy was the traffic, that anyone who lingered risked being run over by a fast moving carriage.

Manuel surveyed the square. It was vast and oval shaped, dominated by the castle at one end, and the bell-tower of the cathedral at the other. In the centre rose a fountain depicting the fabled Phrygian King, standing in a river of gold with his hands to the sky. Out of his fingers gushed flickering jets of yellow liquid, a golden offering by a grateful people to their munificent God.

'On certain windy days' explained Iscar, 'a fine yellow spray rises up to envelop the square in what seems like a haze of golden dust falling down. On such a day even the most wretched man on the island will wish to sing to the glory of his good fortune.'

There was also a story attached to the inception of the fountain, which many swore to be true. When the Romans first landed on the site of the city, its river was infested with millions of vicious, blood-sucking flies, which made the Romans curse the day they had set sight on the island. One day a party of soldiers returned jubilant from a very fruitful trip inland where, not only had they killed off a tribe of natives, in the process they had discovered a natural yellow stream, which they believed to be of gold.

Their hopes proved to be unfounded, but not altogether futile, for someone discovered that if you washed your face with it, the flies stayed away. Imagine their joy! The Governor, who had suffered many a vicious attack by the beastly swarms, decreed that the water be diverted to the city and a fountain be erected, which they called, appropriately enough, the Midas fountain.

To his dismay, the country youth heard no shrieks of children in the square, no urchin's lively calls, no idle chatter of women, no lazy mumble of old men basking in the sun. There weren't in fact any idle people to be seen anywhere. Had there been human sounds, they would have been drowned by the constant clickety-clack of shining carriages, which sped past in glittering convoys of gold and silver.

Behind the fountain was the Big Dragon, looming like a mighty, supervising giant. The Big Dragon was the popular name of the castle's great bronze door, because the Roman eagle cast upon it resembled a huge dragonfly. Below the eagle were cast the initials S.E.Q.S. (Senatus Equesque Sudfaliae), which means: The Senate and the Knights of Southfalia.

Flanking the castle on its right was the palace of the Lemon League, and on the left, that of the Orange League. The latter looked as if put together somewhat chaotically, in contrast to the solid, well-polished facade of its rival on the other side. I say rival, since these were the respective headquarters of the opposing factions of Southfalian politics, or to put it in modern terms, the two parties.

'A man is wooed by Lemonists and Orangists alike,' explained Iscar, 'and he may choose either. All other colours are unsouthfalian, and a mark of those backward nations which are, thankfully, too remote to exercise a corrupting influence on the people of this island.' And noticing Manuel's obvious disinterest he added, 'yes, young Squire, politics are a great bore, I grant you. Come, we must move on before the *Law and Order* notices our idleness.'

V

The Western Flank (or the Right)

'The western flank of the square begins with the Lemon League and ends with the Cathedral' explained Iscar as he took the young man around the square, describing its more important structures. 'The Lemon League palace is truly Patrician in character and style. It was designed by the knights, for the knights; and to remind citizens of this, the four Roman columns on which it stands contain the carved busts of four knights: a Judge, a Scribe, a Merchant, and a Governor; living symbols of all that the Lemonists stand for.'

Next came a very impressive, very formal mansion in white marble built in grand imperial style. Two statues dominated the foyer of its porticoed entrance, one of Octavius Augustus, and the other of a tree, in rare yellow marble.

'That's the Governor's palace,' said Iscar. And before he had time to say more a trumpeter came trumpeting on the foyer. All carriages and horsemen made a feverish exit out of the square and in their place arrived people with banner in hand and children in their arms.

Another round of trumpeting and the iron gates of the palace were opened. From within the palace appeared a most lavish carriage: all white and yellow, drawn by four white horses, escorted by twenty guardsmen, followed by a procession of four other grand carriages.

The whole train did three rounds of the square amid the cheers of especially selected common people, flag-waving children and mothers holding up their babies; then it came to a stop once again in front of the palace next to a permanent marble dais. After some moments of expectant hush there emerged from the carriage a figure whose face was sandwiched between a towering cap topped by tall ostrich feathers and swirls of satin flowing down from his shoulders. On his chest hung a medal as large as a dinner plate.

'Consider yourself the luckiest of men, Squire' cried Iscar 'No sooner you set foot in this city, than you get to see the Governor. That's him: Sir Isaac Garrish Hippocritus. Isn't he magnificent?'

'I can't really see his face with all those feathers.'

'You can see his robes, can't you? And look at all those attendants.'

'What does he want all those people around him for?'

'They are not people. They are the elite of this island, whose job it is to filter the air through their nostrils before it reaches the noble ones of the Governor. Because if he were to come in contact with the people, by breathing in the same air, then there would not be any point in retaining such an august symbol of Roman grandeur. Sir Isaac, you see, embodies the finest, the most rarefied pedigree on this island. Just think, he is related by blood-line to the noble Lady Beth, by proxy to the Emperor, by mutual *simpatia* to the Consul's young wife, by business partnership with Sir Bart, and by common interest to the brewery owners; all excellent reasons why the common people owe a living, not only to him, but to all his entourage.

'One day, my Squire, if ever you reach the top, you may get to do a portrait of the Governor's horse, or even his favourite corgi.'

'Why not him?' Asked the young man.

Iscar snorted.

'Mon vieux, vous manquez vraiment de pudeur!'[1] Come on, let's get a bit closer; you never know, one of those great ladies might take a fancy to you.'

And as he shoved the young man forward, he undid the front of his shirt so as to expose the smooth, tanned skin and strong pectorals. Meanwhile the Governor, who looked so weak that he had trouble standing on his feet, had been helped up the dais and was now propped up on either side by two faithful attendants. A child with fine skin, blue eyes and blond curls was heaved up to present a bunch of flowers. The Governor kissed the flowers and sneezed all over the child. Cheers and smiles all round, as someone quickly handed him a speech to read.

The Governor then wavered on his feet as he tried to read the lines. He really did look unstable on them! Manuel noticed also that his cheeks were red and puffy beneath the thick layer of powder, and that his eyes were glassy. Still, being a well intentioned young man, he told himself that Sir Isaac must have been a lot older than he seemed. It may also be the weight of all those robes that makes him unsteady, thought he, charitably.

Then as he began to struggle with his speech, the Governor stopped dead as if struck by inspiration, braced himself and discharged a resounding explosion which was really too distinct to be mistaken for a belch.

Still, everyone continued to smile. Manuel was truly puzzled.

'Didn't you hear that, Iscar?' he asked naively.

'I heard nothing, Squire. Now be quiet and smile like the rest of us. Here is your chance to show the ladies those strong, white teeth of yours.'

But before Iscar had finished advising his companion, there issued from the noble Governor a succession of bombardments that would have held its own against a barrage of modern artillery. The Governor looked violently shaken, but relieved. Manuel's own reaction wavered between embarrassment and admiration; and he deduced, quite logically, that the Governor's unsteady buoyancy had been due partly to all that excess air—not to speak of the odour—trapped inside him. Yet, miraculously, the knights and ladies of the entourage continued to smile ecstatically, although if one looked closely, one could see that the smiles had attained a thin-lipped wryness, the Roman noses had flared considerably, and the ostrich feathers looked droopy. Such fine display of *noblesse oblige* in a moment of crisis escaped Manuel, who was merely a peasant close to nature, and had not Nature just shown an uncanny disregard for nobility and rank? Likewise the young man was to reveal want of tact (and prudence) as he turned to his companion and said,

'Now if you didn't hear all that, you must at least be able to smell it. Why does he have to read a speech? The poor man is blind drunk!'

No sooner had he finished, than a guard on horseback pounced on him.

'You're drunk, boy! Don't you know it's against the law to be drunk in front of the Governor?'

'Me? Drunk!...' The young man was speechless.

'Do you deny that you.... that you made ungentlemanly noises?'

'I most certainly do, Sir. Listen to him Iscar...Iscar!...Where are you?'

Iscar had vanished.

'Seems to me that you're too drunk to control your tongue. Seems to me you need some treatment. I'll have you taken to Sir Herod, boy...'

And as Manuel was about to be dragged away by two burly guards, Iscar reappeared from nowhere waving a stick and started to hit the young man as far up his back as he could reach.

'Drunk again, you lazy rascal! Here, take this, and this!'

'Is he your son, Sir?' asked the guard.

'My son? If I had a son like him I should have turned him over to Sir Herod long ago. No Sir, he works for me, the useless rascal. Owes me six months' work.'

'In that case, if money is involved, we can't touch him. But be sure, after his debt is paid off, that you turn him in. He's the sort of cocky young toughie that Sir Herod loves to straighten out.'

As Iscar quickly dragged away the bewildered youth, the Governor finally managed to read his speech and then was away with all his attendants, retiring back inside the palace to the sound of trumpets.

VI

The Eastern Flank (or The Left)

'What was the meaning of all that?' asked Manuel when Iscar had finally stopped running.

'Shush! Don't speak so loud!' whispered the panting Iscar, 'it means that I have just saved you from a most horrendous fate. Remember that, Squire, if ever I am in need of you. Do you know what 'the treatment' is for being found drunk?'

'But I wasn't drunk! I am not drunk!' protested the young man, exasperated, 'how can you say that!'

'I don't say it, the guard said it, and unless you're at least a Grandee it pays you not to disagree with the *Law and Order* of this island.'

'The Governor was drunk.'

'Shush, don't you say that again,' cried Iscar terrified, giving his companion a murderous look, 'for I won't be here to rescue you next time. His Excellency was not drunk. His Excellency cannot be drunk. If he were pronounced drunk it would mean that the ruling class of this island was cankered. People in the street might start asking real questions about the whole, complicated fabric of this society. And, of course, no peace-loving society invites turmoil. Whatever happens law and order must prevail. No more of that. Now we will quickly tour the rest of the square then we will take up lodgings.'

'That's a curious building,' said Manuel pointing to a squat little structure, which looked austere, almost humble in fact, next to the grand style of the Governor's residence. On close study, however, it was discovered that its plebeian appearance was part of a deliberate and studied effect. The building in fact had a kind of subtle symmetry, a sophistication, which its neighbours lacked, despite or because of, their bulky grandeur.

'That there, young Squire, is Procrustean House, workshop of the island's Scribes, and if you're wondering why they have not erected a more worthy monument to their power and influence, it's because they have no need to. It is the Scribes' role to record and comment on the events of each day, then convey it to the people through *The Voice of Southfalia*, commonly known as *The Voice*.'

The Scribes were, of course, the forerunners of that unique establishment modern society collectively referred to as *the Media*: a name suggesting something powerful, mysterious and fearful. In fifteenth-century Southfalia the Scribes made it their business to 're-port' packaged prejudice with engaging arrogance. Our friend Iscar, does not sound too fond of them:

'These spurious masqueraders of fact, scourge of uniqueness and truth, makers of myth, and destroyers of men, purport to carry the word of the people, whilst forever usurping it. Like Mercury, their sly patron-god, they employ eloquence not to reveal, but to fake and distort. In the guise of the same god, they are likewise masters of knavery, thievery and invention...'

Chief of the Scribes was, of course, a knight, Sir Matthew McKiavel, in many respects the most powerful knight in the land. His opinions on everything touching Southfalian society, from wars to hunting parties were respectfully sought; for neither portentous Cassandra nor Delphi's mighty oracle could have borne greater weight than Sir Matthew's word. A word from Sir Matthew and dead men were revived, the mighty fell, poets were awarded laurels and grandees contracted mysterious diseases.

By now they had crossed Liberty Way and were coasting Knight's House: a large building with turrets and balconies, from which flapped flags and pennants of many colours. Though not particularly large, it stood alone in imposing aloofness, separated on the other side from the A.L.E.R.T. fortress by the wide Victory Road. The A.L.E.R.T. housed a very influential organization, whose concern it was to fire the heart of all Southfalian youth with the noble spirit of combat, by preaching fear and mistrust of all foreigners. Its entrance was dominated by a towering bronze statue to the god Mars, bearing a striking resemblance to Sir Marc Martial, Southfalia's most decorated warrior.

The remainder of the Western Flank was taken up by grand mansions, banks, exclusive inns and other lavish edifices: the property of knights, senators, merchants and judges. At the back of these, away from the square, were intimate little gardens called collectively 'the gardens of the wasps'. As this puzzled Manuel, the old philosopher went on to elaborate:

'It is said that many a dangerous wasp inhabit the garden. These never touch its august dwellers; if, however, a foreign body ventures into the bowers where the deadly wasps lurk, they will swoop down onto the intruder and inflict a sting, invisible, yet so lethal as to cause the victim either to turn lemon-yellow or perish.'

The cathedral, which marked the far end of the Western flank and the beginning of the Eastern, had once vied with the castle for prominence in the square. Now, it stood almost obscured by a series of buildings which had proliferated around it. The biggest among these was the D.R.L. (Death to Reds Legion), whose foundations originated on the left, but had grown bit by bit toward the right so that now it almost hid the cathedral from view. Only the bell-tower reached up over the top: as vestige of the cathedral's past glory, like the pompous hair-style of an aged prima donna, whose voice and beauty had long vanished.

Iscar and his young master moved on to the left flank, past artisans' shops, plebeians' inns, modest stores and stalls, until they reached the House of Guilds, home of Southfalia's workers, at whose entrance stood a statue of Sisyphus, symbol of serfdom and relentless drudgery. Actually the workers who sat on the lower steps of the statue did not look particularly emaciated. On the contrary they were round-bellied, sun-bronzed and seemed as if they suffered from chronic inactivity. Out of their mouths came constant noises which sounded like something between a burp, a grumble and a rumble.

'Their job is to arouse the compassion of passers-by to the sorry plight of Southfalia's workers,' explained Iscar, 'but, take no notice of the lazy bums, they count for nothing. The man to watch is their leader, Peter the Guild-master, a man of great standing and power; respected by both Plebeians and Patricians, thanks to his unique ability in the fine art of deception. He's a shrewd man that Peter, there's much to be learned from him, if you hope to succeed in this city.'

Now, after going past several more shops and a number of modest dwellings, Manuel's attention went to a large, elegant-looking building with a lush, walled garden.

'Aah! Here we have Ivory Tower University, Southfalia's highest temple of learning,' said Iscar.

'It looks out of place, here with all the small shops around it,' commented Manuel.

'In fact, Squire, you're right. Formerly it stood on the other side of the square next to the Lemon League, under exclusive patronage of the Patricians. It shifted to this side, at grave cost to its status. Once a young gentleman spent several years within its lush precinct, polishing his speech, his finger-nails and manner, courting the right acquaintances. Now all of these will come to him with money. If you have money to lavish about, you can have as many degrees and doctorates as you're willing to accept.'

VII

The People

In order to better appreciate Iscar's concern that his young charge might go astray, we must take a pause and talk briefly about a large but unimportant section of Southfalian society: the people.

All the titled gentry, from the Governor down, were the machinery, which organized the affairs of state according to the principles laid down by the early Roman colonists.

Below them stood the free artisans: a kind of free worker, often self-employed, whose economic strength was not matched by political clout, simply because they were too busy to bother with politics, and too independent to unite with others.

Finally there were the serfs or hired workers. Vociferous and dissatisfied, their ambition was only to disrupt the system, which compelled them to do the most lowly, back-breaking jobs for little reward and no credit. Spartacus was their hero, and their villain Sir Herod, who was always quick to crush their hope of revolt with merciless savagery.

A person unfortunate enough to be a serf was likely to be either an imported serf or a savage indigenous; for not all the inhabitants of the Lucky Island could boast Roman ancestry.

Of the two, the most conspicuous were the natives: a small minority, fortunately, but quite troublesome in their own way; not for anything they did; on the contrary it was their very inaction, their abject passiveness, which for some reason caused Southfalians to experience curious pangs of conscience.

When the Romans first landed on the island, they were confronted by wild tribes of nomads, who, being unacquainted with Roman might, foolishly tried to resist their advance. Naturally the civilized Romans proceeded very methodically to teach the impertinent barbarians a lesson so masterfully executed, that it soon reduced the creatures to near extinction.

Actually, once they were subdued, the natives became surprisingly docile, just like tamed horses; so tame in fact, that they had to be soundly beaten up before they moved out of the way. They sat around the doorsteps of inns and ale-houses, their faces dull and listless, their bodies limp, seemingly unaware of the life that moved around them at a frantic pace, and no amount of Roman discipline or ingenuity would move them. What a blow to Roman pride to feel powerless before the very slave whose head they were crushing!

Less severe, but more pervasive, was the problem of the serfs imported from foreign lands to till the fields, milk the cows, sweep the streets, make the bricks, build the houses...in short, to do work too strenuous for Roman backs, or too lowly for Roman pride, a pride inflated by centuries of domination and mastery.

The great founding fathers of that island, in their wisdom, had decreed that only men and women of pure Roman strain should enter its ports. But Rome had fallen, and with the barbarian invasions the pure Roman was a disappearing race.

To entice the few left, Southfalia offered them a free passage, instant citizenship and other such privileges. But the Romans were unimpressed. Those who finally deigned to come bemoaned their state, criticized everything, refused to work, and at the first opportunity sailed back to their degenerate Roman life. So it was decided that most serfs were to be recruited from the Southern Mediterranean, noted for producing a hardy, stocky type, noted for his ability to work hard and be content with little. The purists objected vehemently to this contamination of the Roman race, but in the end, they too had to conclude that comfort and the purse were more important than genes. After all, if they were to have new homes, new roads, shiny carriages and well-furnished tables, then the price had to be paid.

Once in Southfalia, the serf was 'assimilated', that is, he was given a Southfalian name and haircut, and told to forget the backward way of life of his country of origin, its language, history, customs and such obstacles which stood in the way of his assimilation. If he proved to be the malleable type, soon he would begin to be 'accepted', a great honour indeed. Then he was taught to dress casually, swear profusely and finally, the big test: to drink beer like a man. If he measured up, he was a fully-fledged New-Southfalian, which was the second best thing to being a real Southfalian.

Of course they looked different and spoke differently, which must have been a source of constant regret for them. Still, they did live in the best country in the world, as they were constantly reminded.

Nor were Southfalians happy to see their Lucky Island overrun by scores of foreigners. In the end most learned to reconcile themselves with the unpleasant reality. Besides, there was always the hope that after several generations the stronger Roman strain might prevail and then these serfs too would grow tall and handsome, and bleach to a healthy lemon-yellow. And then there would only be the nose to tell the true-blue from the grey.

VIII

Filippo Grassi

With their future in mind, Iscar set to work at once to upgrade his own appearance and that of his young master. They bathed, shaved, had a haircut in the latest fashion, bought a couple of imported outfits made of silk, then waited around for some lady of renown to notice them and serve them an invitation to her salon.

Garbed like a peacock, Manuel felt uncomfortable and embarrassed. He was also bored with lolling about doing nothing, and took every opportunity to go out on the street, much to Iscar's displeasure, who feared that his inexperience might land him in some serious trouble.

One day as Manuel stood idly at the front of the inn, waiting for something to happen, he saw a serf of swarthy appearance alight from Equality Road pulling at a cart full of fruit for sale. The Innkeeper's wife: a stout, impatient matron, was abusing him.

'Hurry up Grass, you slow coach, you're late. Do you think I got all day waiting fer ya?'

Filippo Grassi, the stocky Sicilian grocer, filled the lady's basket with the worst fruit he could find, then, in a gesture typical of his temperamental race, as he handed it back, deliberately dropped the contents all over her. He moved on, leaving the lady in a trauma of hysterics.

'Don'worry,' he shouted at Manuel, who went to help her, 'let the fat *puttana* picke dem 'erselfe.'

The next day, Manuel waited for Grassi to come by and asked him if he would sit for him, as he wanted to do his portrait.

'Watchiu recken!' shouted the other. I can sit on my bum all day. I gotta worke my frien'.'

Nevertheless he was flattered by the request and after that mandatory display of reticence, his own Latin imagination, and vanity, impelled him to agree to the proposal.

Iscar was furious.

'Who? Him? An imported serf! But Squire, do you want to ruin your career before it takes off? Why, with your looks and talent, who knows? You might well aspire to marry a knight's daughter!'

Aware that he had let down his mentor, Manuel became defensive.

'I came to the city to paint, Iscar.'

'And paint you shall, but not foreigners and serfs who can bring neither money nor prestige. What's the good of that! No Sir, you have a reputation to build. Forget about your Grassi, or we'll be ruined. I'll go and seek out my friend Gay Ganymede, and you can do a portrait of him. His father's the wealthiest man on this island!'

Again the young man felt that he could not fault the soundness of Iscar's logic, but this time he knew that in his heart he was definitely unconvinced.

When Iscar was unable to trace Gay Ganymede, Manuel was relieved and without hesitation he decided to ignore the old philosopher's sensible argument and follow his own desire.

Filippo Grassi watched fascinated as his chubby, swarthy features took over the canvas, faintly at first, like a reflection in a pond. Then the strong jawbones and the sensuous lips floated to the surface beneath black stubborn locks poised over the forehead crossed with lines of experience and the servitude of untold ages. Finally the black Sicilian eyes suffused the canvas with that ancient, penetrating light of the Mediterranean. It was like a miracle. Manuel put down his brush and looked at Filippo.

'Hey, dat's me truly?' he cried choked by emotion, like a blind man who gains his sight and sees himself for the first time. 'Noooh!... Is not me!' he said, pressing back tears *'Ma guarda un po'! Ma guarda un po' chi cosa curiusa é chista '*[2] And unleashing an outburst of Latin emotion, he embraced the young man and sobbed like a child; to which Manuel responded with less abandonment but equal warmth.

Iscar was shocked to discover that neither seemed ashamed of a behaviour that in Spartan Southfalia was regarded reprehensible in children, let alone in adults. He cringed with fear, as he contemplated what might happen if Sir Herod ever got to hear about this.

IX

At Stivaletto

The Grassi portrait proved to be a rewarding opener for the budding young painter, for the little Sicilian came from a very large family and had an even larger round of acquaintances, all of whom wanted to have their portrait done. And what was more to the point, so far as Iscar was concerned, they seemed prepared, and able, to pay handsomely for this concession to their vanity.

Iscar was worried about this turn of events, for he knew that no great lady or knight would dream of having a portrait done by the same artist who had worked—of all the people—for imported serfs. Nevertheless the money kept rolling in (for Iscar, like a good businessman, insisted on prompt payment), and that was after all the most important consideration. Besides, he could see now that he would never make a gentleman out of the wild young peasant. Why, he wouldn't even wear the silken garments he had bought for him! 'Too hot and uncomfortable,' he said. He preferred his old, linen tunic. As a result they had to move out of the Golden Lemon, as no knight wanted to see their exclusive meeting place invaded by peasants.

At Filippo's invitation they moved into the ground floor of his house, in one of the poorer sections of the city, inhabited mainly by imported serfs and for this reason nicknamed the 'Stivaletto' district. Notwithstanding its poverty, it was by far the most colourful part of Southfalia City. There the houses had balconies backed by Persian shutters, bright coloured front doors and shady pergolas cascading with golden vines. There black-scarved old women sat knitting and singing melancholy old songs, children shouted as they played ball out in the street, and card-playing old men argued.

Manuel spent some happy months there. Filippo's wife was a fine woman and a fine cook. Both loved the young man, a love shared by all the people of the district. With each new portrait his circle of friends seemed to multiply. He soon became everyone's protégé. They smothered him, lionized him, idolized him. He accepted and returned people's love, as if there could be nothing more natural in the world than for people of diverse backgrounds to love one another. Iscar, who had travelled enough around the world to know otherwise, found it all very puzzling.

Filippo Grassi had a fruit stall outside his house, to which neighbours came in the evenings to buy and to chat. One warm evening Manuel sat outside chatting with a group of customers, when up the street appeared a black-shawled old woman, limping laboriously on her stick. Timidly she approached the stall, held out a rusty old coin in her scrawny hand and asked for an apple. Filippo took two apples from the heaped stall and put them in the old woman's hand.

'Here, Vecchiona, takke dem, an' don' let de *Law an' Orda* see you, or you gettestick,' he said, refusing the coin.

Fruit, as we have seen, was plentiful in Southfalia, but not cheap by any means. It made business sense to destroy surplus goods so as to maintain the prices high. And in order to protect the business structure of the Lucky Isle it was illegal either to beg or to give freely to beggars.

The old woman returned nightly after that, always wrapped in the same shawl, tendering the same rusty old coin. Taking the apples, she quickly walked off without saying a word.

Then one night as she went to cross the street, she did not see an approaching carriage and was knocked down. The coachman swore as he leapt down ready to drag her onto the path from where the *Law and Order* would come to cart her away; for unproductive old peasants were of no use to anyone. Manuel got to her first. Gently he helped her off the road and then uncovered her face. The people who had come crowding suddenly recoiled.

'It's Old Mary the leper!' they cried, dispersing.

Just then, who should appear up the street but the Black Knight on horseback, Sir Herod Moronus Nero himself.

'Sir Herod!' gasped the coachman.

Hearing this the people scattered on all sides and fled into their homes. As if by miracle, Old Mary revived and scampered away with a speed that would have done credit to a young athlete.

Only Manuel and Iscar were left on the road. The latter, who had first hand experience with Sir Herod's methods, was petrified, while Manuel, perhaps for the opposite reason, looked merely curious. The coachman was about to take off and clear the street, when the rich, sensuous voice of a woman spoke to him from inside the coach. The coachman then called out to Manuel,

'Hey there, Squire, my lady wishes you and your servant to come into the coach.'

The door opened from within, and an elegant, bejewelled hand appeared on the handle and beckoned him in. Old Iscar leapt in, while Manuel, drawn perhaps by curiosity, or by some mysterious instinct, followed.

X

Madam Magdalene

If Manuel felt relieved at being rescued 'in the nick of time' from the clutches of Sir Herod, it did not show on his face which, even in the unfamiliar confines of that splendid carriage, wore its familiar expression of bemused calm.

Iscar, by contrast, sat recoiled in one corner of the carriage still numb, too shocked even to notice his rescuer sitting next to him. But Manuel did notice her, if nothing else because of the richness of her attire and the subtle blend of scents emanating from that voluptuous body.

To say that the lady was beautiful would have been trite and probably untrue. In the fleeting darkness of the carriage it was impossible to see. She was, in any case, a lady of a certain age; that would have been clear even to the young man's inexperienced eye. But then, she was the kind of woman with whom age and flawless good looks are irrelevant. That too was clear to young Manuel. Hers was the kind of beauty that needed no collaboration from the light to shine. It attracted just as powerfully in the dark, filling the carriage with the intense flux of alluring echoes. She communicated through her skin, the warmth of her bosom, the intensity of the silences between one breath and the next.

'I say, Sir, I've not seen you hereabouts for some time. Don't you recognize an old acquaintance?' Her words and face turned to Iscar, but her voice was making a submission towards the young man sitting opposite. It was a voice that well suited the woman. It was full and innately sensuous. A voice familiar to a good many of the males of that fair city, not excluding old Iscar, who in former days had had occasion to know it intimately. It was in fact the voice of Madam Magdalene, grand dame of Southfalia's red-light world.

Southfalia, being a proper Christian country disallowed prostitution, officially. All the same, prostitution was a lucrative business, lucrative enough to deserve the blind eye of the *Law and Order*, the protection of the business sector, the interest of the tourist department and the custom of some of the island's most notable worthies.

Thinking about it, Magdalene congratulated herself on her presence of mind in acting as she had. For, like the professional that she was, she enjoyed her occupation and was ever on the lookout for the kind of experience that extended her ability to give and receive enjoyment, and perfected her skills. To this end she had developed an eye for spotting virile young talent. Now her well-practised eye could tell at a glance that the young man sitting before her was an uncommonly talented specimen.

'And you, young man, who are you?' she asked.

'I paint portraits, Madam. Thank you for the ride.'

She smiled, amused and mysterious. Her skin opened to receive the sound of that steady voice. Her eyes caressed the power of his frame. She smiled, pleased. Manuel too smiled, a smile through which transpired the curiosity, impatience and vigour of youth. Iscar, newly recovered, sighed nostalgically, while the horses, with a snort and a whinny, cantered on toward Madam Magdalene's establishment.

The Spunk and Pot Strip or more briefly: The Strip, as it was known, was the notorious red-light district of the city, frequented—perhaps for different reasons—by pimps, prostitutes, poets, politicians, professors, unfrocked priests and the like. Magdalene's bordello was sited at the entrance of The Strip, known locally as the respectable quarter. Its quality announced itself to the customer at the very outset, in the form of expensive perfume, refined music and soft whispers. No loud shrieks, foul language or uncouth carrying on here. And those who ventured further could see for themselves that the underwear of the girls was of the best silk, that the beds did not squeak and the cushions were well padded.

In this unreal setting Manuel spent many surreal days. As for Iscar, well, it was hardly the kind of place for a eunuch, but he was, after all, an old man now and whatever degree of frustration he endured, it was preferable to the kind of torture he would have suffered at the hands of Sir Herod. So, making the best of the situation, he feasted on the fine wines and the food, and dismissed the rest with a shrug of his philosophical shoulders.

As for Manuel, he was led by his rescuer to her private boudoir. There, in the tremulous reflections of mirrors and chandeliers she held him against her palpitating bosom and knew that her expert eye had not failed her. As the garments fell to his feet one by one, even Magdalene, who had seen a few naked bodies in her time, found herself holding her breath. Manuel's body combined the perfection of Apollo with the strength of Hercules; the sensuous abandonment of Bacchus with a touch of Vulcan's brutal vitality. In the next few days he was to reveal all of these. For an instant they parted, waited, staring into each other in perverse torture till their swelling passion hurt; they searched, they felt, they came to one another, they parted and enjoined once again...for the life.

Whether the earth moved, we don't know. I doubt that they themselves would have noticed or cared, falling as they did in deep slumber almost immediately. If it did move, then The Strip was to experience a formidable succession of quakes in the next few days, as Manuel discovered the subtleties of love-making and Magdalene its meaning.

And to seal the miracle with some sort of visual symbol, Manuel painted Magdalene's nude. Toned with passion and gratitude she posed submissively; both of them oblivious of the other activities in the bordello, unaware even of the succession of days and nights as Magdalene's double took shape on canvas. In the end the little boudoir glowed with moonshine reflected from that mass of reclining white flesh, contorting with fertility and the simple desire to share in each other's life. There were no blemishes on the canvas, just pure beauty, free from lines of obscenity and guilt. Manuel depicted a bountiful body, ready to yield generously, and on her face transpired a hint of the sacrificial offering that tinges the grain-field golden before the harvest.

'It's done,' said Manuel, 'now I can go.'

She cried unashamedly. Then, for some female whim she insisted on bathing him; stroked every pore of his skin with her black, wavy mane; finally she anointed his body with perfumed oils. He submitted to her, as she had done to him, as they had done to one another so many times and once again the two of them were filled with sating power.

They embraced, then parted in silence, without promises, for there was no need for promises.

XI

Black John

The Strip was deserted, but for the street cleaners sweeping away the dregs from the exploits of the previous night. Manuel smiled distantly. At once he was fascinated by The Strip. Every new thing was for him a revelation. The shops, the gaily-painted windows, the people themselves. Everything wore the same somnolence, the deflated nakedness, the intimacy of a woman's face the morning after the feasting. The young man's absorption was total, even while the warmth from the kisses of Magdalene still lingered with him.

How can he forget so quickly and so completely, thought Iscar, incredulously.

'Look Iscar,' said Manuel, 'I could do so much here!'

The old philosopher's heart plunged. That brilliant 'coup' with the island's foremost expert in the art of amorous practices had filled him with pride in his protégé, and given him renewed hope that finally good sense was prevailing in him.

'Take it from me, Squire, you'd do well to put your talents in the service of those who appreciate and pay handsomely for them,' said he hopefully.

'That's probably very wise, Iscar. But we did try.'

'It takes time.'

'In the meantime I must take what there is. And here there's so much...Hey, look, there in the gutter. What is it?'

Manuel ran ahead to investigate. They had just turned the corner past the Blackfellas alehouse and there in the gutter lay what looked to be a corpse.

'It's only a drunk native,' said Iscar dismissively, 'you'll see lots of them around.'

Manuel knelt down by the body and gently turned it face-up. It was in fact a native. His dark face, gaunt and bruised, seemed permanently set in an expression of puzzled helplessness. Manuel studied it with an air of dreamy anticipation, as if he expected the man to get up and walk away with them.

'Leave him there, he'll revive before the end of the day, they always do,' said Iscar.

'But then I wouldn't have a superb subject for a portrait. He really is a beautiful man, Iscar, can't you see?'

As a matter of fact Iscar could not see that at all, and made an eloquent grimace.

'But he is, Iscar, truly. Look, give me a few days and I'll show you, I promise.'

Manuel's eyes flashed with the fire of inspiration. They were happy eyes, glowing with strength and purpose. The old man felt powerless.

'Don't frown, old one, there's time enough to paint the knights and become famous.'

It was no problem for the strong young man to toss the native over his right shoulder and carry him up the street.

Iscar could hardly control his frustration. What recompense could there be in painting the portrait of a penniless drunk! The foreign serfs at least could be relied upon for prompt payment, as for this drunk…why Manuel would have to pay for his keep and lodgings! In his frustration, the old man regretted ever having come to the city again. But then he remembered that since his association with the young painter, he had suffered neither hunger nor indignities. And after all, so long as there was gold to be spent and he was safe from marauders, life could be comfortable almost anywhere.

The novelty of a soft bed soon revived the native. He sat up unsteadily, looked with disbelief at the ceiling and the four walls, and when Manuel pushed a bowl of fruit in front of him he looked positively terrified. Manuel's dark eyes reassured him. He took an apple from the bowl, smelled it and bit into it timidly. Feeling something of an intruder, Iscar went and sat outside on the veranda step. Not a few minutes had passed that the door was flung open and the native bolted.

Manuel explained, 'He asked for money and when I gave it to him, it seemed to put wings on his feet. Not bad for a drunk,' and he laughed, his hearty, happy laugh.

'Manuel, dear Squire,' despaired Iscar, 'you're too simple for the ways of these people. He's probably already reached the ale-house around the corner, and I'll give him half an hour before he is drunk again.'

'Which means, that he will be back tomorrow,' Manuel chuckled.

The next day he did, in fact, return, and the next, and the next. He never said a word, just ate the food, took the money and went. But each day he remained longer, lingering, pacing around the room as if interested in this or that, without saying a word.

One day when Manuel took out his brushes and said he wanted to paint his portrait, the other became suspicious and morose. He obviously knew what Manuel meant, but for some reason found it objectionable. He went away and did not come back for some days. When he reappeared he was almost unrecognisable. He had bought new clothes, cut his hair Roman-style, but had either run out of money or had forgotten about shoes, for his bony feet peered incongruously underneath the fancy new garment.

Manuel said nothing, but in the next few days, as the shape of Black John (such was his name) began to form, it had no fancy clothes or Roman haircut. He worked feverishly on it, both of them did, for John was as engrossed in it as the artist. He no longer went to the ale-house, so they worked at night too, sometimes all night, until it was finished. It was Black John all right, but not the one with the blurry eyes, the Roman clothes and the Roman hair-cut. It was a naked native freed from vulgarities and excesses, a spiritual figure transpiring through its casing of black skin. Nothing but man in his essence: ancient as dreaming, as new as a dream. It fused so well with its surroundings as to appear almost transparent. But a pair of fiery, bloodshot eyes confronted you with an inscrutable mystery. They blazed over a stark background in which he was both slave and revered master.

In all this, even Iscar discerned something noble.

As for John, his expression was the same as that of Filippo Grassi when he had looked at his finished portrait. But unlike the Sicilian, he did not sob or embrace Manuel. His only gesture was to scratch the nape of his head, as if his mind were trying to unearth a memory out of a long-buried past.

XII

At The Strip

The Strip was a place of excesses: extreme ugliness rubbed thighs with refined beauty. There, among street-walkers, artists and opium-takers, our young hero spent many months, coming face-to-face with life's more strongly delineated features.

Into this hedonist cauldron, simmering with life, the young man plunged himself with typical enthusiasm and lack of reserve. He loved The Strip, he loved its people: weak, self-indulgent, romantic and introspective. They, in turn—the pimps, the junkies and the artists—soon discovered the spirit in the young man. His portrait of John, and above all the change it seemed to have wrought on the native's behaviour, brought Manuel a fame verging on idolatry. The Strip dwellers, more than any other people, had to have idols for life to be bearable.

Manuel spent the days in his room, re-named the Blackshop because of John's portrait which made it famous, and because its previous dweller had painted the entrance black. He repainted it, in bright colours of green, orange and ochre, and when his friends criticised it he replied:

'I want to recapture some of the freshness of my village.'

Iscar, whose pleasures could only be of a vicarious nature, often sat outside the little shop watching The Strip pulsating with life. One evening his roving eye caught sight of a graceful youth going by and wriggling his well-rounded buttocks with understandable pride. Iscar's faded heart revived.

'Ganymede, is that you?' he gasped, his voice chocked with emotion.

The young man swung around. He was indeed a divine looking thing, with lovely, baby-blue eyes, flawless skin and a mane of curls crowning his head in captivating elegance.

Heavy tears of nostalgia—and frustration no doubt—ran down the wrinkled old face as Iscar embraced his friend.

'My lovely boy, how good to see you again. What happened to you?'

Ganymede, as he informed his old tutor, was doing quite nicely, thank you. By day he was at Ivory Tower studying comparative anatomy, at night he frequented a few select clubs on The Strip, and in between he cultivated the friendship of several influential knights, including the fiery Sir Marc Martial. A busy boy indeed! And by the sound of it enjoying every minute. Iscar was jealous, despite himself. It was evident that Ganymede's heart was too fickle to remain constant to any one person. And once more the old philosopher was compelled to accept stoically life's sad realities.

'And your father, Sir Bart, has he forgiven me?'

'Who daddy? Oh, he is insufferable, the silly old thing. I couldn't bear his nagging any longer so I took off and have never gone back. Now he goes around saying he'll disinherit me.'

To Iscar's amazement, Ganymede shrugged off the whole thing as quite unimportant. Clearly money did not have the same import for the young man as it did for Iscar. But then, thought he, that's a consequence of being a heavenly-looking youth, for whom rich knights were ready to commit plenty for an hour of his time; whilst for an ageing eunuch getting by was a daily challenge.

'And what philosophy do you follow now, dearest Ganymede,' Iscar asked.

Ganymede's face lit up, not in homage to philosophy but to anatomy, which was more in his line, for his eyes had just set on Manuel.

'Wow,' he cried, 'and who is this scrumptious creature?'

'Come into my workshop,' said Manuel, 'I would like to paint you.'

Hardly had Manuel got the words out than Ganymede's garments had dropped down to his feet and his naked body—which may well have served as a model for Michelangelo's David, as it is of that very period that Iscar's diary narrates—was ready to be immortalised by Manuel's brush.

Ganymede became a regular visitor to Manuel's workshop, which was soon to be a meeting-place of The Strip's artists, entertainers and raconteurs. Among these was Lusty Simon Spurioschenko the self-conscious, middle-aged 'literatus', who wrote poetry whenever he was sober, which wasn't very often. He and others spent entire nights in the workshop and even when they were not addressing Manuel they were performing for him.

What drew them to him none could tell, or at least each would have given different reasons. Some even denied it, as a matter of defence. Perhaps in that chaotic environment of The Strip, Manuel appeared as real, accessible and solid as the stones they saw by the roadside. They observed this strength in the sure strokes of his arms weaving an invisible filament as he spoke; in the stillness of his eyes; in his sense of the absurd causing him to burst into rich, reassuring, contagious laughter. Most likely they came to find their own sense of uniqueness, which seemed to surface as they came into contact with him.

'You know, Iscar,' said Manuel, 'I will always be grateful to you for guiding me to this city. I know now that beauty has an infinite number of faces.'

'Beauty is in the eye of the beholder, as the great philosopher says. But tell me, Squire, how can you bear their endless prattle? It has no meaning.'

'That's not so, Iscar, they have meaning, the people,' he paused, 'you know, their chatter is who they are. Talk is never meaningless.'

Such simplicity confused the old philosopher, accustomed as he was to discuss great disciplines of thought.

XIII

Professor Thomas Equinus

There was one learned man in Southfalia City whose brilliant eloquence would have soon raised the pathless little phrases of our inarticulate hero to the heights of grand rhetoric—had he been there to do it. But, of course, it's pure nonsense to suggest that such a great man would be found in a place like The Strip.

Professor Thomas Equinus, Professor of Histrionics and Humanist, often sat by a lofty window of Ivory Tower, gazing over his intellectual realm with an expression of calm contemplation. He watched the soft fern-leaves fanned by the light breeze, followed the ribbons of sunlight slice through the naked trees, whose shadows wove an intricate pattern on the matted green lawns. He studied his colleagues, who strolled in intelligent engrossment; spotted a bald-headed one wrestling over some knotty intellectual problem with a pretty blond, in the seclusion of a bower; yonder still by the pond, patterned with quivering reflections, students exercised their faculties by aiming a ging with studious intensity at the goldfish, while another group clumped underneath the scented frangipani, passed around an opium pipe, and seemed well on the way to achieving intellectual sublimation.

From all of this the onlooker would no doubt deduce that things could not have been better for Professor Equinus, in that luckiest spot of the Lucky Isle. Not so, alas!

In actual fact all was not well with the great Humanist. For some time now his heart had been saddened, his pride stung, his will for academic pursuit impaired, and all because, like so many great men of genius, he felt misunderstood, misinterpreted, undervalued and unrecognised by his contemporaries.

ANTONIO CASELLA

As a young man he had dreamt of wearing the laurel crown by the age of thirty-six like the great Petrarch. To that end he set out to compose his great Latin epic, 'Africa et Asia', followed by a treatise, 'De Vulgari Inconsequentia,' and capped by the mammoth philosophical critique called 'Metaphysical Nemesis of Thomist 'Essentia'.' The three volumes were thoroughly researched and beautifully bound in leather, with captions in gold letters; ornately hung, with critical accolades from his academic colleagues, and totally ignored by the reading public. Within months works which had taken years to research and compile had lapsed rapidly into oblivion. There was no doubt in the Professor's mind that posterity would eventually discover their true worth. Perhaps like Dante, who was not as smart as his younger colleague, Professor Equinus would wear his crown posthumously. But in the meantime he had to put up with irreverence, even derision, from lesser mortals. Worse still, he could see the Vice-Chancellorship of Ivory Tower going to one of them.

Then, Professor Equinus had an inspiration. If genius alone failed to bring him deserved recognition then he would have to resort to a 'coup de grace' to impress the right people. And the Professor knew exactly what would do the job: a life-sized portrait of himself in formal academic attire, celebrating the physical forms of those intellectual attributes inherent in his great works. Yes, properly conceived, a portrait could not fail to bolster his chances.

Take the present Vice-Chancellor, a proper imbecile to be sure, yet his portrait, where it hung in the Great Hall, alongside the great *illuminati*, shone with reflected light.

Having conceived the idea proved to be only the beginning of his worries. Artists were non-existent in Southfalia. No man was mad enough to spend thankless hours at a canvas, when he could make a fortune speculating on land or exporting precious stones. The two or three compulsive *dilettanti* had to give away their works, for those whose opinion counted, regarded local art, such as it was, as worthless.

One day the Professor overheard Andrew Ganymede rave about Manuel' work. His heart leaped, but only to sink again when he discovered that the man in question was not a recognized artist from abroad. A Professor could not compromise his position by posing for a local dabbler! In the end, however, enthusiastic reports about the young artist from various sources convinced Professor Equinus to take a chance.

XIV

At Ivory Tower

When Andrew Ganymede came with the request from Professor Equinus for a portrait, Iscar was so excited that he jumped up and kissed the lovely youth on the lips. But Manuel did not share the enthusiasm. The prospect of leaving The Strip did not please him.

'I cannot afford the time to go to Ivory Tower. I have so much to do here.'

'Whatever are you saying Squire! This is the golden opportunity we've longed for. Of course we must go to Ivory Tower. You just make sure they recognize your genius. After that, Knight-House is the limit.'

Partly to please his old friend, Manuel agreed to go to Ivory Tower.

Professor Thomas Equinus sat on his great rosewood chair, capped and gowned, his figure almost blending with the high bookshelf behind him. A beautifully bound volume by the other Thomas in his hands, he waited to greet the young artist with some of Cicero's best. Professor Equinus was a firm believer in the value of first impressions.

'*Possum oblivisci qui fuerim, non sentire qui sum, quo caream honore, qua gloria?*'[3] declaimed the scholar, as the artist entered the great study, followed by Iscar.

Manuel greeted the other respectfully, but disregarded the Latin.

'What price do your portraits fetch, young man?' demanded Professor Equinus as Manuel proceeded at once to study the facial expression, the theatrical pose, the room where everything seemed carefully placed to mimic and to pretend.

'My dear Sir,' replied Iscar, 'you ask an impossible question. My young master's portraits are priceless simply because the owners never sell.'

'What school does he follow, pray?'

'Oh! various schools. Paris, Florence, Venice, the lot. But above all, he is his own school, Sir.'

'That cannot be so. Each one of us who strives to further the reaches of human intellect is tied to a tradition...' And the Professor was about to expound some great theory, but seeing the inspired absorption on Manuel's face he refrained from venting his academic windpipe.

'No,' said Manuel, as if speaking to himself, 'here it won't do. Will you sit in the garden, Sir?'

The Professor regarded the very notion un-edifying. On the other hand he was taken by the young artist's self-assurance. Besides, if his ways seemed whimsical, it might just be the workings of a genius. Outdoors, in the midst of all that unreal greenery, made up of tall, symmetrical cypresses, semi-circular ti-trees, delicate roses, masses of ivy throttling dead trunks, of moss-covered buildings, of pale wisterias and pampered ferns, of flower-beds with pansies and rose-bays; in all that stifled growth tyrannized by spade and secateurs stooped the figure of Professor Equinus. His horsy face was dulled and yellowed by too much learning and not enough sun. Only now, as the sunshine poured onto his buttery features, it brought a new glow into his myopic eyes; and a new strength stemming from curiosity and an ego as obstinate as a child's.

It was this Thomas Equinus: the man triumphant over the pompous poseur, that the portrait unearthed, and for that reason the university Dons killed it at once.

'Too informal in composition,' they decried. 'As for the figure itself, it lacks the intellectual *gravitas* of a portrait deserving of a niche in the university gallery.'

Everyone expected Professor Equinus to suffer a series of intellectual tantrums over this reception. On the contrary, he was both delighted and intrigued with the portrait and continued to study it with a glow of discovery on his cheeks. He received the official comment with a wry smile. He was neither indignant, nor offended. He seemed humble almost, perhaps a little amused.

To Manuel he said, 'Thank you young man, you have given me a lesson in sincerity. It's a luxury I can't afford. Not many can. Now at least I know its face.'

Manuel remained at Ivory Tower long enough to do two more portraits, one of Paul the Red, with whom he became very friendly despite Iscar's warnings, and one of Gabbie, leader of the Amazonic Union.

At Ivory tower, whenever the Reds chanted 'Down with the Lemonist tyrants!,' the Amazonics retorted, 'Down with the male chauvinist pigs!'

The Amazonics were females who advocated a world of 'persons'. They denied a person either feminine graces or virile forms. Their leader was a lady, pardon, a person calling herself Gab, short for Gabbie diminutive of Gabrielle. This Gab, had a prodigious talent for swearing like a trooper and for talking faster than a trooper's wife. Manuel liked the Minervan face flushed with fire and vulnerability.

'Hell, a mere male to do my portrait,' she exploded when the young man suggested it, 'not on your bloody chauvinist life. You'd have me all done up like a hare-brained twit.'

Nevertheless she agreed to sit for him and by the time the portrait was finished, after much swearing and imprecations on her part, she was impressed and swore, many times over, that Manuel was the only decent person among all the male chauvinist pigs.

XV

Doctor Leonard Roguefort (Ph. D.Cantab.)

Whilst Manuel was at Ivory Tower, its ever-simmering intellectual pot-pourri was further fermented by the arrival from abroad of an exciting, young academic of world fame: the illustrious Doctor Leonard (Ph.D. Cantab.), exponent of an entirely novel philosophical direction called 'Inverted Logic', or, if you prefer 'upside-down thinking'.

According to that unique genius, the traditional structure of logic had become obsolete, and was being superseded by a new way of reasoning, simpler and more instinctive: Inverted Logic. The way to this fresh realm of pure thought was first of all by means of ten gold pieces. If you had that kind of money, then the privilege of listening to Doctor Leonard Roguefort (Ph.D. Cantab.) was yours, and an entirely new dimension of human intellect was opened to you. We, of course, have access to the precious philosophy at no cost, thanks to Iscar who managed to go and listen to the great man through an invitation from Professor Equinus.

The ingenuity of Inverted Logic, like all revelations of pure genius, lies in its very simplicity. Here is an example straight from the horse's mouth. No, not Professor Equinus, but the Doctor himself.

'Three travellers staying at an inn fell victim to a thief who demanded their purse. The first complied without a word, the second tried to resist and was struck down, while the third put on a bold face and asked the thief for money to pay for his lodgings. The thief soon recovered from amazement, laughed heartily and gave him the money.

And there you have it, gentlemen, Inverted Logic saved the young man's life and his purse.'

'Tell me, Sir,' asked Iscar, 'what if a traveller was unfortunate enough to strike a thief devoid of good humour, who reacted by beating is logic out of him, took his money and left him lying a bundle of broken bones? What then, Sir?'

Doctor was not one to be lost for words—he was not a Ph.D. Cantab for nothing! 'I very much doubt, Sir, that the poor fellow would be in a condition to refute the efficacy of Inverted Logic.' The good doctor paused, enjoying the peal of laughter that his joke had provoked, then proceeded, 'I would not be so presumptuous to claim for Inverted Logic a status of infallibility. No philosophy ever is, nor should it purport to be.'

Then there was the case of a shy young knight with a rather delicate problem.

On his recent return from the Crusade he discovered that his key no longer fitted the lock of his young wife's chastity belt. Should he ask the blacksmith to make another key or cut away the belt? Both solutions involved violating the privacy of the lady in question. Which one would Inverted Logic recommend?

'Neither,' replied Doctor promptly, 'Inverted Logic has the perfect solution to the problem: the knight must learn the blacksmith's lovemaking skills and in future send the latter to the Crusade, whilst he stays at home.'

Towards the end, a cheerful little man in a red felt cap asked permission to speak. To everyone's amusement he produced an egg from his pocket.

'Please, *Dottore*, I have one question for you: how you make dees egg stand on de end?' He spoke with an emphatic foreign accent, aided by theatrical gestures. The Doctor pondered over the question, then proceeded to expound some theory by which he proved that no philosophy could reverse Nature's laws.

'Please *Dottore*,' interrupted the other, 'spare me all de *filosofia*, it hurt my nerves. I show you how is done.' He leapt to the front in the guise of a pixie, raised the egg up to the audience like a magician before the trick, then tried several times to make it stand. The egg kept on rolling down on its side.

The crowd laughed. He then tapped one end of the egg on the table and cracked it. The egg stood on its end. The crowd wavered for a moment, then broke into a mixed reaction of cheers and laughter.

'Ecco *Dottore*, see? De egg stands,' said he with a cheery, roguish grin.

'I congratulate you, Sir,' said Doctor , 'you have learned how to apply the principles of Inverted Logic with commendable speed. May I have the pleasure of your acquaintance?'

'I am Cristoforo Colombo from Genova, by your leave.'

' What is the area of your study, Sir?'

'Eggs.'

'Splendid! And at which university, may I ask?'

'I am not a great *Dottore* like you, only a poor sailor. And I want to voyage to India by inverted logic, sailing west.'

But Doctor was listening no more, for a Ph.D. Cantab. debated only with other Ph.D.'s or M.A.'s at the very least. It was bad for business to fraternize with a Genoese madcap, whose plan to reach India due west had made him the laughing stock of Ivory Tower's shiniest-scalped intelligentsia.

Cristoforo came to visit Manuel in his Ivory Tower workshop. He took a side glance at the young artist and his art, gave out a whistle and said:

'*Deh! Finalmente vengo a trovar el prim uomo en questa terra*[4] You too are stranger on dis island. I see by your arte.'

'And you are no stranger to art, I see,' Manuel replied, very pleased.

The stranger made a grimace, 'For de arte I am an ass, but I know when a man put his soul in his worke.'

Manuel loved the man's inspired, genial face.

'Let me do your portrait, Messer Colombo,' he begged.

The other laughed, with untypical gentleness, judging by the strained lines on his face.

'*Niente affatto giovinetto.*[5] I need my mask of de clown for survival,' then more seriously he added, 'I have no gud news for you *giovinetto*. You put nothink between yourself and de others. Very bad! Very dangerous! We men of *fantasia* cannot let de dreams uncover us too much. More dangerous still is to bare de others to demselves.'

' What morbid fatalists these Italians!' commented Iscar after Cristoforo's departure, 'Take no notice of that, Squire. You have to be positive to succeed. Now, I believe that you're heading for a brilliant future. Why, we've had so many requests for portraits lately that we could spend years here.'

But Manuel had no intention of spending any more time at Ivory Tower, he found it stifling.

'I understood that this was a place of freedom and tolerance.'

'Indeed, Sir, in Ivory Tower you can be decadent, eccentric or plain insane and they will honour you for it. But they will not tolerate genius. *Enfin, mon ami*, I agree, I would not waste my time hanging around here. This is the kind of place, which welcomes morons and churns out plagiarists. There's more fame to be had and more money to be made outside.'

XVI

Off to the Crusade

Manuel returned to The Strip whose atmosphere he found more congenial to his art. There they lived together, the three of them: Manuel, John and Iscar, in the little ground-floor shop. John, it was soon discovered, had astounding artistic talent. He painted, carved wood beautifully and sometimes in the evening while the others talked, he composed ancient-sounding rhythms by ear. He spent a lot of time 'walkabout', sometimes he stayed the whole night and returned in the morning, very tired, depleted, calm. Sometimes too, he would bring home a hungry native child or drunken adult, and he would care for them, just as Manuel had done for him. And so they understood that he spent his nights around the streets, shanties and ale-houses helping his people.

It was a very enjoyable, productive time. Even Iscar stopped talking about returning to the West Flank. More often than not they were joined by one or several of their friends who decided to stay for a time. They worked, conversed, speculated, experimented; became flushed, boisterous, entranced; learned from one another. Above all they felt secure in Manuel's presence, now that he was back with them.

Then, one morning, while The Strip slumbered, the *Law and Order*, which generally kept away, erupted upon it, and amid screams of prostitutes and the curses of the customers, the wails of junkies and tirades by tragedy actors, they arrested all the young men to be enlisted for the war. Only the transvestites escaped.

But, what war? You might well ask. Southfalia, in fact, was at war but that was in another country, and besides it was only against the heretics of Riceland. Riceland was a swampy, malaria-infested, barbarian land to the north of the Fair Isle, whose sallow-coloured people had the gall to refuse to pay homage (and taxes) to Otto VIII, most Christian Emperor of the West. The affront was more than enough justification for the Emperor to organize a punitive holy crusade and subdue the temerarious savages. Southfalians proved their unshakeable devotion by being among the first to rush in support of the Emperor's crusade.

Naturally it was expected that the imperial standard, supported by many Christian nations, would sweep like the flood through the wild marshlands of that country, and its people either converted or crushed. But those barbarians proved more stubborn than anyone had imagined. Their cities seemed inexpugnable, their conduct on the battlefield fierce, their will indomitable; and pagans as they were, they couldn't give a Lucifer for the fact that God was on the Emperor's side.

Years passed and no amount of arms, or number of men, nor cajoling by the Emperor, nor threats of excommunication by the Pope, had prevailed over their primitive will. Now the holy Crusaders were in a dilemma. They could hardly call off the war. The Emperor's pride and Papal infallibility were at stake. So the only alternative was to send in more men, whom the Ricelanders kept on slaughtering with remarkable efficiency. The raid on The Strip, which they well knew would hardly yield good warriors, shows just how desperate the situation was at that stage. The Blackshop did not escape the raid and Manuel was taken along with the rest, but John wasn't. Natives, as we have seen, had become so rare as to deserve the classification of protected species.

The unwilling recruits were taken to a training camp where, to put them in the right frame of mind, Sir Marc Martial gave a great speech, too long to report in full, but which began something like this:

'Fellow Southfalians, your motherland wails for your arms' strength at this hour of crisis. Prostrate she stoops; her pride wounded, her glory tarnished, her dignity craving to be restored...'

SOUTHFALIA

And he went on to remind them all about their Roman heritage, the Roman eagle, Roman might, Roman glory, Roman virgins and lots of other Roman things, all of which, however, failed to impress those unpatriotic bedouins, who would have much preferred that Sir Marc took all his Roman stuff elsewhere and let them return to their decadent lifestyle at The Strip.

Things did not improve when the actual training began. They complained about the food, the coarseness of the linen, the hardness of the beds and most of all the unearthly hour at which they were forced to rise. As for making them wear an armour, there was just no chance. They simply fell down under its weight and refused to get up. Poor old Sir Marc was nearly driven insane and cursed the day when such a mob of shameless cowards came before him.

The sole exception was Manuel, who lacked neither strength nor the self-discipline required of him, and since he believed his country was in grave danger, naturally he didn't wish to shy away from his responsibilities. So he trained hard and did exactly what was required of him, until he realized that he would have to go abroad to fight. This defied his simple country logic. He could see how a man had a responsibility to fellow citizens, if they were being threatened, but failed to understand why he should have to go and attack someone else's country to defend his own.

'Tell me, Sir Marc, how can the Ricelanders pose a threat when there are many seas separating us,' he asked.

'Because, Sir, we are Lemonist Christians and they are Pagan Reds. Ours is the resplendent colour of the sun, of gold, of God's own light. Theirs is the colour of evil, of blood, hell's fire. And it is our duty, indeed our God-given mission to destroy all evil from the face of the earth.'

Manuel was more confused than ever, he really could not understand these subtleties of colour. His simple logic told him that if Southfalia sent men to fight in a foreign country that made them the invaders. Moreover, he thought, that if all young men refused to fight outside their own country, then there could be no invasions and therefore no wars between nations. Having come to this conclusion, he decided not to go to Riceland and informed Sir Marc of the same.

'Do you refuse to serve your country, young man?' roared Sir Marc, his bushy mustachios bristling.

'I cannot go away and kill in the service of anyone, or anything, Sir.'

Sir Marc was speechless.

'But…that's sedition. Do you know that?'

Manuel didn't see it that way, but there was no point in arguing. His silence only served to further incense the knight.

'Do you wish to lose your life, young man?'

'Certainly not, Sir, I love life, and that's the other reason why I don't wish to go Riceland.'

'Listen here, young Squire,' said Sir Marc, barely containing his rage, 'because you've shown yourself to be a man of courage and strength, in short, a natural-born warrior, I will give you a few days to get over this madness. If you act sanely then, there is no doubt that you will do your country credit. However, if you persist in this act of treason, then Sir Herod will make such an example of you, that no one in future will dare try the same thing.'

He was taken to a dark cell where amid the screaming of other prisoners, the sound of rats running in the darkness and the frightening prospect of having to face Sir Herod, Manuel pondered on his decision.

It would be wonderful if we could say that the young man faced his destiny with calm fortitude. In reality he was very much afraid of what was to come, and more than once he was tempted to call the guard and return to Sir Marc penitently. But terrified though he was, the more he thought about it, the more certain he became that the decision he had taken was the right one. If there was any justice—and Manuel fervently believed there was—then the man who followed his conscience must ultimately triumph. This thought calmed his mind enough to allow him to fall asleep.

SOUTHFALIA

During the night he dreamed. All around him the air was thick with exotic scents wafting from a lovely rose garden, in the middle of which stood a little old house. Its door stood ajar and from within a fine hand beckoned to him. Manuel, however, fearing something evil, refused to move. He called out to the lady to let him be.

He woke with his head drunk with perfume, and a voice whispering to him, a voice like a song that came from afar. It was a woman's voice. He took a couple of deep breaths to reassure himself that he was awake. In the dark he could not see her, but he recognized the scent, the voice and the touch of her hand upon his. There was no mistake, it was Madam Magdalene.

'Listen carefully and don't speak,' she commanded, 'I've arranged for your escape this very night. A vessel's waiting to sail you off to some far off land, but you won't be able to ever return to us. Or if you wish, you can go to Riceland, not as a soldier, but as a member of a peace mission that's due to leave very soon. Which do you choose, Sir?'

Oh, what luck to be loved by a Madam! She obviously lacked no friends in high places! Imagine being on the verge of the most terrible tortures and to be given a choice of escapes.

Manuel chose the second, not merely out of gratitude for the good-hearted Magdalene, whom he planned to recompense at some later date, but also because he loved Southfalia and loved his friends and he didn't wish to part with either forever.

Iscar came to farewell him.

'Goodbye, Squire, and don't worry, this may yet prove to be a blessing in disguise. You are young, strong and courageous, go and earn as many medals as they can pin on your chest. That's one way to earn a knighthood. As for me, should I survive until your return, I will serve you well once again. So, *in bocca al lupo*.[6]

XVII

A New Sheep for the Flock

The so-called peace mission turned out to be something quite different from what Manuel had imagined. Apparently pious optimists had been suggesting for some time the sending of a party of missionaries to Riceland to spread the good word, hoping that religious fervour might triumph where force had failed. And so Manuel found himself accompanying the missionaries, who needed a strong young man to carry their things. They also hoped that his darker skin might work to soften the initial resistance of the savages towards the fair-coloured missionaries.

On arrival, they set out at once for the wild interior, travelling for months through thick jungle and marshlands, encountering every now and again remains of villages which had been burnt down or ransacked. Not a soul to be seen alive, for the crusaders were known to do a thorough job.

They arrived at a village called Yu-Lai. The fire was still smouldering in the dampness of the jungle, the smoke billowed indolently to the sky: terrestrial offering to the heavens in the aftermath of a recent battle, and from the trees the carrion birds swooped down onto the sacrificial corpses in a frenzy of feasting.

The missionaries knelt down to pray for souls of the dead, just in case there were any Christians among them, because in that desolation of mud and ash, skin colour and racial features were no longer distinguishable. While the missionaries prayed Manuel inspected the village. His face, once serene, had the pallor of death, and his eyes were cavities to a nightmare. All about him were remnants of bodies half-eaten, half-crushed, smeared with a paste made of ash and blood, like grotesque wax-figures in a charred pyre. From the remnants of a hut came a feeble whimper, like the sound of a dying wolf. Trapped in it was a woman with a child to her sunken breast. Manuel rushed to her with his water-sac.

'To her, to her,' she whined, taking the baby from her nipple. The child's head swivelled back to the nipple that was yellowed and ulcered for having abided too long inside a dead mouth. For days she had nursed her, clasping the inert body close to the palpitations of her heart, finding signs of life in the faint tremor of a tuft of hair, unfurled by the breeze. Now the presence of another live being gave death too strong a delineation to be denied. She let the tiny body slip down her side, while her own frame, no longer held rigid by the nerves of a lie, fell limp.

Manuel freed her from the log, her legs were crushed and burned. He poured water over them, gave her a drink, washed her. Then she became responsive and told her story in broken, but good Southfalian, which she had learned from her Southfalian lover, father of the dead child.

The story was often incoherent and broken by long pauses, but then, details were superfluous when the sight all around was eloquent witness to it. When the village was taken, all red banners were ripped down and replaced with the cross of the Crusaders. One morning a red flag was found on top of the commanding officer's tent: a bull-like type called Brutus Callous, who was naturally furious at the affront and swore publicly by the Almighty that he would punish the culprit before the day's end. All the suspects were brought to him and the interrogation began, but although he tortured them until they died, none would own up. Driven by frustration and rage he rounded up all the villagers and had them slain, assuring himself in this manner that his vow to God had been kept, and the honour of the Crusaders avenged. The woman and her child escaped the slaughter by hiding in one of the huts, but were trapped inside when the Crusaders decided to finish off the job properly by burning the village.

Having finished her story the woman slumped back and fainted. The missionaries, meanwhile, their prayers done, came looking for

Manuel and when they discovered that the woman was still living they were filled with joy. At last they would be able to administer the baptismal rite and bring their first pagan to the fold. The head missionary, a man of rubicund features and sky-blue eyes, put on his robe and started the ceremony.

'Pardon me, Holy Father,' interrupted a young novice.

'What is it my son?'

The head missionary tried hard not to betray his vexation at this untimely interjection. The young man flashed a decorous glance at the woman's bare breast.

'Should not the new sheep be modestly clad before she enters the house of Our Lord?' asked he, blushing down to his pious pink lips.

'Indeed my son,' replied the head missionary, with a grateful smile perspiring down to his wholesome white neck; and after covering the offending breast, they proceeded with the ceremony.

The woman meanwhile came to, and seeing the strangely robed figure leaning over her, became hysterical.

'See, dear brothers,' said he to his companions, 'she's possessed by the devil. He always chooses to abide in the weakest bodies.'

The woman was certainly weak. She was now delirious; with each spasm she bled more from her side, and soon she would bleed herself out of life. Manuel tried to pacify her, while the missionary first exorcised, then baptized her. But though her spiritual gain may have been great, neither ritual managed to relieve her of her physical agony and she wailed intermittently.

'Well, brothers,' said the head missionary, 'we have saved one soul, but let's not sit here complacently. We will journey forth to where many more desperate souls are crying for salvation, just as this new Lamb of God did.'

'Do you mean…leave her?' protested Manuel.

'There's little else we can do now. Hopefully she will be in Purgatory before night comes. As for us, we came here on a mission. Each minute lost will make our quest more arduous.'

It began to rain, pouring down as it does in that land. The woman awoke, her face contorted in the rain. She beckoned for Manuel to come near and tried to say something, but could not. Her bony arm rose slightly reaching for something on his hip: the curved jungle knife, which Manuel handed to her without hesitation.

'Grab it off her!' cried the head missionary, horrified, 'can't you see that she intends to kill herself!' And seeing that Manuel wasn't going to act, he rushed to the dying woman, but Manuel, who was quicker, held him firmly back, while she, with a strength driven by agony, sliced her own throat. The missionaries were beside themselves.

'You've let her take her own life,' said the head missionary in disbelief, 'now she'll go to hell and all our work was for nothing. Why, don't you know that only an inquisitor, a soldier, a judge and God can take a person's life?'

Manuel felt that as far as his own life is concerned, a man ought to be in that select group too. Anyway, he had seen enough to put him off pious quests for good, whereupon they parted company.

The missionaries did not stay to bury the woman.

'It would mean a further unnecessary delay,' they explained, 'Unnecessary because it's a sin to bless the corpse of a suicide.'

XVIII

His Finest Hour

We must leave the path of adventure trodden by our hero and return to the Fair Isle to record a very special event. Southfalians did not indulge in festivals and celebrations, unless it was in honour of some great man or battle. Most important among these was the day commemorating the massacre of Pappagallis, in which thousands of young Southfalian men perished trying to capture a fortress by the same name in some far-off land.

Dawn broke, on that day, upon the Midas Square in an atmosphere of intense and decorous formality, attended by organized files of chesty men of war, venerable old soldiers, and splendidly decorated knights on horseback. Floating over proceedings was the Patrician voice of the Governor Sir Isaac, intoning a most moving speech, equating the valorous massacre to the immortal Greek Leonidas and his thousand heroes. What joy to behold! The Midas came aglow faintly, as if reluctant to disturb the sea of soldiers with impassive, solemn expressions, while bugles played Land of Wealth and Glory. It was enough to stir a coward's heart onto foreign soil, to fight any foe.

Sir Marc was there, of course, as was his friend Sir Herod—scourge of thieves, adulterers, and Reds—munching away at peanuts. Yes, peanuts! In the north of Southfalia they all grew bananas, except Sir Herod, who would have none of that phallic symbol. He devoted his lands to growing peanuts, to which he himself became addicted. In moments of tension, he devoured peanuts in voluminous quantities as a substitute for torturing victims.

After the dawn service, it was traditional for the high-ranking officers to head for the Golden Lemon, where the latest news and opinions on the war were discussed, and if you were really lucky you might find a place in Sir Marc Martial's select group for expert assessment of the war situation. But let's first read what Iscar has to say about this extraordinary man:

'Stories of this knight's heroism are too many to recount. Suffice it to mention that even such expansive front as he possesses, cannot accommodate all the medals and crosses, badges and ribbons—to say nothing of the many a great swords—accumulated over a lifetime of service in the defence of war. It is said that he keeps life-size wax busts of himself, on which to attach the lesser spoils won on the great battlefields of our age.'

As Sir Marc strode into the Golden Lemon, all eyes turned to him with due reverence. For this was his day, as everyone could tell by his sombre, resolute expression, by the splendid glitter of his iron chest, by his ostrich-feathered helmet, worthy even of divine Achilles.

Like a man accustomed to creating an aura of admiration all about him wherever he went, Sir Marc threw up his hand in sign of recognition in the direction of one or two prominent knights, then strode stiffly to the head group where everyone made room for him. In a husky soldier's voice ordered a goblet of ale which he downed in one prodigious gulp, to the delight of all. Finally he wiped away the froth from his luxuriant mustachio and ordered a refill. He could not have made a more splendid entrance.

A stranger could well be excused for thinking that Sir Marc was the biggest man he had ever encountered, such was the power of his bearing and of his voice. In fact, on close inspection, he was quite short, though what he lacked in height he compensated for in roundness.

Soon there was around him a sizeable audience, enthralled as he recounted some deed out of his glorious past. And the noble actions could not find better expression than that voice and that face. Rosy-cheeked, puffy-browed and shiny-eyed; his pomaded mustachio twitched stiffly to the resonance of the words. Often at a crucial point he would interrupt his story to down another pint, inviting his listeners to do likewise.

'And so it was, gentlemen, that we saved our Christian *Condottiero* from the hands of the pirating Moroccan dog and escorted him safely back to Genoa.'

Amid the cheers and gasps of admiration, someone asked him how he came to be in possession of that unusual-looking sword which he carried always with him.

'This, Sir, is no common sword, but a scimitar once hanging from the flank of the famous Abdul Caliphant Eliphant, surnamed *El Vampiro* by the Spaniards. I met him in mortal combat during the siege of Granada, whilst in the service of the Most Christian Ferdinand.

'We were camped outside that city, when one morning came the surprise attack led by the savage *El Vampiro* himself. I was then in my tent taking a meal with a promising young soldier. Hearing the commotion I rushed outside practically naked—as there was no time for putting on clothes, let alone my armour—and there before me in Moorish flesh was *El Vampiro* himself, scourge of mighty Christian warriors.

'Experience told me that my only recourse was to seize the initiative. So I gave a tremendous roar, the like of which was not heard on a battlefield since Haladin, enough in any case to terrify the horse which neighed, reared, convulsed and shook *El Vampiro*, down on the dust and galloped off berserk as if taken by the devil.

'With lightning speed, I was on top of the mighty infidel, drew his scimitar that had slain so many Christian warriors and smote him thus,' concluded Sir Marc drinking down another pint.

This was received with thunderous cheers and cries of 'Hear! Hear!' and a new round of drinks was called for. Then Sir Marc began to muse aloud. 'Ah, Gentlemen! No doubt about it, those were the days of adventure, of daredevil feats and undaunted courage. Now we've become soft-bellied. These pith-less Ricelanders should have been subdued long ago. In a flash!'

When he was asked how soon he thought the Ricelanders would be crushed, Sir Marc's tough face gave a pained expression, he sighed and drank deeply.

'Not soon enough. It's those up top you know, blunting the whole thrust of the crusade, blocking the soldier's path to glory. Too much division, too much irresolution. Time and time again, I've said this dilly-dallying will do nothing to subdue the stubborn foe. We just give it time to lick its wounds and bark us back into retreat. Meanwhile we keep losing men, arms, horses, and most of all our glorious reputation. Since we've set out to do the job, there is only one way: storm in there with metal and fire, and raze the lot to the ground. Never you mind what the world will or won't say, all the world loves a winner, and when all is said and done, the world will be only too happy to applaud our triumph.'

Again the applause came crushing down, accompanied by a chorus of 'quash the pagan dogs!', followed by a series of toasts, the first to the Most Christian Emperor

Otto VIII capped by a rousing chorus of 'God bless our Fairest Roman Soil' sung with great passion and gusto, albeit not exactly in harmony.

When the singing subsided, fresh pints were ordered to quench the hoarse throats, whereupon a timid young lad approached the group and appeared keen to say something. He was a thin young man with nervous eyes, pug nose and pimples, all of which made him appear even more conspicuous in the midst of mature knights, oozing self-confidence and virility with their close-razored cheeks, trimmed whiskers, round bellies and feathered helmets.

Always the great soldier, Sir Marc was tough and yet he was also gallant and chivalrous, ever prompt to rush to the aid of young lads in distress.

'Come, young squire,' urged he with an encouraging nudge, 'what is it you wish to say? Speak out your heart, don't be afraid, this is a free country. Oh, you're a shy one!'

Sir Marc stroked the smooth nape of the youth's neck ever so gently. But all to no avail, the ungrateful youth winced away haughtily.

SOUTHFALIA

'Stand up and defeat your shyness boy, or you'll never be a brave soldier. Come, say your piece,' he commanded, ordering a pint of frothing ale for him, 'Here boy, drink this, it'll put hairs on your chest.'

The youth tried to dodge the persistent stroke of Sir Marc's hand and refused to drink, but finally gathered up courage to speak.

'I was wondering about what you said before, you know, storming into Riceland and that...Well, wouldn't it be better for everyone to leave them alone and recall our men?'

A shadow began to show on Sir Marc's Mercurian features, while the feathers on his helmet hissed.

'What's that you say, boy?'

His tone portended little good.

'I mean,' continued the rash youth, I mean...after all, if they don't want to be converted it's their jolly business.'

Sir Marc drained the contents of his goblet at lightning speed and put it down with a bang.

'What is it you do, boy?'

'I'm a scholar, Sir.'

'A scholar, hey! And pray what is it you scholarize in?'

'I study philosophy.'

'Philosophy, hey! And pray which philosophy do you phil... phil...philophize in?'

'Why, the ancients: Plato, Aristotle...'

This was too much for the proud soldier.

'Just as I thought, one of them pagan heretics,' roared he, crimson with rage, 'the Holy Bible, Saint Augustine, Saint Thomas are not good enough for you, hey? You prefer the teachings of pagan heretics, hey? There, gentlemen, there you have the canker that rots our society! There's the worm that feeds on cowardice and turns to discontent! When I was his age, I was on the plains of Abyssinia fighting through my third war, and mark you this, the point of my lance had pricked the flesh of more infidels than I could count. This gutless little scum spends his time reading books. And what's the good of books? I ask you. Books never won wars. Books never made a great soldier, nor earned a single medal on the battlefield neither. Books indeed! Come with me you cowardly corruptor of our fighting spirit,' cried Sir Marc, seizing the youth by the cape of his cloak and dragging him towards the door, 'I'll put you on the first ship to Riceland, or else by the god Mars, and mighty Jupiter and fiery Vulcan too, I'll see to it that your mouth will not utter another sound.'

And as he dragged the bedraggled youth, Sir Marc was suddenly seized by a strange contortion, he gasped, brought his hands to his throat, his mouth opened wide and…oh dear! Here our friend Iscar gives a detailed description of what follows; however, in deference to the delicate stomachs of the modern readers and Sir Marc's pride, we'll omit all detail. Suffice it to say that all those badges and medals, crosses and ribbons were splattered all over with mustard substance. And if this were not humiliating enough, before he had time to recover, a further more powerful seizure overcame him, and this time Sir Marc Martial was down flat on the floor to the dismay of all present.

Poor, proud Sir Marc! The harshness of combat, it seems, can finally break even a Titan's spirit. It would have, no doubt, consoled him to know that both great Alexander and mighty Caesar were known to be victims of seizures too.

XIX

'In bocca al lupo'

Things may not have been as peaceful as one might have thought on the Lucky Isle but they were assuredly in better shape than in Riceland.

The missionaries had travelled through a depressing countryside where the only sign of life was corpses, burning and devastation. Finally, one day, through a clearing, appeared a native village whose huts were still standing and, by the sound of children's voices, inhabited by living beings.

The missionaries stood by nervously as half-dressed savages approached with their lances, cautiously at first then, reassured that the newcomers were unarmed, they became excited. They confabulated in their language, as others joined in, attracted by the clamour. The village chieftain, Wil Choo, came forward, approaching with confidence, smiling even, through his strong sharp teeth as he compared the bodies of the fair-skinned, well-nourished missionaries with their own thin, sallow ones.

Encouraged by such interest, the missionaries got down to business at once with fervour and efficiency. Producing icons and crosses, they took turns to deliver some impressive sermons, confident that where language could not reach, mysticism would. They accompanied their words with telling gestures, frequent signs of the cross, beating their heart in vicarious repentance, rising pious eyes upwards and inviting the villagers to do likewise. These continued to take it all with interest and with increasingly pleased stares, while the missionaries rounded off the sermons with a few psalm verses, which they sang with the nervous excitement of choir boys singing their first mass.

Little did they imagine, the well meaning souls, the cruel fate that was awaiting them, or else they would have at least chosen less rousing verses!

'Be not far from me, for trouble is near. For there is none to help.'
'Many bulls have compassed me.'
'I am poured out like water, and all my bones are out of joint.'

The chanting created a buzz through the crowd. The elder men deliberated, the younger approved, children raced around joyfully as everyone's eyes shone in pleasurable anticipation.

Taking all this as signs of imminent conversion, the missionaries hurried to set up a makeshift font in readiness for mass baptism. I won't attempt to describe their shock when, in a sudden change of mood, the savages produced long, sharp knives, tied all the missionaries up, then seized the fattest—who happened to be the head missionary—and proceeded to put into effect their macabre design. They killed him as if he were a fat pig, chopped him up into a cauldron, cooked him and treated themselves to a meal of man-soup before the very eyes of the other prisoners, most of whom died of terror before suffering the same unfortunate end.

Consider the cruel irony of life: to set out with all pious intentions to save a man's soul, only to finish up in his cooking-pot as nourishment to his body!

XX

Among the Cannibals

Having given proper burial to the woman and her child, Manuel started on the road back to the coast, carrying with him a heavy heart. In his mind, paralysed by horror, there hovered only one thought: to return to Southfalia and tell everyone of his experiences in the hope that it would turn them against the Crusade.

But Fate had reserved more tribulations for him; for just then up the thick jungle track appeared a company of Crusaders who accused him of deserting and gave him such a hiding that would have all but finished a normal man. Then they tied him to a tree trunk and left him there to die at the mercy of mosquitoes, snakes and other beasts of the jungle. Paradoxically it was these which saved his life, especially the mosquitoes, whose relentless stings continuously put to test his strength and miraculous will to live.

How long he lasted this way no one knows. Some days must have passed, for when tribesmen found him and took him to the village, the people were cooking the last of the missionaries.

Some days later Manuel awoke to an excited gibberish, reaching his hut from the centre of the village. He was too ill to make any sense of it, but he had the distinct impression of hearing the voice of his faithful friend Iscar.

'Illness can cause some curious hallucinations', thought he, in semi-conscious stupor.

When Manuel had recovered enough to learn of the hair-raising experience of the missionaries, he was overcome by pity and horror directed at all involved in that macabre victual. Soon, however, pity and horror took a more poignant direction as he realized that his own scalp might well find itself in the cooking pot at the next cannibalistic orgy.

However the village chief decreed that Manuel could not be chopped up in his sick state for fear that he might carry diseases, the cannibals took no health risks.

So began a period of convalescence which Manuel, knowing what was coming at the end, was not in a hurry to see pass. Never has a man been less inclined for his body to heal than Manuel was. Helping him to recover was the chief's daughter: a lovely creature with fleshy lips, flawless, zinc-coloured skin and two cups of breasts capped by large brown nipples. Lyn (such was her name) had been educated in the city, changed her name to Lina and regarded her father, who doted on her, with haughty disdain. Lina tried to comfort her terrified prisoner.

'They will not touch you yet. You are unwell', she said by way of encouragement. 'Besides, they have since captured a new batch of missionaries and there are still a few of those left.'

This was hardly any consolation for the young man, especially as he knew that the brief reprieve he was enjoying was being gained on the flesh of other unfortunates. Nevertheless he was relieved that the cannibals' hunger was temporarily appeased and their patience extended.

Being civilized, Lina naturally abhorred cannibalism, despite the fact that, indirectly, it allowed her to have more rice to herself; and aware that Manuel was averse to man-soup, she made sure he got ample supply of rice each day.

'Anyway,' she said, 'man-soup is a delicacy for these savages. They could not let you have it unless it was plentiful, like after a battle or something like that. As it is, there are only a few bowlfuls left which are reserved for my father, the witchdoctor and the Southfalian priest.'

'A Southfalian priest among you?' asked Manuel astonished.

'Yes, one of a new batch that was captured two days after you were. The others were readily disposed of, but this particular one was found to be castrated. In the tribal lore they castrate all priests to make sure the vestal virgins stay that way.'

'So they didn't kill him?' asked Manuel.

'Not only that, but they've made him a tribal priest.'

This news nurtured the seed of suspicion already implanted in Manuel's mind.

Iscar here in Riceland! But no, how can that be? The young man pondered over it all night.

The next day Lina came accompanied by someone. Manuel's heart faltered. 'Is it you, Iscar?'

The other by way of reply threw his arms around him.

'Alas, yes, it's old Iscar right enough: misfortune's lackey.'

'But...how? Why?'

Then Iscar told his story.

'I joined a monastery thinking it to be the best way to stay alive without a patron. How was I to know that they were going to post me to this forsaken jungle? But so it happened, Squire. I had not been with them a few days when the Abbott approached me.

'You speak many languages! Indeed you must have been sent to us by the Good Lord, Brother Iscar,' says the pious *cornuto*. 'You shall accompany a small party to search for our lost brothers in Riceland.'

'*Merde!*' I thought, 'the Good Lord could leave me alone for once! But there was nothing to do. I escaped the military, and got nabbed by religion instead, *Che sfortuna balorda!*' Iscar spread his arms helplessly.

'And have you been fed on man-soup?'

'I'm a priest, they say, and I must feed on man-soup. It's either that or they'll turn me into man-soup.'

'What about the missionaries?'

'They've long passed the entrails of these savages. I would have too, if I were not a eunuch. Surely there must be hidden order in the universe, when a man comes to be glad for being without bollocks. But, *veniamo a noi Paesan*,[8] how do you hope to escape from this nightmare?'

'Oh, we'll escape, Iscar, don't doubt that.'

'How?'

'How, I don't know. But I do know that I don't hate the tribesmen. I know too that I've not done enough to die yet.'

Lina nursed the young man's bruises and rubbed his sores, while he showed his appreciation to the young woman rather skilfully, considering his state. As it inevitably happens in such cases, she fell passionately in love with him and expressed her wish to take him for a husband. Manuel had no objection to the proposal and at any rate he was hardly in a position to play hard-to-get!

After some deliberation, in which the chief was torn between feasting his stomach and providing a husband for his daughter, parental responsibility prevailed and he consented to the marriage on the condition that Manuel swear faith to Sol the Sun-God, to which Manuel had no objection, feeling that the sun was as divine an object as any. Secondly he was to prove himself a worthy member of the tribe by capturing a Crusader and bringing him to the village for general consumption at the wedding banquet.

Well, it may be easy enough to swap gods, but it is something else to change one's diet so dramatically. We don't know what he would have done had he been faced with the dilemma of choosing between death or survival on the body of some other unfortunate.

The resourceful little Lina, in collaboration with Iscar, had the answer: eloping. And the three of them drew up a plan of escape. But it wasn't necessary. As luck would have it, on the day prior to the set date the village was attacked by Crusaders, led by Brutus Callous. Manuel, his sweetheart, and Iscar were freed and the cannibals massacred.

More death, more screaming children, more wailing women, more burning, more orgies. Manuel was shattered, while Lina, who wasn't particularly proud of her people, and thoroughly fed up with that monotonous village life, got over it quickly enough to capture the heart of Brutus Callous, for whom she experienced an irresistible attraction. Brutus made love the same as he made war, violently, which apparently suited Lina very well. So at his request she became a Christian, married her new suitor and accompanied him on his trails of destruction.

PART TWO

The Prophet

XXI

The Fist Followers

Manuel and Iscar returned to Southfalia even sooner than they had hoped. The gruesome story of the missionaries, and Brutus' subsequent rescue of Manuel, reached Southfalia. As the story was passed around from person to person, it became more fantastical, the Ricelanders more savage, the feat of Brutus more glorious.

So, Brutus Callous was recalled to the Fair Isle to receive a hero's welcome, and with him came Manuel and Iscar, living witnesses of his courageous deed. The people were in the Midas Square to give them a welcome reminiscent of a general's triumphant return from a victorious campaign. All of this, of course, could not have happened without the approval of the *Law and Order* and the patronage of the knights. And what interest did these have in promoting such a welcome?

For some time there had been a growing disenchantment with the Crusade among a wide cross-section of people, embracing such diverse types as Paul the Red and the Proles, students at Ivory Tower, serfs and natives. Their peace rumbles could not fail to reach the responsive ears of those mothers and wives whose men had either been killed or were risking their lives every day in Riceland.

Sir Herod was called upon to act; arrests were made, executions were staged. In the past that would have been the end of that. But now with daily reports from Riceland of more dead, people became incensed and vocal, their fear blunted by anger. Now a few of the guilds began to give support to the pacifists, as they came to be known. Southfalia's establishment were worried.

The story of the missionaries contained all the elements of good-versus-evil so familiar to the people. It was enlarged and adapted by the Scribes, to enflame popular feeling against the Ricelanders and draw support for the Crusade.

From the raised rostrum in front of Procrustean House, Brutus struggled to give an account of the events. Unfortunately Brutus did not look a hero, less still did he speak like an orator. Evidently he was more adept at flinging screaming children in the air than in the art of rhetoric. Moreover, his hate for the Ricelanders was so intense, that he only managed to frighten the crowd.

It was left to Manuel to do the job. There were many in the Square who had known the young man and loved him. Now they were perplexed. They did not understand what connection there could be between his soulful eyes and the hate of Brutus. Could war have changed him so much? As soon as he climbed onto the platform, their fears receded. Changed he was: the eyes had lost their innocence, but not their strength. The face had aged with lines of experience, its cheerfulness was gone; in its place was a great sadness, free from rancour, but marked with determination.

'Dear, dear friends, I've seen it all; all the lambs on the sacrificial stone; and there is really nothing more to say and everything to do. We've been bleating for too long but, no more. We will tread on the tiger's tail if that's what it takes to save what's left of the lambs.'

And the people said, 'What does he mean? The poor man, the experience was too much. It crazed him.' But there were many who knew the meaning of his words.

Iscar, back from a session at the Golden Lemon where he had gone to test the mood of the Patricians, was elated.

'I've heard that many great ladies are keen to make your acquaintance. It augurs well. Some of these multi-chinned dames will pay anything to have themselves flattered in colour. At last you're on your way.'

Iscar scratched his belly gleefully, but he saw that Manuel was no longer thinking of his art. He looked absent and pensive. The youth was made man by experience.

'There is no time for painting, Iscar,' said he, 'I can no longer afford self-indulgence, not after what I have seen.'

'I told you, Squire, not to place too much stake on human happiness. You've been disillusioned eh? Do you still believe that men can be happy?'

'I believe happiness.'

'You're still young then.'

'And you must be older than you seem.'

'What about money? If you don't paint how do we eat?'

Manuel smiled.

'Follow me old man. You won't go hungry, I promise you.'

And so he started the *Peace for Life* movement and went to the most squalid parts of the city to preach.

By a fountain where women went to fill their pitchers, a crowd clamoured around a man. He was a wild-looking native with rusty feet, long beard and so thin that he must have fed on grubs, grasshoppers and tree roots. Lying inert before him were two drunken natives whom he had dragged to the fountain.

'Wake up, you black bastards,' he yelled, 'I'll take you back to dream-time land,' and he poured water over them. The drunken natives woke and, judging by their state, they were already in dream-time land.

Manuel approached and said, 'Give me a drink, John.'

Black John shuddered and turned on his lean frame. His eyes were marked by bloodlines.

'You've come back, Manuel!' John cupped his bony hands under the running water and opened them to Manuel, who drank from them. Then he ran his hands over the young man's face, with a delicate motion of his skeletal fingers. The two men were filled with love.

'You teach people,' said John.

Manuel said 'I see from the colour of the dust on your feet that you've been to the land of your fathers. I can teach them much less than you, now.'

Together they went to the harbour looking for Peter the Guildmaster who was involved in some delicate mediation between port-workers and ship-owners. Peter came out of the conference surprised not to be besieged by scribes. He wondered at the commotion around the tall young man.

'Welcome, Peter,' said Manuel, 'I've been waiting for you.'

'Do you know me, Sir?' asked the other, pleased at being recognized.

'I know you, Peter. I know all of you. Together we will feed the hungry, teach the ignorant, heal the sick; then we can begin to hope for peace.'

Stirring the port-workers was Paul the Red, whom the people had nick-named 'the Zealot'. Since he had left Ivory Tower he had spent his time waving red flags, shouting 'long live the workers', and running from Sir Herod. Hearing Manuel's words he came and joined him.

And now there were John, Peter, Paul and Iscar. They followed him as he went around country hamlets, drawing large crowds wherever he went.

As Iscar records:

'*Manuel spoke of a world free of poverty, oppression and greed; and the hearts of the people were aflame with joy and their spirit was enveloped in dreams.*'

Manuel went from village to village carrying a message of hope, inspiring the peasants to believe that one day they would be able to cultivate their own garden in peace. With them he discussed crops and animals, helped to work their land, ate of their offerings. He spoke to the people with passion.

'*If you want peace, you must believe that it's possible...*'

'*Those who believe are strong. We are gaining in strength each day..*'

'*Don't be afraid to lose a little. A man may be at his strongest when he is prepared to lose all...*'

'*Peace means more than freedom from war. It means to be in harmony.*'

The people listened and even if they didn't understand, they believed. There were, of course, the doubters.

'There'll always be wars,' they said, 'as one ends, the other will start.'

Manuel said, 'See that stone, I can fling it to wound or kill, or I can cut it to build a house, crush it into clay; use in a multitude of ways. I believe in human goodness.'

SOUTHFALIA

One report reaching the city said that an old man who had welcomed Manuel and his friends into his home, woke up the next day to find his trees laden with fruit, the hen's nest full of eggs and the cow heavy with milk.

Once he led a whole village up the stony slopes of a hillside and told them to disperse around the passes, the outcrops, the flowering broom-bushes.

'What will we do?' they asked.

'Breathe the air, drink the torrent water, look, feel, listen, let the sun saturate you, then lie back in all this immensity to dream.'

When they gathered back in the village square in late afternoon, Manuel scanned that mass and said, 'Nature teaches that there is no life without struggle, but only in peace can you give form to the energy you have.'

They travelled on, sleeping where they could. One evening they went down in a peasant's barn and Iscar complained miserably at having to sleep below the cock's roost. Hardly the kind of bed for a cultured eunuch!

'*Per Bacco*! Little do I fancy what might drop from above as I sleep!' he declared.

'Be sure to breathe through your nose, Iscar,' warned the others.

It was a night of full moon and they had not gone down half an hour, when the door opened, flooding the barn with moonlight. A hooded, stooping figure slipped in silently to where Manuel was lying and stroked his tunic.

'Who's that?' cried Manuel, waking.

The figure slipped away quickly, but Paul the Red seized the figure by the arm and dragged it back. Manuel said,

'Leave her, Paul. I know who she is. Old Mary, what do you want?'

Old Mary fell to her knees crying.

'Old Mary's dead, must be her spirit,' whispered Iscar.

'I'm no spirit, Sir.'

'What were you doing here, Old Mary?' asked Peter.

'I was going to wash Manuel's tunic in the stream down yonder.'

'You're a leper, Old Mary, would you give him your sickness.'

'No, not him, Sir,' then turning to Manuel, embarrassed, 'I believed I would be healed by your touch, Sir.'

Manuel smiled, not a happy smile.

Iscar noticed the smile and said, 'You see, Sir, I warned you about playing the Messiah. Now they'll have you perform miracles, whether you like it or not.'

'Well, I can't work miracles, Iscar, but I'll try the next best thing: love.'

He bade her to lie next to him, outside, under the full moon, as the cows ruminated. In the morning he led her down to the stream where she shed her rags, stood naked in midstream, washed her body clean, and took the sun.

Old Mary, as it turned out, was no leper. Her body was blotched by age, lack of food, sun and water. In fact leprosy did not exist on the island.

'Leprosy is a myth!' charged Paul the Red, angrily, 'perpetrated by the rulers to banish from their own homes those too old and too infirm to work.'

But peasants are never content with simple explanations. In no time news reached the city that Manuel had cured Old Mary of leprosy, and the people from Stivaletto to The Strip rose in one cheering voice.

'This is indeed the luckiest isle in the world!' they cried jubilant, 'not only have we the best beer in the world, but now we have a Prophet all our very own.'

XXII

An Urgent Meeting

News that Southfalia's countryside was fast becoming converted to the Pacifist Movement worried the Lemonist establishment. Sir Matthew, the Scribe, along with the others, cursed the day they had recalled Manuel from Riceland and thus had unwittingly contributed to his fame.

The situation became serious enough for the Aulic Council, the most powerful body on the island, to call a special meeting.

First to arrive in the splendid Aulic hall of the castle were Sir Matthew, and Sir Bart, the merchant. The latter was by now well established as the richest man on the island. It was natural, therefore, that the two should become the best of friends. Like all lasting friendships, theirs was based on mutual dependency. Also among the first to arrive were Sir Lucas, the Chief Justice, and Lady Britt Romula Augustula.

Search as you would, you could not find two more noble specimens. Fair, portly Sir Lucas had greying hair combed down Roman style, Caesarean nose, blue eyes, finest yellow skin and the kind of Latin to make Cicero envious. Add to this the fact that he was born into a dynasty of judges, that his six sons were on the way to becoming judges, his nephews were lawyers and his servants court-room ushers and you have a figure firmly entrenched like no other in the power structure of the island.

As for Lady Britt, she could trace her family tree to none other than Romulus Augustulus himself: last of the Caesars. Her forebears fled Rome to escape the Barbarians, settled in Southfalia, but behaved as if they still lived in the shadow of the Colosseum. Lady Britt too, spoke virgin Latin, understood only by those familiar with Virgil. She dressed with the austere sobriety of a Cornelia, set her hair higher than Messalina's, while her virtue was no less suspect than Caesar's wife. Her father, Sir Romulus Augustulus, had such delusions of grandeur that often he believed himself to be Octavius Augustus. One day, as he raged through his palace halls crying: 'Varus! Varus! render me my legions!' he crushed his skull against a pillar and died a Roman death.

The meeting was attended also by Monsignor Macdomus, Southfalia's best-loved prelate. Monsignor was blessed with good humour and a fond heart, and enjoyed the good things of life such as good food, fine wines and other pleasures, as attested by his lively eyes and well-groomed body.

Sir Pepin Cretinus Dodus, the Consul, looked like being late again, to the irritation of all. Their irritation turned to envy as they began to suspect that his beautiful French wife, Princess Sybilla, might have something to do with his tardiness.

Earlier in the year, the Princess, known as 'Europe's most fashionable woman', had arrived on the island as guest of honour at a charity ball. Her arrival had caused a social earthquake. Her figure was so perfect, her clothes so chic, her accent so French that the establishment, determined not to lose her, ordered Sir Pepin to marry her. And so, that glamorous specimen of European blue-blood was now one more feather in the island's cap.

Sir Lucas adjusted his wig, cleared his throat and said, 'Punctuality is a great virtue, punctuality above all!'

Sir Herod who sat irritably next his friend Sir Marc, masticated peanuts at a voracious rate; Sir Bart jangled his gold; Lady Britt wriggled her little finger, and swallowed at nothing, while the cheerful Monsignor tried in vain to interest Sir Marc in a discussion on the efficacy of the chastity belt as a cure for frigidity.

At last Sir Pepin rustled in, in full Consular regalia, looking something of a dressed-up mouse with his short legs, long ears, round little belly and protruding lip.

After Sir Pepin declared the meeting open and sank back out of sight, Sir Lucas took to speaking in that formal, phlegmatic tone so natural to a man born into a dynasty of judges.

'Noble Lady and fellow knights, it has undoubtedly come to your attention that a certain eccentric has had the temerity to make highly inflammatory speeches within the walls of our peace-loving city, stirring the simple hearts of the citizens into open defiance of those principles laid down by our noble ancestors, of which we are the rightful keepers.'

'And pray who is this bold creature?' demanded Lady Britt, who, living as she did in her lofty realm, had not heard of Manuel.

'He calls himself Manuel and has no title. Which suggests something equivocal, perhaps disreputable about the man.'

'Indeed a man without worthy ancestors is worthless. I don't believe, Sir Lucas, that we need waste precious time discussing some upstart.'

'Quite so, Lady Britt, quite so, except that the considerable following he has managed to garner among the plebeians could undermine our God-given authority.'

'What daring impudence!'

'Indeed Lady Britt, what shameless temerity!' echoed the voice of Sir Pepin, reaching for the floor with his short legs.

All the others were equally indignant.

'Put him on a galley to Riceland,' suggested Sir Marc.

'To Riceland, yes, but extract his tongue first,' suggested Sir Herod.

But sagacious Sir Matthew, who knew a thing or two about what is liberally called nowadays 'public relations', did not agree.

'Undoubtedly, gentlemen, that would be the most expeditious solution. Nonetheless I ask you to consider the wisdom of such action at this stage. Through neglect and ignorance we've allowed this man to become a hero in the eyes of the people; to eliminate him now, would mean antagonizing thousands of his irate supporters. At this stage we can ill afford that. Let us never forget the lesson of that renegade Spartacus.'

Lady Britt sniffed and spoke. 'I should very much like to know what rhetoric he employs. Most Plebeians are incapable of grasping the most elementary Latin, let alone the complexities of high rhetoric.'

'That's precisely it, Lady Britt. He speaks to them in their rustic vulgarism, which, though lacking in finesse, does allow them to understand what he is saying,' explained Sir Matthew.

'Damn all words and speeches and rhetoric! I'll tell you what, when the chips are down, there's only one language everybody understands,' and here Sir Bart jangled his gold, 'promise them gold, and they'll sell you their soul. Whatever this upstart's promised them, we'll double it.'

'So far as I know,' said Sir Matthew, 'the man is poor, he delivers only a message of peace. A very skilful politician you'll agree. No other word arouses more the people nowadays.'

'What! What! Speak against the holy crusade, that's sacrilege!' cried Sir Marc, 'is it not, Monsignor?'

Monsignor Macdomus, whose pastoral duties allowed him too little time for sleep, had temporarily dozed off. Hearing his name, he woke with a start and cleared his throat.

'The position of the church on this matter is very clear,' he declared rubbing his numb jaw.

'Justice demands swift excommunication,' demanded Sir Lucas, the Chief Justice.

'Excommunication yes, but pull out his tongue first,' insisted Sir Herod in a tone suggesting that one can never be too careful.

'Hands off the holy crusade; the Red Peril must be crushed!' chanted Sir Marc.

Again Sir Matthew cleared his throat.

'The spirit of the crusade cannot be questioned by any clear thinking Southfalian, and deserves our fullest regard. Nonetheless I urge you all to take notice of the current of popular feeling running against it. It would be dangerous to disregard it. Let us remember that it has gone on for years and the end appears as elusive as ever. What I mean is, the signs of discontent were there before this man's appearance. He merely capitalized on it.'

Sir Bart said, 'Well spoken, Matt. There you have a point. A war is a capital venture, the returns must be worth the risk. The price of raw materials, that should have increased, keeps coming down, while our costs go up. Our profits are a fraction of what they were at the beginning of the war. This war has long become a one-way loss and no gain.'

Sir Marc was getting ready for an outburst, but before he could strike the right pose Sir Pepin's voice squeaked through the murmur.

'But, what about our allegiance to the Emperor, Sir Bart, hey! What about that?'

'Sir Pepin!' burst in Lady Britt with such vehemence to send the little Consul recoiling in his chair, 'Sir Pepin, as I recall it, Southfalians owe allegiance only to the Caesars who, unfortunately, no longer fill Rome's imperial halls, else we should not be involved in this absurd crusade. As for this ridiculous upstart sporting the pompous name of Holy Roman Emperor, this barbaric German, whose fathers roamed the savage woods of the Black Forest, how dare he claim the same title of the mighty Caesars!'

'But Lady Britt, what about the Yellow Peril and the Red Peril what about them, hey?' cried Sir Pepin with more energy than he was wont to have.

'Fiddlesticks, Sir Pepin! Every thinking person knows that the real reason for this war is so that Otto can get his hands on the rice fields of Riceland, and to impress the Pope. The German is a pretentious fool, a vainglorious madman and we the greater fools for supporting him. The sooner we get out of Riceland the better.'

'I could not agree more, Lady Britt,' said Sir Bart, 'while the war lasts my ships are sailing the seas unprotected from pirates and the riches destined for our shores go to fill the coffers of Turks and Jews.'

'Soon our ladies will be without silks, or jewels, or rich perfumes,' lamented Sir Lucas.

'And our streets without shiny new carriages.'

'And our tables without French wines...'

General silence, as everyone contemplated with dismay this frightful prospect.

'The French wines above all, Gentlemen,' sighed Sir Lucas, 'to distinguish us from the Plebeians.'

'This war's a dead loss, I see no reason to go on with it,' persisted Sir Bart, and everyone seemed to be in accordance with him. But they had forgotten about Sir Marc, whose fury had hitherto been checked by his disgust.

'Reason? Do I hear the word reason? Since when must there be a reason for war? Gentlemen, Lady Britt…' cried he disconsolately, 'I cannot believe mine own ears. It's unreal, nay, it's insane. What are we, men or prancing damsels? Whatever happened to the fighting spirit of our forebears? Are we not sons to those immortal heroes who marched off to battle, chanting behind the Great Eagle? Oh, Scipio! Oh, Mutius! Oh, mighty Julius! Shield your eyes with blackest gauze so as not to see the depth of cowardice to which your sons have fallen; or else draw your moribund sword and….'

In his rage, Sir Marc had drawn the famous scimitar captured from the savage *El Vampiro*. Heaven knows what tragic act might have ensued had not the terrifying silence been broken by a rustle of satin, accompanied by a sensuous whiff of French perfume and peering around the door was the elegantly coiffured head of Princess Sybilla, Sir Pepin's beautiful wife. There she paused timidly with a sweet child-like expression as if to ask, 'May I?"

All the Council was speechless, mesmerized by so much radiance, next to which Helen's face would be lucky to launch half a dozen gigs.

The first to recover his presence of mind was Monsignor Macdomus, who, with surprising agility for a man of his portly frame, rushed to the rescue of the gentle lady.

'Come, enchanting creature, come forward. Is it your Lord you want? Oh, the fortunate man! Why certainly you will speak with him. Here, take my arm, I shall lead you to him.'

But sour Sir Pepin did not seem as appreciative.

'Princess Sybilla…we are in conference.'

Sir Pepin's voice betrayed his annoyance. But she was too sweet-natured to take offence and encouraged by the prelate's solicitude, she proceeded,

'You are not ready, Monseigneur?'

'Ready? Ready for what, Madam?' Little Sir Pepin looked uneasy.

'Why, that which you promised me. You are so forgetful.'

This time Sir Pepin seemed positively dismayed and blushed down to his fingertips.

'Whatever did I promise you? I've never promised you any such things.'

'But you did promise...all of the week I have awaited...' And Sybilla could not continue, for tears glazed her eyes and fell like dewdrops down her cheeks. This poignant sight was more than any red-blooded Archbishop could stand. He took her cold little hand and said, 'Don't cry, gentle lady. Whatever your wish, it shall be accorded, I'll see to it personally.'

'The hunt; my Lord promised to take me to the hunt and he has forgotten.'

A somewhat relieved Sir Pepin said,

'As you can see, my dear, the conference has lasted longer than expected. I'm not permitted to leave important affairs of State...'

As Princess Sybilla's forehead again began to furrow, Monsignor intervened,

'Nonsense, Sir Pepin, the conference is all but over. I suggest we adjourn it and complete any unfinished business at the next sitting. What do you say, Gentlemen?'

The hunt was the sport *par excellence* with which the Southfalian knights amused themselves, and it would have taken much less than Sybilla's perfume to lure them to it. Everyone promptly acquiesced, except Lady Britt, who, not caring about such things, gathered the folds of her stole and left.

'A splendid resolution!' cried Monsignor, euphoric. And being such a fine day he decided to take a break from his pastoral cares and joined the hunters.

Thus the gay Monsignor led the knights out of the hall, frisking cheerfully about the princess. And all hearts were glad, and the spirit joyously sang in praise of the happiest isle of all.

XXIII

In the Desert

'When are we returning to the city?' asked his followers, to which Manuel replied, 'The time has not come yet.'

Then turning to John he said, 'Lead me to the desert, John. I have many questions to ask.'

And so they journeyed, the two of them, through hamlets and farms, crossed rivers and forests, and, further still, they walked to where the trees thinned out and the last sturdy trunks slung lanky limbs to the sky, until there were no more trees, nor any other vegetation except blue-bush and spinifex over the flats and rocky outcrops. And there was the sun, inexorable in its realm. They were in the desert. They searched for wood and lit the fire on the newly settled dust and they drew their bodies to the flame. The two men drew closer to the warm ashes. Silence huddled them together and they slept just as the desert dwellers had done for millennia. And they felt the mystery of their own nothingness.

All night the desert lay stretched, invisible, expectant for the sun. Towards morning it slowly came aglow, advancing through a frosty quiver, tearing away from the face of the sun a final greyish smear. The dew slid down the striated backs of the rocks, the thorns of the spinifex thawed and flexed, reptiles uncoiled and slithered numbly into the sun. The two men awoke with ashen backs and fiery eyes. They hunted the landscape for berries and grubs, and they felt good.

The journey resumed. For days they trod the red dust, cleansing their feet to climb the Sacred Rock. They reached a wide valley, in the middle of which a wall of jagged rock plunged into a gorge carved by water snaking its way down to a pool. Around it a clump of massive eucalypts stretched over the raw landscape with wanton arrogance.

They went down to drink and wash their bodies. Above the cockatoos screeched a frenzied song at the red sun. In all that garish show of life the men themselves felt a craving for sustenance. They had travelled a long time where nature offered little, and the sun consumed their bodies.

'What will we eat?' asked Manuel, aware that even the stars could not blanket their hunger.

They both looked at the face of smooth rock above the pool. Despite the vegetation, it all looked impenetrable and unyielding. John's eyes were alight with renewed faith.

'I look you for tucker.'

Together they followed the water's course down the gorge. John's movements were swift and shadowy as if he knew the way from ages past. At the next turn the gorge opened out to a wide, shallow stretch, thick with reeds. John froze on his toes and Manuel moved up to see over his shoulder. Over the water's gurgle came the bleats of a young, stranded goat.

John's eyes took on a wild glimmer. Quickly he picked up a sharp stone and took a few stealthy paces closer. Sensing danger, the animal ceased its drinking, sharpened its ears, sniffed at the air nervously, then noticing the hunter, took to flight. Too late! With reflexes sharpened by hunger, John swung his arm wide and threw the rock. The young legs had barely left the ground when the weapon hit the animal in the neck and it fell down.

John ran to it. He held up the dead animal and showed Manuel. Standing on that ancient rock, polished by years of floodwaters, his dark frame aglow, the wall of the gorge behind, Black John looked huge and powerful like a god.

In the burning ash they cooked the animal and ate it, listening to the mournful bleating of the mother goat. Even in the desert, in all that vast expanse of red dust, nature imposed its intolerable pantomimes.

'Might be tomorrow we get to the Big Rock,' said John.

The Big Rock rose in the centre of the island's desert region, like a tumescent umbilicus. The natives had used its caves as burial grounds and there were countless legends connected with it. It was said that the man who dared spend a night alone in one of the caves and came out the next morning alive would be endowed with great powers.

Manuel spent three days by the shadow of the Big Rock, fasting. On the third day he went down into the dark cave and Black John waited outside anxiously.

The Big Rock floated through the heat of the day, then paused precariously for an afternoon rest. It stirred with the sun, then changed from golden to orange to red. For a long while it glowed purple then settled to a harsh grey.

Night fell. The outline of the Rock sharpened as it rose to meet a descending sky. The outcrops, the caves, the dips and the crevices donned fantastic costumes. Mouths gaped from drowning heads, arms grappled and flailed the dark, wings flapped blindly.

Black John passed a sleepless night under an empty sky muted by the brooding struggle of the spirits. The desert lay suspended, as if listening to the wild dogs for some clue.

Toward dawn the dogs were silent and Black John fell asleep. When he woke up, Manuel's huge frame shadowed the dust. He looked up, but could not see the face for the sun.

'Are you ready John?' asked Manuel.

Black John said,

'Now you're every man. Time to go back.'

XXIV

A Ride on the Ass's Back

On a cold spring dawn as the dew still clung to the grass, and the sky, ashiver in purple-grey, stood in wait, a peasant convoy rolled slowly towards the city, taking goods to the market. There, amid the rolling wheels, barking of dogs, and the excited chatter of peasants, were Manuel and his followers.

As the convoy passed beneath the eastern gate, all noise stopped. The peasants chatted no more, and even the dogs and chickens were quiet. The city made its own noises, arousing to the din of the first carriages, the hurried footsteps of merchants, the curses of port workers. Smoke blackened the dew. The sun crept high, timidly now, as the fog slipped down the stony surfaces, exposing white marble columns, high towers, the whitewashed facades of the buildings.

Filippo Grassi, atop a cartful of apples drawn by a donkey, spotted Manuel's tall outline against the background of peasants.

'Hey, Maestro Manuele!' he yelled, surprised and cheerful. He skidded down like a happy urchin, ran to his idol, overwhelmed him with kisses on the cheeks, then, in a mood for celebration, distributed apples for everybody as the convoy moved into the city between rows of cheering crowds.

The number of people out in the street staggered Manuel. They chanted, 'Long live Manuel, Southfalia's saviour! Bring peace to Southfalia!'

The procession advanced through the deserted Strip district. Madam Magdalene and her girls, up early that morning after a quiet night, were drawn outside by the commotion and tried to catch some early business.

'Come up and see me sometime, Sir,' called Magdalene, 'I will wash your feet and anoint them with scented oils, the very best.'

The cheer rose to a crescendo as they went through the district of Stivaletto where Manuel's name sent those excitable people into a frenzy.

'*Riportaci i nostri figli,*' they cried. '*Ristoraci la dignità.*'[9]

Inspired by all the excitement, Filippo Grassi unhitched the cart which was now empty, left it in front of his shop, then, with others from the crowd, urged Manuel to ride the donkey to the city centre. The procession moved thus, with the crowd following Manuel, as he rode on the animal's back.

When they finally reached the square, Professor Thomas Equinus emerged from the Ivory Tower. He noticed the large crowd, recognized Manuel and at once concluded that the latter must have returned from abroad with a doctorate and a brand new philosophy. Professor Equinus well knew that an academic must always be up with the latest trends, so he too, decided to follow.

'Manuel the saviour! Manuel the peacemaker,' shouted the crowd as it poured into the square.

Anyway, this sort of thing did not cut any ice with Sir Herod, who, forewarned about Manuel's coming to the city, waited impatiently as he and his followers entered the square from the Orange League Avenue. When he saw Paul the Red carrying a red flag, his fury could no longer be checked.

'Haaa, Reds!' he roared, and his terrible cry echoed down the avenue, as he charged towards the crowd. 'Round 'm up, the Red demons, round 'm all up,' he commanded, 'don't let a single one escape. By Satan I'll scalp you all if you let one go.' He charged at full speed in the direction of Manuel.

'Run, Manuel, run!' yelled the people, 'you'll be trampled to death! He'll give you *the treatment.*'

The young man held his ground, erect and determined.

'Look, look!' they said, amazed. 'Manuel is not going to run. He is not afraid.'

SOUTHFALIA

'Why, you faithless people!' cried Paul, 'didn't he cure Old Mary and convert Black John? Did he not go among the cannibals and return unscathed? Goodness is mightier than tyranny. We've been cowards for too long. I'm staying right here to fight,' said he, brandishing the baton of his flag like a fifteenth century Mutius Scaevola. The students and proles closed ranks around Manuel, to protect him, or for protection.

Eventually Sir Herod's horse was able to break through the barrier. 'Got you, you evil scab,' he roared. 'You anti-Christ! You, you... Red!' And with his whip he lashed at Manuel's head.

Blood dripped from his ear. Manuel was a country boy, his strength and agility were those of a forest-dweller. He sprang high to seize Sir Herod's whip even before the latter had time to react. The frightened horse reared high and Sir Herod—perhaps for the first time in his life—found himself whipless and with his rear in the dust.

Minus his horse, the Black Knight looked small and vulnerable. His faded blue eyes, no longer fierce, blinked opaquely before the gleaming black ones of his opponent.

'Kill him! Whip him to death!' shouted the people, while knights and patricians—aware of the danger to their precious selves—slipped away quickly.

Sir Herod was left alone, encircled by the mob, which formed a wall between him and his guards, and seemed ready to give vent to all the hate accumulated over years of oppression.

Trying to regain his composure, the Black Knight reached into his pocket for peanuts, filled his mouth and started that terrible grind which had terrorized so many in dark torture cells. The people shivered. Manuel suddenly burst into laughter. The echo dispersed all around the narrow avenue, soothing away the anger from the faces of the mob, and for an instant the act they contemplated seemed absurd. Taking advantage of this moment's hesitation a guard went to the rescue of the cadaverous Sir Herod.

'Don't let them have him,' yelled the people. 'We'll murder the savage bastard.'

And they would have lynched him had not Manuel waved them back.

'No, that's not the way,' he said, 'we must seek a new way.' Then, turning to the guards he bade them to take away their leader. The guards heaved the stooping figure onto a horse and so the Black Knight made a quick exit, amid the jeers, abuse, and curses of the crowd.

The people couldn't understand why Manuel had spared the ogre. Still, they were too happy to wonder for long. They headed straight for the nearest inns and drank to their victory, and to the health of the young peasant who had dared to take on the terrifying Sir Herod and won.

XXV

On Wealth and Greed

Suddenly the indolent capital of Southfalia found itself animated with discussion and exulted with new hope. Manuel's name was in every person's mind, even if it was still risky to bandy it around.

'Did you see how he squared up to Sir Herod?' they whispered, 'did you see the Old Tyrant's face? He looked like death warmed up.'

Influential men of foresight in the Orange League saw in the young man's popularity an opportunity to increase their following, and took him under Orangist patronage. This allowed his Pacifist Movement a degree of official recognition. It meant also that he was able to preach, unhindered, from the Orange League steps. The Orangists, though always ranked lower than the Lemonists, were still a formidable outfit.

Such a turn of events could not fail to arouse anxiety among the Lemonists. They instructed Scribes and Priests to publicly question and embarrass the young man. If they could not match his appeal, they could try to demolish him by argument.

'Why do you preach peace, young man? Don't you believe in the ideals of the Holy Crusade?' Asked Sir Matthew Mackiavel.

'Whatever the ideals, the Crusade's methods are no longer acceptable to the people, or else they would not have given me the welcome that they did.'

'Don't you wish the Pagans to be converted?'

'It's they who do not wish it.'

'They are savages and don't know any better,' proceeded Sir Matthew.

'I have been there, Sir and I know that we have as much to learn ourselves.'

'You don't really believe that men can live in peace, do you?' asked an academic.

'I do, Sir.'

'History teaches that men need to go to war, just as they need to...to marry and have children.'

'I trust that the people don't see them as alternatives, you seem to do, Sir,' said Manuel laughing. Then he turned to the crowd and said,

'What is history, my friends? The actions we perform today are tomorrow's history. Today peace is our most pressing need, but only attainable as part of the whole. Our aim is a society free from violence; a mature society, in which Justice furrows its course in tolerance, and sustains itself through a lucid vision of the ideal.'

On another occasion Paul asked, 'How can there be justice when a few have so much?'

'Greed is fear of hunger: real or imagined. If no man goes hungry, fewer will experience greed, though you will still have those who will measure their worth in wealth.'

'Don't you believe it is possible to abolish wealth?'

'No, not in this country, and in any case I doubt that it would be wholly desirable. An active pursuit of wealth is better than none at all. However, we can try to minimize its relevance.'

'You mean, there is no alternatives to putting up with these wealthy parasites.'

This caused Manuel to smile.

'I would put it differently: we can make allowances for people's weaknesses and even try to exploit them. After all, there is room enough in this world for the greedy, just as there is for the ascetic. Our job is to ensure that the dross the wealthy leave behind does not clog up the way too much. It's a delicate, laborious role.'

XXVI

The Emperor Comes...

'It appears that unruly elements have been allowed free rein, leading to disorder in our streets. One wonders whether such tolerance, on the part of those responsible for peace in the streets, is justified in the present climate. It is to be hoped that His Imperial Majesty will not be exposed to any kind of public discourtesy during his official visit. '

Manuel's following at this stage was disturbing enough to deserve a comment in 'The Voice' from the lofty plume of Sir Matthew. Normally such a strongly-worded comment would be taken as an order for the *Law and Order* to comb the streets of the city and arrest any suspects, but the imminent arrival of the Emperor did place undue strain on the Squad.

The Emperor's visits were always marked by feasts, balls, parades, jousts and hunts: the culmination of months of feverish preparation. The great ladies employed all their allure, plus whatever cunning they could muster, to procure for themselves the most exclusive, most stunning imports in clothing that money could buy. Books could be filled with the squabbles, the rivalries, intrigue, threats, promises, the profound crises and the sweet triumphs, which went into the creation of a hairstyle or a gown that carried the label of exclusiveness.

The knights too, fought to the bitter dust for the acquisition of a more splendid helmet with feathers one or two inches longer than their rival. And, after all, in a society which had everything, how else could one's superiority be asserted if not by the length of one's feathers?

Preoccupied with these affairs, the Patricians found it more convenient to turn a blind eye to popular restlessness and to the triumphs of the young man from Belpied. They hoped in their hearts that the splendid arrival of the Emperor might work on him much the same miracle as Pope Leo's appearance did on barbarous Attila.

When the day finally arrived everything was meticulously prepared to give the Emperor a triumphant welcome: country peasants were given the day off to travel to the city, as were school children. Even the convicts were encouraged to wave and cheer as the imperial train passed the prison walls. It was as if the Patricians, seeing their power waning and their authority challenged, wished to reassert themselves through this lavish welcome of the Monarch.

The Midas was abrim with expectant masses, headed by the knights and their glittering ladies among whom Lady Britt was the only notable absentee. Monsignor dominated, with his corpulent figure clad in a mass of gold-embroidered robes and a mitre towering over his large head.

As for the knights, they were just splendid, but none of them could match Sir Marc Martial for sheer regality of aspect. Not one hair of his florid mustachio, not one feather of his Achillean helmet, not one medal, cross or ribbon on his Mercurial front was out of place. As he stood stiff and erect next to his wife, Lady Virginia, a stranger could be excused for mistaking them for the Imperial couple.

At the head of it all should have been the Governor Sir Isaac—had they been able to sober him up. But perhaps it was just as well; after such hectic preparations the mere possibility of something going awry—like giving a windy performance in front of the Emperor—was too daunting to contemplate.

However, his place was more than deservedly filled by Sir Pepin, the Consul, and his beautiful wife, Princess Sybilla. The former was not quite visible due to his small stature and because the helmet he wore was too big. The princess on the other hand, having no faults to hide, had chosen something rather scant, revealing thus some of the reasons why she had been named Europe's most fashionable woman.

Suddenly, trumpets blared and everyone in the square held their breath. Then to the sound of fast-approaching carriages a cheer rose. It soon grew to a tumultuous roar as the imperial coach rolled up

Victory Road, drawn by four white steeds, and came to stop at the entrance to the square in burnished resplendence. From it alighted His Imperial Majesty, a man no longer young, but virile in appearance. His face was covered by thick gingery growth, while the small blue eyes shone with passionate light. With him journeyed Her Majesty the Empress, a delicate, ageing woman, born of the bluest lineage in Europe. There was no Monarch or Prince who did not boast of some blood link with the Empress: small wonder then, that she was consumptive. A rarefied constitution such as hers was ill-furnished to resist the cruelties of this world.

As she was unable to bear the Emperor an heir it would have been a simple matter to annul the marriage. The Pope offered a dispensation, but the Emperor, engaged in that costly crusade, could not afford the price. Besides, as Otto himself declared publicly: 'We leave such conduct to the barbarous English.'

There was an instant of magic as the Imperial couple stood on the makeshift throne especially erected for the occasion and smiled condescendingly to a hushed mass, suspended in one breathless moment. But alas, this life is cruel and unpredictable! Just at that moment of sheer delight, not far from their Imperial Majesties a clamour broke out. The people recognized Manuel surrounded by a group of students, serfs, peasants and natives. They had produced something and raised it above their heads. It was a white flag with a blue circle at its centre, the standard of the Pacifist Movement.

The crowd turned away from the Emperor. Even before they realized what they were doing, they began to cheer the protesters, instead of the Emperor. Everyone was caught off balance, including Sir Herod who looked stunned by the daring act. His indecision was taken for weakness, because the chanting began in earnest,

'*Two, four, six, eight,*
Put an end to the Crusade!'
And
'*Peace now! Peace now!*

Imagine the anger, the embarrassment, the consternation! Even Sir Lucas Pompous Curse lost his judicial equanimity and snorted, 'Run over the bastards!'

Naturally Sir Herod would have liked nothing better, had he been able to get to them. But his movements were restricted by the crowd and he could do nothing, adding frustration to his anger. Luckily he had ample supply of peanuts or else he would have minced his tongue to pieces.

Otto VIII was affronted. His whiskers bristled like a lion's before the kill; and heaven knows what would have ensued had he unleashed the full force of his titanic fury. But rescue came on the very brink of disaster in the shape of that custodian angel, Princess Sybilla. As her divine form struck the Emperor's eye, his ready-to-explode rage turned into ready-to-burst passion. He looked at the white shoulders, the naked arms, the swan neck adorned by a rich pendant, which sat between her rising bosoms, like apples on the forbidden tree. His eyes stroked the contour of her hips, down to where a slit in her gown revealed a long velvety leg. His rage was frozen, his voice was muted, his heart enflamed and his blood flowed not up, but down.

Refusing all help, he took the Princess in his arms, swept her up into the coach, and together they rode through the crowd into the castle. The cheers managed to drown out the chants of the Pacifists, much to the relief of the knights.

XXVII

...And Goes

The demonstration against the Emperor shocked Southfalia's establishment and unleashed The Voice's rage against the Peace Movement, calling its adherents 'Enemies of the State'. The Orange League, whose growing importance made it sensitive to criticism, decided to send Manuel on a mission to the country for the remainder of the Emperor's stay. It paved the way for the *Law and Order* to make several arrests and to warn that all further agitation would be the death of the instigators.

The Emperor had a jolly time during a visit marked by pomp and circumstance, befitting his august personage. But alas, too soon, it was time for leave-taking, much to the dismay of the island's *bonne-société*, who were faced with the daunting prospect of another dull season of provincial non-events. In his final speech Sir Pepin reiterated once more Southfalia's unflinching support for the holy crusade, promised more arms and men for 'the common weal', and concluded with a ditty he composed in a moment of inspiration from the heavenly muse:

'We saw you once, but fleeting by,
For thee in combat, we yearn to die.
So all the way we'll march or wade,
For Holy Otto's great crusade.'

And to match words with actions, several demonstrators who had affronted their Imperial Majesties, were executed in the square as part of the farewell ceremony. Among them were: a lady of some notoriety whose excited shouts 'Make love, not war', were regarded morally corruptive as well as seditious; an old man with a wooden leg unable to move out of the way was arrested for obstruction; a young lady whose dress was torn in the fray was found guilty of indecent exposure. An imported serf who pinched the bottom of a forty-year-old belly dancer, was charged with molesting; and a drunk who shouted ' 'ang the 'ole bloody lot!' at the Imperial train, was executed for seditious incitement.

When Otto VIII saw the inert corpses hanging from the gallows, he was naturally touched by the gesture and, overcome by emotion, he gave Lady Sybilla a final embrace before mounting the Imperial coach. As the train moved out of the square the Emperor mused that no European Vassal State could have matched the tributes accorded to him by the people of this remote Roman colony.

It was customary, in those days, for the bodies of the executed to be left hanging in the square for a day or two as a woeful warning to criminals, dissenters or heretics, contemplating mischief. On his return to the city, Manuel was met by his despondent followers, who led him to the square where the bodies hung from the scaffold next to the Big Dragon.

'Why were these people executed?' he demanded, and before anyone dared reply he roared, 'why did you let it!'

The people eyed one another confused. Finally Iscar said,

'What could we do against the Law and Order, Sir? You can't blame a man for wanting to save his skin.'

Manuel turned to him, his face suddenly calm.

'You're right, old man. Still, the people of this island deserve better and it's time they took some risks.' He paused, then, 'tonight we will not go to sleep with those bodies hanging over our beds.'

'Take care, Sir,' cautioned Peter, 'the Lemonists will not tolerate open defiance.'

But Paul the Red had had enough.

'What the hell, Peter, we've suffered oppression, slavery and the useless slaughter of our men on foreign soil. Enough is enough! Time to take up sword, face the tyrant and free ourselves once and for all.'

'Forget the sword, Paul, it won't be necessary. Disperse, all of you, go to every part of this city and call all the supporters of the

Peace Movement to the square. There is a better way than the sword, and that's the one we will tread.'

They went to the port, The Strip, Stivaletto, the market place, to the farmhouses and hamlets outside the city, and took the message of Manuel's summons.

As people began to pour into the square, news spread that Manuel had been arrested. Some turned back in panic, but many more marched on, dodging the blockades of the *Law and Order*. By noon the square was full.

XXVIII

Transition

People assumed that Manuel would be given 'the treatment' by Sir Herod, and then executed, but Sir Mathew cautioned against it.

'A martyr is too heavy a burden to bear at this time of discontent and popular unrest,' he said.

Indeed, the resourceful Sir Matthew had a plan by which he hoped to clip the wings of the intrepid young peasant. He called an urgent meeting at Knight House, of the big four of Southfalia's establishment: himself, Sir Bart, Lady Britt and Sir Lucas.

'The young man's following is such that we can no longer afford to ignore him, and even less to antagonize him.'

'Good heavens, Sir,' exploded Lady Britt, 'we are the ruling class of this colony. We cannot appear to fraternize with a peasant.'

'He has the support of the people, transient though that may be. He is too dangerous to be left to his own devices.'

'What have you in mind for the upstart, Sir?'

'I would feel a good deal more comfortable if we could keep him on side. Tie him down, as it were. Something we have to offer: a knighthood may be necessary,' he said, a little too rushed. The others were outraged, none more than the Lady.

'Have you lost all reason, Sir Matthew? Why, the man has literally no name to speak of!'

'Yes indeed, and no nose,' said Lucas.

'And no money,' added Sir Bart.

It took all of Sir Matthew's patience to calm down his colleagues and all his diplomacy to persuade them. Finally they agreed reluctantly.

'Good,' concluded Sir Matthew, satisfied, 'I shall have him brought before you directly, if I may, for you to probe and question.'

If Manuel felt overwhelmed, as well he might, to find himself before the four great Patricians, he did not show it. He remained calm and somewhat distant, receiving their condescension with dignified reserve.

'As you can see, young man, we mean no harm,' began Sir Matthew.

'I expect none, Sir.'

Sir Matthew gazed outside into the garden where the wasps were feverishly abuzz in the heat of the late afternoon.

'It has come to our attention that you have gathered many followers,' continued Sir Matthew.

Manuel remained impassive.

'What the hell have you promised?' asked Sir Bart. 'You've got no money.'

'They don't need money. They need reassurance, hope.'

'And are you able to give them hope?' challenged Sir Matthew's arched brows.

'If they believe I can, I have to.'

'Are you what they say you are, a Messiah?' asked Lady Britt.

'I don't even know who my mother is, Ma'am.'

Sir Bart's patience had reached its limits.

'Now come on, Matt, let's quit all the la-di-da nonsense and get down to business or we'll be here all day.'

Sir Matthew cast a tolerant glance towards his friend.

'You display exceptional talent, young man,' he said, 'and despite your appearance, you have the temperament of a Patrician. That is why, after some careful thought, we have decided to offer you what every young Plebeian dreams of...Sir Lucas, if you please.'

Sir Lucas inflated his chest, stretched on his high-heeled boots, and declaimed,

'Sir, I shall be brief to the point of bluntness. We have unanimously decided to award you an investiture of the Order of Silken Suspender. Indeed, yes, they...we are offering you a knighthood, Sir.'

SOUTHFALIA

'Thank you all,' Manuel replied promptly, as if he had expected nothing else. 'But these are honours I neither deserve nor do I seek.'

It took a while for this to register on the four noble brains.

'Good God! Do you mean you refuse a knighthood?'

'I am a peasant, Sir Lucas.'

'Have you no ambition, young man?'

'I have indeed, Sir Matthew, I have many. The first is to bring peace to Southfalia.'

'That's quite an ambition. And how do you propose to attain it?' asked Sir Matthew, amused.

'I believe, Sir, I am destined to become Consul of this island.' Manuel spoke this slowly, clearly, the size of his pupils did not alter. The four great nobles laughed a nervous patrician laugh, exchanged bewildered glances, followed by outraged exclamations.

'Why, you're merely a peasant, an unknown upstart!' said Sir Lucas, livid 'Why, Sir Matthew, how could you! This is an outrage, an outrage, indeed!'

Manuel kept silent, and as if to fill the silence he turned towards the balcony shutters from behind which ever-increasing cries arose. All heads turned with his.

'Down with cruel Otto! Down with servile Pepin! We want Manuel!'

Sir Matthew turned away from the balcony door and said, 'Tell me, young man, should we recall our army from Riceland, in defiance of the Emperor?'

'The people who follow me have expressed no allegiance to the Emperor, only concern for the dying.'

Lady Britt found herself in agreement although she refrained from expressing it.

'Do you know, Manuel, that without our consent no man ever enters the Big Dragon in any position, especially in the robes of Consul.'

'Then I will ask you to give me backing.'

'Never!' said Lady Britt, 'the impertinence of it!'

'Why not? What have you to fear?'

'You're a Plebeian and an Orangist.' Lady Britt turned her nose up as if she smelled something putrid. 'You have no family and you fraternize with natives and serfs.'

'You'd give to the poor by taking from our pocket.'

'I've already said, Sir Bart, that money is not what the poor need.'

'You'll help the Plebeians and neglect the Patricians.'

'I will help whoever seeks it.'

The voices in the square were becoming more belligerent. Sir Matthew went to secure the shutters but what he saw put fear even in his phlegmatic temperament. The square was overflowing with a loud, angry mob. Near the Orange League steps was Paul the Red, flushed face, eyes shining, red hair blowing free and rebellious, his aspect inciting the crowd as much as his speech.

'They've abducted Manuel because he spoke for peace. They will murder him so that your sons will continue to be slaughtered to appease the pride of the German tyrant. Say 'no' to Otto, say 'no' to the Crusade, say 'yes' to peace. Down with Sir Pepin! Long live Manuel! Manuel for Consul.'

Meanwhile dusk was fast approaching. The crowd's attention was drawn to the castle, where, on top of the Big Dragon a guard walked across the drawbridge to the scaffolding of the gallows to light up the torches on the bodies. Normally the act would have been enough to cool down animosities, but now instead it did the reverse. From Paul's chest issued a strident roar.

'Come on, fellow-Proles, let's demolish that monster!'

And he ran to the base of the scaffold followed by the crowd and they all started to push and heave at its base, trying to bring it down. But the beams remained firm. Inspired by his own hysteria, Paul scuttled up the tower with the speed of a mountain cat and started cutting the ropes. The first body fell with an awful thud. The crowd roared as each corpse was freed from the ropes and fell down. Presently they turned to see Sir Herod and the Squad men on horseback, come to restore order and round up a few for 'the treatment'. The people instinctively went to escape through the many exits, but

Paul, remembering Manuel, did not run; instead he waved a threatening arm towards Sir Herod and that gesture was enough to incite the crowd to surge forward, pressing against the Squad in the face of all danger. The horses panicked and for the second time Sir Herod found himself running for his life.

Now that the crowd became aware of its own power, it became like the heavy swell of an angry sea. A cart was obtained from somewhere on which the corpses were loaded and led out towards the Castle.

'Murderer! Murderer!' shouted the people. 'Down with Sir Pepin! Free Manuel! Manuel for Consul'

The sun was fast moving below the horizon and night approached, and with it the fearful prospect of mobs running wild and ransacking the city. The cathedral bell rang and Monsignor came out to deliver a sermon that no one heard.

Sir Bart turned to Manuel and said:

'I want to know one thing; if we make you Consul, will my ships be free to sail once again?'

'Sir Bart, you can do what you please with your ships, once they are back from the Crusade,' replied Manuel.

It was the reply they all wanted.

'Well Matt,' said Sir Bart, 'what are we waiting for? As far as I'm concerned our best bet's the only bet.'

Sir Matthew agreed. In the circumstances there was neither time nor scope for disapproval. The others were silent, except for Sir Marc, 'What, what?' he roared, 'a non-knight for Consul, never!'

But in the end reality prevailed and even he had to agree that an insulting precedent was preferable to the danger of anarchy.

'To the balcony then, Sir, to speak to the people,' invited Sir Matthew with as genial a smile as he was capable of.

'Not from here,' said Manuel promptly. 'Down in the square I'll speak with the people.'

The scene which followed is memorably recorded by Iscar.

'*The door of Knight House opened and Manuel was ushered out to a surging crowd. Many could not see because of the poor light. The cheering subsided to a murmur.*

'*Is it him? Did you see?* '

A space cleared in the crowd, growing, like the mouth of a dragon, to the left of the Castle toward the Orange League. It led up the steps and there a figure rose, very tall and composed: the figure of a Prophet. The crowd responded with reverence, fell silent as he turned to them with outstretched arms and began to speak. And though many knew not what he said—for his voice was much subdued—they felt his strength as it spread from man to man in ever-widening circles. Thus it was carried to all the people, and a calm settled over all. And there was no more anger, nor bitterness, nor hate. And they could see clearly their own folly, while the bodies of the dead piled high on the cart became one black giant in the dusk. And all the shapes in the square fused and dispelled and fused again with nightfall. And everyone, even Manuel, was enveloped within its folds.'

'Matter of survival and interest of purse require that we forsake Sir Pepin, rescind support for the Crusade and come to terms with the young Plebian,' said Sir Matthew.

'I cannot bear to stoop to that peasant. It's improper,' lamented Lady Britt.

'It's not a matter of propriety, but of strategy.'

The term is 'expedience', as any politician who values his survival will tell you with sly self-satisfaction, as if he were its inventor. In fact with Signor Machiavelli alive and well, extolling its virtues to the Medicis, expedience was in a phase of renaissance at the time of our story.

Southfalia City, notwithstanding its wealth, was no Florence, and though it abounded with Machiavellis, they lacked the Florentine's finesse and aspirations. But then, Southfalia, unlike Italy, was not a divided country. The expedience that they practised was a highly moral affair dressed in hypocrisy; for in Southfalia, people expected propriety, which is, after all, the mother of hypocrisy.

The next day all over the walls of the island appeared a copy of 'The Voice'.

'Sir Pepin erred in pledging so much to the Emperor,' it said. 'It shows insensitivity to the people's plight, subjected as they have been for years to shoulder the ever-growing burden of the war. There is no argument with the high ideals upon which the Crusade was undertaken, but it makes no sense to continue to support it merely on principle, when it is reducing our Fair Isle to its knees. Sir Pepin has a lot to answer to the people for persisting in his support of Otto's war.'

Sir Lucas, the Chief Justice, during court proceedings had occasion to make comments pertinent to the political situation in Southfalia: 'Those in a position of authority are deemed by law to abide by the traditions of our Fair Isle, a tradition based upon fairness, justice and the pursuit of peace. He who contravenes these principles oversteps his mandate.'

And Monsignor Macdomus in a special sermon spoke of untold misery and hardship suffered by Southfalian soldiers at the hands of barbarous Ricelanders.

'The position of the Church is very clear on the matter: It opposes all wars, though the Church, like all bodies of society, must take heed of the decisions taken by the temporal leaders. It's the people's right, indeed their duty before God, to oppose those decisions which they believe ill-taken.'

After which, Sir Pepin was left no other recourse but to sail off into exile, taking with him Sybilla, much to the distress of her many admirers, who felt that fate had been too cruel on one whose involvement in the harsh world of politics was merely by way of a feather mattress.

And so the way was clear for an Orangist to be elected Consul. On advice from Peter, the Orange League presented Manuel's candidacy at the next sitting of the Senate, and he was unanimously elected Consul. Following the election Sir Isaac Garrish Hippocritus, the Governor, managed to sober up long enough to present him to the people of the city. The people were delirious; the knights hailed him politely; and the sick, the children, the old, the poor and the suffering felt certain that a new dawn was rising over Southfalia.

PART THREE

THE STATESMAN

XXIX

A Plea for Unity

'Manuel seemed not touched by fame, sensitive though he was to the love and trust of the people. And indeed he did love them, claiming this to be a 'self-indulgence to which all men are entitled'. Yet, even in his love, as in all things, he maintained an equanimity which some took for indifference.'

Iscar tells us that Manuel performed his role as Consul with wisdom in the face of many challenges, wrought even by those who purported to be his followers. One of these was Paul the Red. 'The Zealot' maintained a bellicose stance against the Patricians. When Manuel decided to adhere to protocol, that required a newly-elected Consul to receive the Great Knights in formal audience, Paul's reaction was typically vehement.

'Let's have no more ridiculous relics of a past dead and buried. Everyone is equal now. We'll strip these fat pigs of their lard and feed it to the poor.'

'I'll take issue with you on that, Paul,' said Peter, 'it's complete nonsense to suggest that everyone is equal. No organization can function without some kind of hierarchy. Take us at the Guilds for instance. Men of ability, drive and charisma will get to the top; others just haven't got what it takes. It's like this Paul. You've got to have your princes and your paupers. That's nature.'

'I believe,' said Manuel, 'that in some things we must strive to improve on Nature. There is no gain in antagonizing the Patricians or any other group in our society. Much more constructive is to invite as many as we can, to work with us.'

The knights came, bringing with them smiles and rich gifts worthy of their position. Lady Britt presented him with a mantle, said to have been worn by Tiberius. Monsignor gave him a Byzantine rosary chain with beads of precious stone. Sir Marc: an ancient eye-band which he took from the Black Corsair. Sir Lucas: a copy of Lex Romana with S.E.Q.S. inscribed in gilded lettering. But the most splendid gift of all came from Sir Bart: a glittering coach, white and gold, drawn by four Arab steeds.

'Good Lord, Sir Bart,' Manuel exclaimed at the sight of so much magnificence, 'what would the son of a carpenter do with a coach fit for a Monarch!'

'Whatever you may have been, Sir,' said Sir Matthew, 'you are now Consul of Southfalia. You must do the position honour. Sir Lucas has another gift for you, far more precious than any.'

The 'gift' turned out to be Lady Penelope, Sir Lucas' delicate daughter, a girl whose Patrician pedigree made her a fit match for a Prince. She had everything: birth, title, money, even anaemia. None of which, it seems, impressed our hero, for he said,

'Thank you all. Your gifts overwhelm me. I will accept the coach, but will not use it personally. With Sir Bart's permission we will sell it and use the proceeds to build a hospice for the old. We will call it the Saint Bartholomew Rest Home. I am certain the arrangement will please you, Sir. As for the gentle lady, well gentlemen, a man as ambitious as I, would do a lady an injustice to ask for her hand. Put simply, I'm not for marrying.'

The Patricians gave one another an uncertain glance before all eyes centred on Sir Matthew for some kind of lead. But that knight was too wise to stick his neck out, so he opted for a cautious silence, for now.

'Gentlemen...Lady Britt,' said Manuel, 'we know how much work there is ahead of us. We must try to restore peace and harmony on our island. Now, we know that little can be achieved without the people's trust and the co-operation of the Patricians. The first I believe I have. As for your co-operation...I appeal to you, humbly.'

A pause followed in which Manuel was the recipient of guarded glances, then Sir Matthew said, 'We've already supported your election, Sir.'

'And how much can I take that to be an undertaking for the future?'

'We can't give guarantees,' put in Sir Bart, 'everything 'll depend on what measures you take.'

Sir Matthew elaborated.

'Your Orangist followers will expect you to take certain actions which may conflict with traditional Lemonist interests…'

'Conflicts of interest, gentlemen! If we dare look far enough it will be seen that the interests of one man are the interests of all, and vice versa. I suggest, gentlemen, that we abandon so-called positions and start dealing by way of principles. I suggest further, that we abandon confrontation for its own sake in favour of sensible debate. Who knows? Perhaps, having discovered that it works, we may make a habit of it.'

'That's very idealistic, highly commendable, of course,' began Sir Matthew with an amused smile.

Manuel interrupted.

'Well, Sir Matthew, why should we continue to be afraid of ideals? They are, after all, the ones which give us hope. It is true that compromises are often the only way, but we should never lose sight of the ideal.'

The Patricians looked at him blankly. Manuel continued.

'The highest possible is somewhere on the way to the impossible. Believe me, gentlemen, there is enough God in us to try.'

There was so much fervour in Manuel's voice that it plunged the Patricians into silent reflection. Suddenly, Lady Britt saw herself seated next to the young Octavian riding back into Rome from Actium upon a triumphant chariot. Sir Lucas gave judicial advice to wise Solomon. Monsignor's elaborate imagination flew him to Canossa, as Henry's knees snapped and bent on the icy floor and his frostbitten brow bowed before the mighty Pontiff. Sir Marc rode in a dust-cloud of glory at the head of half a million men sweeping in from Tartary. Sir Bart gave the Consul a long, inquisitive stare from the tower of a gilded mansion.

Now as the silence lingered, Sir Bart slapped his own knee, stood up and said,

'This looks like taking the whole day and I got things to do. Well, Matt, to be truthful, I haven't got a clue where this whole business will lead us. But the lad's got a tough job ahead of him and I reckon we ought to give 'm a fair go. What do you say?'

Sir Matthew said, ' I must say, Sir, my colleagues and I admire your style. I can only trust you will not be too flamboyant with it. There are traditions and conventions to be observed.' Sir Matthew paused, 'Yes, Sir Bart, I will follow your line: it's your money. At any rate, good-will comes cheap.'

SOUTHFALIA

XXX

The First Steps

The beginnings of Manuel's Consulship must have been impressive enough to stir Iscar's stoical plume to record it in a tone of unrestrained enthusiasm.

> *'It is a measure of the efficacy of his manner, that the youthful Consul should so quickly overcome the fortress of mistrust which the Patricians had erected around themselves. Now he has successfully recruited the advisory skills of Sir Matthew, Sir Bart and Sir Lucas on matters of Diplomacy, Finance and the Judiciary. Their acceptance lends the new Government much-needed status and propriety in the eyes of those for whom such qualities count.'*

This success was even more significant in view of the fact that other members of the Advisory Council included people like Peter, Paul the Red and even Filippo Grassi. It was a way of ensuring that many disparate views were heard before decisions were taken. In addition, it gave the opportunity for individuals to challenge one another openly, rather than to secretly plot against each other. At the same time Manuel never let them forget—by action and by words—that the people had elected him on a desire for change.

'We will abolish the *Law an Order* as it now stands,' he announced, 'I don't believe we will hear too many objections to that.'

'And Sir Herod? What's to be done with the Black Knight?'

'Starve the bloody murderer, and feed his dying flesh to the rats!' Shouted Paul the Red.

Manuel dismissed that with a resolute wave of his hand.

'I won't be Southfalia's executioner, Paul. This is a good occasion for putting into action the new way that we have been preaching. We will send him off to where he can do no more harm.'

'But the man's a monster!' insisted Paul.

'Don't throw stones,' admonished Peter, who was trying to assert his rational approach.

'It isn't simply a question of stone-throwing,' Manuel said, 'we have enough to do without taking on God's role as well. Let Him judge and punish. We'll be content with denying the man the opportunity to harm any more people.'

Like Paul, the people could not understand such leniency, but they had enough faith in their young leader to allow him his whims. In the euphoria of the times vindictiveness lost its sharpness. Only Sir Matthew persisted in calling 'for just punishment'.

'Sir Herod was, and remains, a dangerous enemy to leave free.'

'He won't be free, Sir Matthew,' argued Manuel, 'he will be a prisoner in his own castle in the far North.'

'Still dangerous. Execute him now and the multitudes will cheer. No newly-elected leader ever had a more propitious occasion for eliminating an obnoxious enemy.'

Manuel became very serious.

'It's still wrong, Sir. What you advocate belongs to a past I want to leave behind.' Then he added, 'Anyway, you must agree that so long as I have the people on my side, the Black Knight is safely out of the way.'

'So long as the people continue to support you.'

'Hell! I wouldn't wish to lead this country on any other condition,' exclaimed Manuel with a good-natured smile.

Sir Matthew smiled too. It wasn't the same kind of smile. It was urbane and condescending.

Later, as Sir Matthew was discussing the above conversation with his friend Sir Bart, the Scribe was struck by a novel thought.

'I believe I've got it,' he exclaimed with uncharacteristic excitement.

'I wouldn't have a clue what you're chasing, Matt,' said Sir Bart. 'It's to his advantage to let Sir Herod live.'

'How do you mean?'

'The thing is that while he lives, Sir Herod is both a reminder of the worst aspects of the former regime, and a warning of what could follow if Manuel were ever ousted. It's a masterstroke. Very clever! I tell you, Sir Bart, that young peasant deserves greater respect than we've been prepared to bestow on him.'

Sir Bart was amused.

'No doubt about you, Matt, black and white's too simple for you. Bores you to tears. You spend all your time working out new shades. Well, as far as I can tell, the lad's doin' what he thinks 's right, that's all. What's the good of makin' a ballyhoo over that peanut Herod, anyhow.'

XXXI

A Visit to Spudsville

'How dare he, the peasant upstart, affront our Majesty thus! How dare he withdraw from a Crusade financed by the Jews and blessed by the Pope!'

So enraged was Otto VIII at the news of Manuel's decision, that he decapitated the envoy, called on the Olympians to hurl curses upon Manuel's head, and swore swift revenge.

Meanwhile in Southfalia the soldiers returned to a joyful welcome by wives, mothers, and Sir Marc's fine speeches. The old soldier was there at the waterfront to welcome the men, praise their valour and stir their hearts.

'Let us hope,' he would conclude with a wink, 'that soon sanity will prevail once again and you will be permitted to return to where every soldier craves to be: on the battle front.'

But the men, intent as they were on embracing their loved ones, did not hear his words.

So began for Southfalians the happy times, not only because the spectre of that devastating war was over, but because Manuel's youthful aspect gave strength and hope to the down-trodden, the guild-workers and Patricians alike.

Daily he left the castle and explored the city, visiting homes, inns and shops; speaking to artisans, inquiring about their business, their problems and hopes. In the street, it was the children and the old that he especially noticed. With the first, he shared the sense of fun and imagination, from the old he loved to hear stories from Southfalia's past—myths which belonged to the days before the coming of the Romans. Sometimes he rode beyond the city walls through fiefs and hamlets, to see the peasants who tilled the land. It was their struggle that he especially felt deeply with. This pleased Paul the Red, but not Iscar, who knew that there was more to be had by frequenting the Patricians.

'I am Consul of all the people,' said Manuel by way of justification. 'If I show more concern for the peasants, it's because their needs are greater.'

His concern for the peasants took him to Spudsville: the centre of the potato region of the island. The Grandee, Alfred Murphy, was its biggest potato grower. He was a tall, thin, myopic man, known to be a wizard with figures and statistics. He seemed delighted to be able to show around the Consul and Iscar, who accompanied him around his huge potato complex.

According to the statistics, quoted with self-assured precision by the amenable Grandee, Spudsville boasted the highest number of carriages per capita, the highest rate of violent crimes, the lowest birth rate, the highest suicide rate and the highest number of private baths in the country.

'And say Sir, what is the secret of your success?' asked Iscar.

'Very simple Gentlemen: specialization plus reward produce efficiency. I pay eighteen per cent above the award. The margin gives me the pick of the labour market, lads who can be moulded into a specialist's job more easily. Take the ploughman, for instance, he needs to develop powerful biceps and thighs and a strong voice to shout at the bullocks. The potato-washer, on the other hand, can sit all day, but must have nimble hands with skin like hide that'll resist immersion in water all day.

'Efficiency may mean turning a disability to advantage. For example, the man who can't smell makes an excellent manure spreader and since a manure spreader is highly paid, many agree to have their scent nerves burned out for the sake of extra money. Of course, specialization can only work in a climate like ours, where continuous crop rotation is possible. We're really lucky in that way,' concluded he with a self-satisfied beam. 'But do come, gentlemen, let me show you inside.'

SOUTHFALIA

In the huge potato complex, which was like a long tunnel, there were no human voices to be heard, only a great din of mechanical sounds of machinery working with split-second precision. Manuel tried to speak to one or two people unsuccessfully.

'You're wasting your time, Sir,' Alfred explained, 'they're trained not to communicate with anyone on site. It wastes time and breaks the pace. Besides, most of 'm are imported serfs and wouldn't know what you're saying, Sir. They haven't the time to learn our language.'

They came to a row of women intent on sorting potatoes from a large vat into three different baskets according to size. Their movements were nimble and accurate. Leading them was an older woman, dressed in black, who performed her work with mechanical speed. Staring at nothing, her fingers knew where each potato went.

'You wouldn't read about it,' said the Grandee, noticing his visitors' astonishment, 'blind as she is Philomena is still my champion potato sorter. But, I'm afraid she won't last,' he added tragically, 'arthritis in the fingers, you know. They all get it eventually. She'll be finished before the year's out. And she won't be easy to replace, I tell you.'

Manuel's expression already gloomy, darkened further.

'Couldn't the sorting of potatoes be done mechanically?' he asked.

'Yes indeed, Sir, and more efficiently too. But the Potato Workers Guild would have none of it. Their policy's to try and preserve the jobs of their members at all costs. '

Manuel was about to retort when his attention was drawn to the portrait of a hunchback hanging above the doorway to the crib-room. It bore the inscription: 'In memory of Gobby, the greatest!'

'Now, there was a man worth a gold mine. That's Joe Gobbo, my all-time champion potato picker. In one day he had one hundred and forty eight sacks raked up and bagged. That's an average of just over twelve sacks an hour. And I reckon that'll take some beatin'.'

'And what happened to him?' asked Manuel.

'Well, Sir, it's funny really. The day he broke the record was a real scorcher. So, along with the prize I chucked in a cask of freshly brewed ale; which he drank by himself that same evening, then went to bed and never woke up again. I gave him one hell of a funeral, mind you.'

They hurried along, past men and women on both sides of the track, busy at some monotonous chore or other, with faces engrossed and a comatose brain.

XXXII

A Different Crusade

The visit to Spudsville revealed to Manuel that the life of the peasant on the land was idyllic in comparison with that of the hired labourers. Soon he discovered that throughout the island a hired labourer was first and above all a worker. That he may have been also a husband, father, a member of his community or whatever was of no consequence to the employer. The worker was hired for his skills and was expected to render them at the time, place, or manner required. There was no coercion applied as such; slavery had been outlawed in Southfalia, but there existed an infallible method to get a worker to do whatever was required of him: money.

It might be imagined that in a country where money was relatively abundant, its importance would be diminished. In effect the opposite was true. It was part of the island's tradition that a man was justified in rendering whatever service he was capable of, so long as the money offered was enough to satisfy his greed and appease his conscience. In its favour, it must be mentioned that money was a powerful leveller; even the rich Patricians were ruled by its prerogatives and were its victims no less.

'It seems to me that one of the aims of work ought to be give a sense of accomplishment,' said Manuel in a discussion with his Council, 'people may perform miracles, if they felt that the result met with their notion of achievement.'

'As a matter of policy I always pay my best workers something extra. It's good incentive to others,' commented Sir Bart.

'I've heard it before, Sir Bart. Everyone talks about money; no one mentions purpose or dignity. Money is a poor reward, it's also inequitable. We reward handsomely the lawyer's eloquence, the judge's justness, and the canny of the pawnbroker. Yet, the good man who serves society by example; the wise mother who provides it with fine children; or the man of spirit who inspires it; these may receive no monetary reward.'

'How else can you get people to work if not by money incentive?' asked Sir Bart.

'We should ask ourselves first: why do we compel an individual to work?'

'Nobody wants to work, if he can help it,' said Sir Bart.

'I am sure you don't mean that that, Sir. Still, I agree that too many look on work as drudgery; and that's what it is often: a wasteful and unnecessary drudgery. We send people to work to save them from themselves; we tempt them with trinkets to create more and more work. We have some three quarters of our island busy at keeping one another busy. As a result our cities are bursting with people frantic and frustrated, and our administration is in disarray. Believe me Gentlemen, we could improve our existence on a fraction of the effort we expend now.'

'How would you save people from themselves, and each other, with all that free time to kill?' argued Peter.

'Yes, people are untrained to cope with freedom,' concurred Manuel, therefore we need to move cautiously. We can free them from the tyranny of work only when they have learned to live without it. Then they can begin to learn, to teach, to discover, grow...to live.'

'Allow me to ask, Consul,' intervened Sir Matthew ceremoniously, 'in the ideal world that you envisage, who would sweep the chimneys?'

'Many of us can sweep our own. It does us no harm to put up with some soot occasionally, it makes us better able to appreciate the warmth of the fire-place.'

'And for those who never use their hands, it is good practice too', put in Paul.

'To force a person to sweep chimneys all day, every day is society's crime and loss,' Manuel continued. 'Give people the chance to experience the pleasure of passionate striving, and much resentment will be erased from our society.'

'What I want to know is, how's business going to be affected,' asked Sir Bart.

'You trust me, Sir Bart, and I promise to take care of business. When business is healthy, the people will gain. And that's my concern.'

'You help me, and I'll help you,' said Sir Bart, pleased to be able to conclude the airy-fairy discussion in territory in which he felt comfortable.

XXXIII

The Prosperous Times

The Patricians had much cause to be satisfied now that the ships sailed freely once again, bringing riches to the island. All kinds of clothing and jewellery were again available to the fashionable ladies, while the knights sat grandly in their latest imported carriages.

Lady Britt was still getting used to the incongruous notion of a peasant of doubtful ancestry as Consul; but this was partly compensated by the fact that he had stood up to the Emperor, whom she regarded as a usurper.

Sir Herod brooded at Rookery Castle—his forbidding fortress up North—waiting to be summoned back to the capital for a series of reprisals which always followed a change of Government. But, as there seemed little prospect that his expertise would be required in the foreseeable future, he escaped abroad—to Emperor Otto.

With the soldiers home, and Manuel's enlightened leadership, Southfalia prospered.

'Sir Bart, at what stage are the plans for Bartholomew House?' Manuel would ask.

Of all the great knights, Sir Bart was the most kindly disposed toward the new Consul, 'You'll see, Sir, I'll build you the flashiest hospice you have ever seen. If it's gonna' carry my name, it's gotta be good.'

For Sir Bart it wasn't merely a question of pride, but also of ethics. Thanks to Manuel's decision to withdraw from the Crusade, his ships were doing a brisk trade. It was just that a reward should be paid, according to the rules of the game. Sir Bart's philosophy had no complications.

What Sir Bart had in mind was something akin to a grand house for a country Gentleman, complete with marble staircases, gilded candelabra and onyx mantelpieces. Manuel had other ideas.

'Good Lord, Sir, if you are going to spend that much money, why not build an orphanage as well? In fact, I have another idea: let's build a structure large enough to house both the aged needy and the very young.'

In a country where people were educated to think in blocks, Manuel's idea seemed very strange, especially to the experts, 'Why that's absurd, their needs are so vastly different!' they argued.

But Manuel believed that the two extremities of a person's age is a meeting point.

Sir Bart, who did not pretend to be an expert in human relationships kept out of it, and to cut out all argument he said, 'It's your money; you do what you like with it.'

Bartholomew House was built—not in some far off corner of the city, as many had expected—but right near the centre, where the pulse of life throbbed with enough strength to reach those usually ostracized to the edge of society. It gave its dwellers, both young and old, not merely shelter, but dignity, comfort and the opportunity to be of use. Manuel had been right: the patience, wisdom and experience of the old perfectly complemented the strength, irascibility and the urge-to-know of the child.

Sir Matthew the Scribe, whose Roman nose was able to sniff the direction of the wind even before it started, did a great service to Bartholomew House and, of course, to himself by painting an idyllic vignette of the hospice for the readers of *The Voice:*

'A visit to Bartholomew House reveals an extraordinary spirit of co-operation and ingenuity at work. Such spirit makes it possible for elements of our community, formerly of a parasitic nature, to create for themselves an environment that is both happy and productive. To see the old man nurse the infant, the boy lead the blind to fetch water, the old woman distracting youngsters with ancient stories; these are eloquent witness to the success story which is Bartholomew House.'

Encouraged by this success, Manuel summoned Sir Bart and some of his wealthy friends and said, 'I have in mind a new project, Gentlemen...'

'Hell! Not more money!' Fumed Sir Bart, 'at this rate you'll have us turn into charitable institutions.'

'As they say, 'charity begins at home'. This is for the health of the people, including the workers. So you see, it's really a form of investment from which you gentlemen, who employ so many, will benefit more than anyone...'

'We already got a hospital,' argued Sir Bart.

'And overcrowded it is too. We need a house of health to which we may go for examination, regular rest and above all, expert instruction and practice, to improve body and mind. It will keep us healthier, prevent many illnesses and extend our life. All of which must benefit business. Perhaps it will save us the cost of having to build another hospital.'

Charmed by the young man's brashness, rather than persuaded by his argument, the merchants followed Sir Bart's lead and agreed to a less-costly initial project, with the promise of financing another pending the success of the first. Manuel was happy.

'That's very fair, gentlemen. The people will be grateful to you.'

The ease with which Sir Bart gave in once more, left Sir Matthew wondering whether his friend was succumbing to the Consul's charm to the detriment of his own interests. His first impulse was to bring it up with Sir Bart, but then the Scribe was not an impulsive man and his acute timing instinct, refined by years of diplomacy, decided him in favour of silence for the time being.

XXXIV

A Night for Fishing

It was Sir Bart's habit to invite prominent Southfalians aboard his luxurious vessel which was equipped to provide guests with whatever pleasure money could afford. Of course, no one was under the illusion that Sir Bart was running a floating charity. His guests, therefore, were never surprised when, at a particularly congenial moment, he would casually let drop a criticism, a suggestion, a comment or recommendation. It was common knowledge within the 'establishment', that these trips had been instrumental in Sir Bart's rise to the position of wealthiest man in Southfalia.

Since his election, Manuel had on several occasions refused invitations.

'With such a lot to be done, I couldn't justify that kind of pleasure to the people, less still to my conscience,' he would say with a pleasant grin that disarmed Sir Bart; but not Sir Matthew.

'Of course he won't accept,' said the latter, 'as *the People's Consul* his image cannot afford that kind of luxury.'

'He's a good man, Matt, say what you like, but he's a hard worker and knows how to treat the people,' said Sir Bart.

'Of course, he is a natural politician,' agreed Sir Matthew, in a tone suggesting that there could not be a greater compliment. 'His image is impeccable: an admirable young man indeed. What a pity he isn't a Lemonist!'

One day, some of Manuel's fishermen friends from the Stivaletto district came to the castle to ask whether he would sail with them one night.

'Dey 'ave terrible catches, lately,' explained Filippo Grassi, 'dey tink you will bring good luck to dem.'

Visibly pleased to see his former friends again, Manuel said, 'Well, when you place so much faith in me, I guess I have no right to refuse. All the same, let me warn you that I make a poor fisherman and a worse sailor.'

Iscar was very unhappy about this.

'Heed the words of a wise old man: don't lean too heavily on the side of the people, court the friendship of the Patricians instead, they are strong and their loyalties more constant, because they have more to lose. These others are too fickle. You'll be their idol one day, a villain the next. Take these fishermen here, if their faith proves to be unfounded they will think less of you, if they have a big catch, they will demand a miracle a day.'

'I know the fishermen, Iscar,' said Manuel, amused by the old man's gloom, 'they're my friends. Their earthy humour is one of their endearing gifts.'

'What about Sir Bart, he's sure to take offence.'

'Ah, Sir Bart! He too can laugh at many things, except money. Sir Bart may wish to come along too.'

Sir Bart, who had a passion for fishing, did go. They spent a crisp night on the sea with the fishermen, under a sky faint with stillness and shadows. The men's shouting—pitched higher than usual—struck the frosty air, as they called to one another, excited by the Consul's presence among them.

Manuel did not fish, he preferred to let his mind float in that intense calm. He savoured the air and said, 'So thin! So bare! Reminds me of the desert. Sir Bart, how can you not feel all this greatness?'

Sir Bart did not hear.

Sir Bart took fishing as seriously as he did making money, and performed both tasks with equal intensity. Manuel watched him pull them in, yelling, cajoling, urging or cursing. His expression was absorbed and excited. It seemed as if Sir Bart had never seen fish so big or so numerous.

The fishermen too began to show interest, and soon each new catch was welcomed with shouts of exultation from the surrounding boats.

'Hey, Sir Bart! You better leave some for us,' they yelled. And in their hearts they hoped that it was a prelude to overflowing nets.

When the nets were finally pulled in, the catch proved to be no larger than normal. Still, the fishermen insisted that it was an excellent catch, and the quality of the fish—they all agreed—was far superior to any previous catch. They argued, swore and laughed over inanities. They feasted Sir Bart, and teased him good naturedly.

Sir Bart smiled happy and proud like a child. He looked tired, sated.

Manuel said, 'You see, Sir Bart, you can enjoy good fishing from a boat without the gold trimmings.'

Sir Bart was too much at peace with the world to argue one way or another.

As the fishing fleet edged in toward the harbour it was late morning. On shore there appeared to be a large waiting crowd.

'Look, look how many people!' yelled one of the fishermen.

Sir Bart, who was travelling with Manuel on the first boat, saw it too. He turned to the latter and said:

'Now, I wonder what the commotion is all about?'

XXXV

A Protest

Causing the commotion were The Strip people, and the signs on their banners expressed the purpose of their gathering.

IT'S NO CRIME TO BE DIFFERENT!
SAY NO TO OPPRESSION!
WE'RE ALL GOD'S CREATURES!
LEGALIZE OPIUM!
*MAKE LOVE **ANY WAY**!*

On the day of Manuel's election, some of the loudest cheers had risen from The Strip. All his friends who had known him as a young artist, and loved him, viewed his election as a storm of enlightenment that would sweep away intolerance from the island.

Manuel, in fact, had been to The Strip several times in the hope of drawing attention of 'respectable' Southfalia to the positive aspects of a life-style which it continued to fear. Prejudice, however, is in the habit of taking root all too easily, but is near impossible to eradicate.

'Those people are guilty of the most debauched sins ever devised by men!' protested Lady Virginia, the virtuous wife of Sir Marc Martial, self-appointed defender of public morals.

Most people tolerated the Consul's friendship with 'those people', blaming it on his bohemian days at The Strip, but hoped that it would not 'undermine his responsibilities toward the rest of the community'.

Freed from the oppression of *The Law and Order*, The Strip had grown defiant to the point of displaying publicly some of its more esoteric practices. Lady Virginia and her friends fumed and threatened to take the law into their own hands, 'if that scar on public decency did not cease at once'. And to match words with action, she and her virtuous friends instituted the B.A.D.S. movement, which stood for Bastion Against Degeneration and Sin, and whose motto became Continence, Honour and Chastity.

On the night Manuel was at sea, a troop of soldiers led by Sir Marc Martial raided an 'opium festival' at The Strip, badly beat up many of the celebrants, and quickly brought them back from their aery trance. Now the crowd had come to air its outrage, directly to the Consul.

By night 'The Strippers' could be pretty wild, but there on the wharf, in the soft light of the morning, to which they were unaccustomed, they looked pretty tame. It seemed rather strange, therefore, that when Sir Bart recognized them from the boat, his jolly mood altered.

'I'm not goin' down there among them pimps and queers,' he spluttered. He was nervous, terrified almost. Manuel reassured him.

'There is nothing to fear, Sir Bart. They're much gentler than they seem.'

'I'm not afraid of that cowardly lot!' he protested, and yet he became more agitated the closer they got to shore. 'The lazy, low-down scum! They should all be stripped and caned.'

Such hatred was uncharacteristic of Sir Bart.

'They're criminals. Worse than criminals. They're animals.'

'They're quite harmless you know, Sir Bart...'

'Listen, sooner or later you're gonna 'ave to stop playin' everybody's Godfather. If a man's bad, he's bad and must be dealt with. Harmless you say? I had a son, the only one...'

'Andrew, I know him well.'

'Yeah! And so does everyone of them freaks there. They've turned him into a proper queer that would make me ashamed to be seen walking down the street with him. These people are nothin' but trouble. Many of them 've never earned a penny in their life. They just go around stealin' from honest people to buy opium.'

'Yes, it's very sad but not hopeless. It takes more energy to steal than it does to do most things. Their imagination needs a positive direction.'

Manuel went down to meet the crowd alone.

'They broke up our gathering and beat up our friends,' complained Lusty Simon Spurioschenko. His voice faltered, self-consciously, despite a studied exterior of bravado. 'We had plenty of opium and were enjoying ourselves. They can't stand anyone having a good time. We demand the basic freedom to burn the candle the way we choose to.'

The Strippers cheered, supported also by seamen and wharf labourers, who seemed rather partial to them.

'Very well, Lusty. Seems a reasonable enough grievance. I promise to look into it.'

Having been reassured, the crowd dispersed.

Not long after, the Government decreed that it would no longer be a crime to read certain books, follow certain practices, make love in a certain manner or smoke opium.

'It's not the Government's role to tell adults how to live, so long as their behaviour causes no harm to others.'

Most people found no quarrel with this, though controversy remained as to what constituted 'harm to others'.

XXXVI

Winds of Freedom

In the wake of official recognition, one or two of the more classy bordellos moved their premises into the city centre. Madam Magdalene acquired a cosy little position near the west end of the square, formerly the site of a massage parlour patronized exclusively by members of the Senate. These gentlemen had a record of spinal injuries due to a curious habit of sleeping in their senate chairs.

'Can we sink any lower?' asked Lady Virginia. 'Think of all the temptation, the sin, the corruption of our sons!—not mine, to be sure, for they have been properly trained to love only God and the noble art of war.'

But the real outcry came with the legalization of opium.

'It will kill them! They will kill themselves!' argued Peter, airing thus the opinion of many. But Paul did not agree.

'It's their choice. I don't think it's wrong to allow a man his choice of death. Few have any choice of life, exploited as they are by every fat pig in this country.'

'Some are too far gone to be able to choose,' insisted Peter, 'for them it's no choice at all, but a condemnation to die.'

'Let them die in dignity then, not in some street gutter,' said Paul.

Lady Virginia was against the legislation as a matter of course, nor was Lady Britt happy about it.

'Restraint is still the best tonic for a healthy, strong nation. Remember the tragic fall of our glorious Motherland!' she warned.

'What about self-restraint?' retorted Paul, 'isn't that better?'

Lady Britt seethed.

'If you, Sir, are an example of what self-restraint achieves, may Jove shield us from it!'

The Strip dwellers were not the only outcasts of that society, as we have already observed. The natives and the foreign serfs were also identifiable as fringe groups. But there were many more: the feeble, the sensitive, those who did not conform to standards of morality or ideologies, grappled on the outskirts of Southfalian society like clusters of barnacles on the bottom of a ship. The ruling classes of the past had found it convenient to ignore their existence, while they served the interests of those powerful enough to secure their position. The young Consul was determined to rescue as many as could be rescued. To these people he devoted much of his attention, whilst continuing to cultivate a friendly rapport with the powerful knights.

'The failure of a system is proportional to the number of outcasts it creates,' said Manuel. 'Our competitive system favours the ruthless, the hardy, the adaptable; but at the same time it stunts the creativity of men of fine talents, who do not possess any competitive qualities. Their failure is our failure, their loss of self-esteem is our loss of creative energy, their recovery our responsibility.

'We must accept differences, not merely from person to person, but between groups. Variety fosters creation.'

'Unity is strength!' Paul cried.

'Unity of purpose, yes. Let's all aim at discovering more and better ways to live through a variety of approaches.'

He went to Stivaletto to urge the serfs to revive their old customs, their language, religion and skills.

To them he said, 'Cherish what is different in you. Be proud of it. Pass it on to your children, and share it with those enlightened enough to value it!'

The natives were urged to return to their ancient lore and recapture its mysticism. Black John called on them to return to the desert. At first it was with little success. The natives feared the desert and had no faith in John's ability to lead them back. After all, had they not been taught for years to trust only Roman ingenuity and to fear Roman might?

Slowly he was able to convince a small party to return with him to the ancient tribal lands and begin anew. The others, those too contaminated by Roman civilization were helped to find a place for themselves in the complicated structure of Southfalian society. The success was spasmodic, initially at least. Undaunted, Manuel crusaded with vigour.

'We cannot rest until the outcasts of our society have found some dignity. We cannot call this society just until it is free from the resentment which inhibits the spirit of so many.'

Hearing this Lady Britt's Roman hairdo bristled.

'Really! At this rate our Roman heritage will be superseded by barbaric cultures, our lineage bastardised by inferior blood, and our Government infested with inept foreigners. It will be the ruin of our country, just as our ancestors sealed their own fate when they allowed influxes of Barbarians into Rome.'

Lady Britt could not conceive life in constant change, adaptation and renewal.

More ominous were the words of Sir Bart, expressed to his friend the Scribe over dinner, 'If the Consul thinks I'm gonna play Good Samaritan to every drunk, queer and every other lazy bum in the country, he's got somethin' comin'.'

XXXVII

Changes in the Square

Now that the fear of the Squad was gone, people began to venture into the square to meet and converse with their friends. Country folk, coming to the city for Mass on Sunday, lingered in front of the cathedral chatting, while the Patricians took the opportunity to display their bright new outfits and shiny new carriages.

What spoilt it was the spray from the Midas, which inevitably reached them, and their clothes attained a yellow tint. For this reason the Patricians came to find the Midas as much a nuisance as did the ordinary people.

'Divert the water away from the square!

'No more golden spray?' demanded some people.

But others were still afraid, 'The square has always had the golden spray of the Midas! The fly curse will swoop down onto us.'

'*Les mouches? Ce sont les Erinnyes, les Déesses du remords*' [10] mumbled Iscar.

Manuel laughed.

'Really, we couldn't be cursed with many more flies than we have now. There just wouldn't be anywhere to put them.'

Eventually, when enough people were able to laugh off their fears, the fountain was dried out. The fly epidemic they had dreaded did not eventuate.

'See!' they cried, 'that tyrant Sir Pepin had us duped all the time.'

And they cursed the former Consul, forgetting that the fly-myth had begun long before Sir Pepin's time.

Now that they could see its full length, the square did not seem so formidable; on the other hand, without its haze of gold, old Midas revealed himself in all his oppressive ugliness.

'Demolish that horrible monster, that ugly symbol of slavery and give the square a new name,' cried Paul the Red. But Sir Bart did not agree.

'Leave it alone, the old fellow's brought this great country a good deal of luck.'

'Indeed!' expostulated Professor Equinus, 'if one were to interpret the Midas in its mythological context—or should I say *convention*—the values it personifies are anathema to those whose want defies their reach. Nonetheless....'

'Bull and shit!' broke in Gabby, the women's advocate, who wasted no opportunity to show that she could swear like a man, 'it's just another monument to male chauvinism. Knock the bloody thing down!'

Sir Matthew turned a judicious glance toward Manuel and said, 'I don't believe we should destroy the past, if nothing else it can serve us as a lesson.'

'Well spoken Sir Matthew! I couldn't agree more,' said Manuel.

'If the Consul agrees, another monument can be raised...something to express the new spirit,' suggested the Scribe.

'An excellent suggestion, and if the people wish it we will divert the traffic away from the square so that they may stroll through it undisturbed.'

The people were asked also to nominate the person they wished to have immortalized in the square, and because it was Paul the Red who commanded the support of the most vocal section of the city, they decided on the Gracchi brothers.

'Poppy and cock!' exploded Gabby, ' another monument to male chauvinism.'

The Council agreed that Gabby's outburst, though not necessarily in good taste, was well received. So they decided to erect a female figure as well.

SOUTHFALIA

'Let it be a woman to encompass the beauty of Venus, the wisdom of Athena, the fortitude of Diana and—why not?—the capricious genius of Juno,' declaimed Professor Equinus.

'Give us a statue of Sappho; our patron,' demanded Gabby.

However, not all of her sisters agreed with her, which led to much Babelic babbling, and it took no less than the diplomatic genius of Sir Matthew to break the impasse with an acceptable compromise.

'Why not a statue to the three Graces. The first with the features of Sappho, the second as beautiful as Venus, the third: wise and strong like Athena.'

Gabby let out a string of expletives to record her opposition to such symbols of femininity, but finally gave her approval, consoled by the fact that three females in the square were better than one.

When it came to looking for an artist to do the figures none could be found.

'We will send abroad for a sculptor,' they said, just as they always had in the past. Manuel was amazed.

'I can't believe that in the whole island there is no one capable of using the chisel.'

It occurred to them that there probably was, but since works of art were always commissioned overseas, they just had not thought of considering a Southfalian.

'But of course!' exclaimed Paul, hit by the sudden realization, 'this is the best country in the world, it follows that we must have the best sculptors.'

However, no sculptor came forward until Manuel, whilst on a country journey with Filippo Grassi, chanced on a stocky, dark man intent on breaking stone with a tomahawk by the edge of the road. Manuel tried to speak to him, but the other appeared not to understand. Grassi spoke with him, and after some gesticulation he explained.

'His name is Bottinculo and he work for Sir Bart to make de bricks. In de evening 'e collect stone to build a 'ouse.'

'I tell you trou' burst in Bottinculo, suddenly finding his words, 'brick is rubbish! Shit!' He spat on the ground to illustrate. 'You 'ave very much beautiful stonne. Stonne very strong.' He flexed his biceps.

Manuel was radiant.

'Would you come with me signor Bottinculo? I've got a job for you, which I think you'll like.'

And taking him by the arm, they went together back to the castle.

Though everyone was relieved that a sculptor had been found, Sir Bart complained bitterly that his best brick-maker had been taken away from him.

'At this rate there'll be nobody to do the dirty work.'

'Cheer up Sir Bart,' Manuel reassured him, 'if he is half as good as I believe he is, you'll be able to adorn your gardens with priceless masterpieces. Remember, artistic patronage is the mark of a true gentleman.'

XXXVIII

A Battle in the Square

The Gracchi square became the living heart of the city. People came to it to buy and sell, to stroll, to talk, argue and gossip. Children came to play, chasing one another around the tables set up in front of inns and ale-houses. Families came to take their meals by the retiring sun, while on the steps of Ivory Tower eminent philosophers and their pupils debated, explored, speculated above the shouting of the vendors, the yelling of housewives, the cries of children, the beating of the coppersmith and the hammering in Bottinculo's shop.

Lately Bottinculo had become a source of controversy due to his risqué figures. His nude Gracchis had shocked and offended some Southfalians' sense of decorum, defined by centuries of Christian precepts.

'The Church cannot tolerate such flagrant indecency,' protested Monsignor from the pulpit.

Still, when the Graces were installed in all their nakedness, Monsignor's voice did not raise in protest.

'Evidently the female nude is not so offensive in the eyes of the Lord,' Paul said.

But if the Good Lord chose to turn a blind eye to them, Lady Britt didn't.

'They've turned our heroes and gods into erotic monuments. This sort of thing may be tolerated in decadent Florence, but we, who purport to exemplify Roman sobriety, we should display a responsible sense of decorum.'

Iscar, who found the nudes a source of solace for his frustrated senses, said: 'Et bien! Eros was a very respectable Olympian before Christianity quashed him down to hell.'

Needless to say, the nudes gave Lady Virginia convulsions. One day Bottinculo was enjoying a plate of pasta in the open air at the Muse's Inn, when Lady Virginia arrived supported by a retinue of ladies. She stood directly in front of him and gave one of her speeches in which she condemned his work as scandalous, offensive, corruptive of public morals and so on. As Lady Virginia's oratorical fervour reached more refined altitude, so rose Bottinculo's temper until, unable to contain it any longer, he stood up waving his arms and shouting down the lady without regard to chivalry or rank, 'Gettaway mad woman, you kno' notink about de arte! *Avanti, via, vecchia folle!*'

Lady Virginia ignored him and persisted with her speech, while Bottinculo looked down disconsolately to the pasta he wasn't allowed to enjoy. Rashly he balanced the dish on the palm of his right hand and.... Lady Virginia's majestic head found itself crowned with red worms wriggling down her face, as if to escape her fiery breath.

Still, a virtuous woman has a lot of dignity to defend and a multitude of ways in which to do it. Lady Virginia chose the most direct one. She fixed her foe with a terrible stare, then strode to him majestically, without upsetting the fretting strings of pasta on her head, raised the baton which she always carried and brought it down on the ribs of the terrified little man.

(Yes, I realize we've sunk down to the level of *Commedia dell'arte*: more *commedia* than *arte*; but Iscar swears by this incident, and historical authenticity—of a sort—is what we're after. *'Enfin mes amis,* 'writes he, *'what is history? Is it not the story of men who, like you and I, spent a portion of their existence sitting on toilet seats?'*)

Bottinculo recovered from the ordeal to finish his next work: a naked Apollo whose genitals he enlarged to spite Lady Virginia. The statue depicted the Sun-god on the point of awakening. His face—vaguely resembling Manuel's—was still puffy from the night's sleep; but the eyes were alert in eager expectation for what the day was about to reveal. It was placed on the foyer of Ivory Tower, where it was acclaimed as a thing of great beauty.

SOUTHFALIA

Lady Virginia did not get to see the Apollo. Her husband forbade it, fearing that the sight might stain her purity. But Sir Marc did, and his reaction was predictable.

'Filth!' he shouted, 'downright filth! Are we going to expose the eyes of our virtuous women to this kind of filth! And what about our children?'

Actually the children thought no more of it, once their initial curiosity was sated. Then one morning the city awoke to find Apollo emasculated. Some said that Sir Herod was back in Southfalia and had done it to keep in practice. Now the children who passed pointed and enquired after the missing genitals.

'Never you mind, gods are not meant to have those things,' they were told.

'That's all very well for them,' writes Iscar acidly, *'for gods in their perfection have neither desires to sate, nor impurities to release.'*

XXXIX

Athens of the Southern Seas

At the end of Manuel's first year as Consul we find Southfalia peaceful, secure and cautiously optimistic. The people seemed not unlike the prisoner who, having served a long sentence, hesitates in front of the open cell door.

Manuel had been aware of the risks he was taking and in any case there was no lack of warnings.

'Southfalia is moving too fast, too soon on the road to so-called freedom. The people are not ready for it!' wrote Sir Matthew.

For his part Manuel appeared to have limitless faith in the ability of the people to respond to a new challenge. He encouraged open debate and ensured that innovation and originality was rewarded. New work ethics were adopted.

As people were able to gauge the extent of their freedom, they searched for possibilities, embraced new directions. All that creative energy so long repressed gathered force and was channelled through innovative outlets. Increased restlessness and public debate accompanied this cultural awakening. Conservative organizations such as A.L.E.R.T. who reviled the wave of liberality (which it called 'decadence') warned 'of the perils of a soft nation'. It lamented 'the days when austerity and discipline gave us an assurance of survival', and warned 'Remember! It was Sparta the victorious one in Peloponnesus.'

To which Manuel was reported to have replied, 'Sparta may have won the war, but it was Athens which prospered…and went on to teach the world the meaning of beauty!'

Lady Britt said, 'In Rome we already have the perfect model. It has served us well since this nation's inception.'

'What Rome! What Athens!' cried Paul, 'this is Southfalia: the best country in the world. Be ourselves!'

According to Iscar, jingoism had always been a mark of the Southfalian character; but it was jingoism utterly devoid of cultural self-esteem. Lady Britt's ancestors had created it, and Ivory Tower's snobs had perpetrated the myth that Southfalia's soul resided abroad, as Iscar writes,

> *Everyone competed to outdo one another in the exploitation of the island's material wealth. Few reached for its spirit; a spirit buried by centuries of prejudice, greed, affectation and hypocrisy. Naturally the island was a magnet for all kind of pretentious mountebanks, rogues and poseurs. Naturally anyone unfortunate enough to possess a shade of originality was arrogantly put down. Naturally critical praise went to the worthless, the conceited, the confused and the opportunist. Naturally, the most lauded figures of Southfalia's golden age were not the fine artists, musicians, architects, writers and thinkers; but poets of mediocre talent whose works, enigmatic and mannered, became fashionable in Southfalia's best salons. Suddenly, it became 'a la mode' for the rich ladies to be 'intimately cognizant' of local poetry churned out by poets poor in talent and rich in effrontery.*
>
> *In the art world the story was identical. Popularity, among the rich anyway, went to the artist who could best cultivate the image of an eccentric in manner, clothing and speech.*
>
> *Soon the great ladies found themselves playing an exciting new game: to secure for themselves the services of the most popular young oddball regardless of cost. As a consequence, the price of opium reached new heights and young plume-holders raised enough dust to envelope the literary milieu of the island with hazy affectation.*

Thus, Lusty Simon Spurioschenko, who claimed that his mother was a gypsy, his father a Ukrainian and his brother a Buddhist monk, could not fail to become the heartthrob of every woman with enough money to subsidize his outlandish tastes.

Spurioschenko called himself the Alley Hermit, went about barefoot, wore a cassock and an ear-ring, curled his hair, plucked his eyebrows and kept two mistresses. His poetry always dealt with two subjects: Eros and himself. He read in a husky, soulful voice; and his rendition was so stirring that listeners inevitably forgot to listen to the words, which suited Spurioschenko very well. It is our fortune that Iscar treats us to a typical example of this bard's versifying:

THE FALL

Before a million eyes
The jaundiced plantain tree
Rises alone.

It fears the West
Above the rest
Whose footfalls
Of renovating rains
Of eternal life
And profound abandonment
It seeks.

Soon they will open
Its jaundiced flower-tongues
To the phallic seeds castrated by the sun
Like seamen on the earth
The savage lips will crave in vain.

Aah! My jaundiced soul
Tormented
Like the rising plantain tree
Unweathered
Has lost.

The academics of Ivory Tower declared his poetry the work of a genius. Iscar quotes the example of the enterprising young scholar who, sensitive to the direction of the prevailing wind around Ivory Tower, wrote a three-hundred page thesis entitled *'Orgasm of Sense and Sensuousness in the Poetry of Spurioschenko'*.

'*Spurioschenko's poetry,*' he wrote, '*marks a departure from traditional verse structures, whilst at the same time retaining a translucent and vital link with classical poetic expression. Like a liberating wind, it evokes the spirit of the age, sustained by a diction unshackled yet deliberate, sensitive yet virile, which gives birth to a poetry pregnant with meaning and infused with objective correlatives.*'

Then he went on to dissect the pregnancy of the meaning and the objectivity of the correlation like nobody's business, drawing on quotations from no less than one hundred and eighty renowned critics. Result: a permanent niche among the celebrated critics of the island, and a comfortable chair on the university staff.

Despite that, a cultural flourishing did occur, thanks to the inspired leadership of the young Consul. For a time, freedom, tolerance and truth triumphed; philosophical enquiry was neither affectation nor a joke, and art, that whiff of a passing god, stirred the ashen embers.

'I charge you to replenish our libraries, theatres and museums with real works,' urged Manuel, 'for too long they have been sanctuaries for the mediocre and the snobs. Let us not confuse trend with innovation, vulgarity for realism, obscurity for depth, mannerism for art.'

'What qualities should the artist nurture?' he was asked.

'Sincerity and skill. Sincerity above all. It's too easily affected, rarely attained and even more rarely recognized.'

As word spread abroad that Southfalia was experiencing a creative renaissance some of the foremost artists and teachers of that time—together with many disillusioned expatriates who had formerly left—flocked to the island. Manuel welcomed them and offered his patronage, despite the inevitable objections of those who feared that they would lose their jobs, or that the island's emerging culture would lose its uniqueness. Manuel begged to differ.

'Originality does not mean rejection of what is already there, but building on it. True style reveals an implicit respect for others and presumes a debt to their work. True style is humble.'

Works of astonishing originality were produced by a cluster of gifted men and women, which established Southfalia's reputation abroad. Foreign critics praised the works, foreign merchants sought Southfalian merchandise and Sir Bart's businesses thrived. His ships carried Southfalian artefacts made of wood, iron, silver, gold, ceramics, wool…and sold at the most prestigious markets abroad.

Art, music and literature flourished. All three found a common source of inspiration which hitherto had gone unnoticed: Southfalian landscape and native lore. A few inspired artists captured the spirit in their works then, as always, the plagiarists moved in to take the credit. Architecture did not escape the creative surge. New landmarks were erected: simple structures, elegant and harmonious, as well as practical.

'Art transcends the sensual world and sublimates passions,' said the Consul, 'I believe it renders us free and opens out to possibilities.'

Manuel believed in art for the people. To that end he established a special fund for public performances by actors, musicians and orators. Iscar records that one day the funeral cortege of an influential Grandee found the way blocked by a performing group. The leading coachman began to shout for them to get out of the way, whereupon Manuel, who attended the funeral, approached the dead man's relatives and said, 'I beg you to let the actors finish their play. It will be the last that your beloved will be able to enjoy among us.'

XL

On War and Peace

Southfalians, like their Roman ancestors, had always lived by the motto: *If peace you seek, be ever ready for war.* The policy had successfully managed to keep warfare out of the country, and though Southfalian corpses had strewn foreign battlefields, the stench had never reached its happy shores.

Surrounding Southfalia were many states always at war with one another. The poorer they were, the more belligerent. Southfalia, being so rich, found little cause for war, but if war started, its leaders were wise enough to pick the stronger side and furnish it with ships, arms and mercenaries. It was a very convenient arrangement that suited the majority because it kept the numbers of the starving masses down, satisfied the pride of Princes, kept the forges busy and the economy buoyant, eliminated the weak and reduced the power of the stronger neighbours. In short, it had a wonderful levelling effect, and it rejuvenated fifteenth century society. For that reason, the people looked on war in the same way as they saw floods or earthquakes: with fatalistic acceptance.

Manuel had been elected on a promise of peace, but then so had every other Consul before him. It wasn't long before the realities of politics forced them to undertake 'a programme to strengthen defence for the preservation of peace'. That, in turn, alarmed other nations and the cycle of mutual fear and mistrust would begin anew.

So far the Consul had been able to keep to his promise with comparative ease, despite warnings from the A.L.E.R.T. of red and yellow perils.

Then a brand new war flared up between Roaresia and Tremor, two of Southfalia's northern neighbours and from each came requests for support.

'As you all know,' explained Sir Matthew MacKiavel at an emergency meeting, 'Roaresia is the lion and Tremor the lamb. As far as the former is concerned, the whole thing is a take-over exercise in order to silence a potential nuisance. Our interests will be served best by showing support for Roaresia, while secretly supplying weapons to Tremor. The annexation of Tremor by its larger neighbour is both inevitable and desirable, since it eliminates an element of instability from the area; on the other hand it is in our interest to try and blunt Roaresia's victory. It isn't very comfortable, I'm sure you'll agree, to have an overconfident lion grunting on our northern borders.'

Sir Matthew had spoken the idiom of pragmatic diplomacy, which had proved disastrous by millennia of wars. He knew no other and Manuel did not blame him, but felt certain that there must be another way. 'Thank you, Sir Matthew,' said he, 'the situation could not have been better assessed. However, the people of this island do not wish, nor have they the right, to interfere in the conflict. In fact we should protest to Roaresia and align with Tremor.'

Sir Matthew smiled patronisingly.

'If I may say so, Sir, that kind of moral stance will achieve nothing positive. The reality is that Tremor will be crushed and unless we accept the situation Southfalia will gain a powerful enemy.'

'But a clear conscience.'

'Conscience! It counts for little in politics. The rules of the game are set by the reality.'

'We're part of the reality. We can change the rules.'

Manuel's earnest eyes made him seem very young.

'In the end, Sir, people don't give a fig what rules we adopt, so long as we're on the winning side.'

Unaccustomed to such bluntness coming from Sir Matthew, the Council fell silent as it pondered over the words.

Manuel said, 'To my ideals I subordinate everything.'

SOUTHFALIA

'Including winning?' asked Sir Matthew.

Manuel dodged the question.

'The people have voted for me because they are sick of wars and more wars.'

'We have survived.'

'Survived, yes! But I believe we can do better; and the present vigour in our society is an indication of just how much better we can do.'

'All the more reason why we need to keep a close watch on envious neighbours.'

'I know, Sir Matthew, I know that we must keep our doors bolted. That's a pity, for in the end security, real security, can only be gained through fairness and trust. Now, you will say, *it can't happen*, *it's all a dream* and history is there to support you. But I say let's try, perhaps we've come of age and are ready to begin trusting one another.'

'That can be fatal,' warned Sir Matthew.

'Yes, it can be, but the alternative: the never-ending game of rivalry and mistrust has not worked. So I suggest that we adopt a position of neutrality and put all efforts into initiating a dialogue between the two sides. We need a good diplomat to handle this delicate situation. Frankly I think there is no better man for the job than yourself, Sir Matthew. Come, Sir, we'll thrash it out over dinner.'

XLI

A Journey Abroad

As fame of the idealistic young ruler spread throughout the Southern world, persistent invitations arrived for him to visit neighbouring countries. So, no one was surprised at the news that Manuel was going to travel abroad. What did surprise many was that one of the countries Manuel intended to visit was Riceland, where peace had recently returned following the withdrawal of the Emperor's crusaders after years of unsuccessful invasion.

Sir Marc was furious. Nor was Sir Marc's the only voice of protest.

'The Church deplores, in the strongest possible terms, any contact with those barbarians who rejected the holy sacrament of baptism and ate our missionaries,' protested Monsignor.

Opposition or not, Manuel was determined to go on with the visit. Iscar warned him of the risks.

'You know, Sir, wise is the man who bends with the prevailing wind, especially when it's a strong one. As for a statesman, a supple back is essential.'

'There's danger in that too. The power-wielders are the first to cut you down if a decision taken to appease them fails. No, Iscar, I'll just have to try persuade them, and if that fails I will ask for their trust.'

He went to the Senate first, and then directly to the people in the Square and spoke to them about the wisdom of dispelling mistrust among the nations of the South.

'And what better place to begin than from Riceland, to which we owe a great debt?'

In Riceland he was received with restrained cordiality, by a proud people who let it be known that they sought no sympathy.

'We are not here to dwell on the mistakes of the past,' Manuel assured them, 'but to build on what they taught us. We intend to repay whatever part of our debt that can be repaid.'

The Ricelanders studied the young man with puzzlement. Christians expected conversion in return for help and the Ricelanders had just fought a ten-year war for the right to retain their religion and culture. But this Christian was not like the others. His face was open, his eyes were honest, he did not spin words. They remembered that he had been the first to recall soldiers from their country.

'Thank you, Sir,' they said, 'there is much destruction in our country. We need food, material, boats; but most of all we require arms so as to stave off any more crusades.'

Manuel smiled. Their suspicion could hardly surprise. He did the only thing possible in the circumstances: reassured them of his good intentions, promised what he could, appealed to trust, and planted the first seeds of friendship. He visited the other states and, wherever he went, each claimed to be seeking peace through strength, meaning that they were more interested in Southfalia's minerals and arms, than in building trust. They listened to his talk of peace, made perfunctory observations, excuses, reservations, all nicely coated in platitudes ending with vague promises.

'Now, about that shipment of arms...' they would say.

'That's not why I am here,' he told them tersely, 'speak to me of ways to grow more food, build better schools or dispel suspicion among us and I will hear you; but on the subject of arms I will be deaf!'

They recognized the mark of his candour, and in the clear reflection of those black eyes they glimpsed a world seen in fleeting childhood dreams, long buried in dust of ambition, fear, prejudice and scepticism.

'If our enemies can be talked into it...we will not be the ones to stand in the way of co-operation in our region.'

It was a beginning.

SOUTHFALIA

He went to other countries and he met them all: the wise, the tyrant, the pragmatist, the ambitious, the weak. By the simple weapons of sincerity and passionate beliefs he demolished their resistance and elaborated his vision.

He visited a wise old Rajah who said, 'I too was drunk with vision as a young man, but age has sobered me up and showed me a chasm separating the vision from reality.'

'If we can be free from the burden of fear,' Manuel argued, 'and raise our eyes so that we may perceive the single in the whole and the whole in the single; what's between should make more sense.'

'You aim high, young man, and you'll find that demands you make cannot be met by mere men. For most of us survival depends on being able to get away with daily deceptions: to others and to ourselves.'

'How so?'

'You see, the difference between the ancient societies and contemporary ones is that their gods were imperfect beings who, though powerful and loving, could also exact revenge, vent their fury, deceive, fornicate…in short, resemble human beings. Unfortunately for us, our more immediate ancestors burdened us with a perfect God. As a consequence the people expect perfection from their public figures, whilst knowing full well that there is no such thing. In essence, the people actually want us to lie to them, though of course they would never admit it.'

Manuel had too much faith in human goodness to subscribe to such a cynical view of humanity. He studied the older man's lines about his eyes and wondered what experiences had led him to such disillusionment.

'In the society that I envisage,' he said, 'it should be possible to tell the raw truth—about the world and about ourselves.'

'Such idealism,' said the old Rajah to Paul the Red, who was accompanying Manuel on the journey, 'as if he were dealing with saints. I fear he won't last, your Manuel. They never do.'

A rich Sultan, whom they visited the last, welcomed his Southfalian guests with a lavish feast. Near the end, the Sultan introduced his prize piece: a veiled French 'Chanteuse' covered all over in swirling silk.

She began to sing a series of French songs in a silky voice. Paul, who had not been able to take his eyes off her, wanted to speak to her, get to know her better. Imagine his joy when, having finished her repertoire, the girl brushed past him and whispered.

'Monsieur, would you like to see me in the vestibule?'

With passion surging inside him, Paul followed the beautiful woman. In the darkroom she lit a candle, then let the veil fall away from her face. Paul's leaping heart stopped.

'*C'est moi, Paul*, do you not recognize me?'

The name choked in his throat: Princess Sybilla!

XLII

Adventures of a Princess

In the dim light of the room, between sobs of despair and tears of joy, the Princess spoke of her travels. Not long after leaving Southfalia to go and join Emperor Otto, the first and greatest of her misfortunes struck; she lost her dear Sir Pepin. He disappeared one stormy afternoon, while she rested in her cabin, in the company of a young sailor. With Pepin gone, the crew took it into their heads to change course and head for the Greek islands instead.

On a dark night, when the crew were drunk and brawling, the boat was grounded. In the morning they waded ashore only to fall into the hands of Sicilian bandits who killed the crew and took Sybilla prisoner back to their hide-out in the mountains.

Their leader was a fat brute called Lucky Capon who was the most fearless of bandits. This Lucky, who was ugly as well as fat, made her an offer which, he said, she could not refuse. But she did. Subsequently the Princess found herself locked up and on a ration of bread and water. Soon, however, a handsome young bandit made her a much better offer, as a consequence of which she agreed to escape with him back to the coast.

They took a small boat and sailed for Greece, but before they got anywhere Lucky Capon's henchmen had caught up with them. They killed the young man and left her stranded on the high sea. After days of wandering, just when she began to fear that she would have to suffer a dreadful end, she sighted land.

It was a craggy Greek island all white and spotted with caves from which smoke rose into the blue sky. Sybilla began to wave and call. No one answered. Though exhausted she managed to clamber up the ridge and, on reaching the top, she discovered a group of people lying by the fire. Again she called, but they did not hear her cries. A dreadful fear that they might all be dead overcame her. This fear, coupled with thirst and exhaustion, weakened her and she fainted.

She woke up inside a white stone cave, surrounded by strange faces. She thought she was in delirium but no, she found herself in the midst of a Community of Dreamers, mostly young, and all of them disillusioned with the state of the world. Hence they had retreated to this remote Greek island to dream of ways to change it. Sybilla had caught them in one of their day-dreaming sessions; that's why they had not heard her cries for help. Unfortunately, they were having problems co-existing, as Sybilla discovered when she attended one of their communal meetings.

First to speak was a tough-looking herdsman who, since his recent arrival from somewhere or other, had wanted to run the island. He stood up and confronted his arch-rival, a grizzly bear type, and accused him of wanting to run the island and of spying on everybody. Then he mumbled, 'This 'ere island ain't big enough for the two of us. We can't co-exist no more.'

The other stood up in his huge, ugly frame and rumbled, 'Who says that we must co-exist on your terms?' And nobody argued.

A fanatical young Palestinian yelled, 'It's all the fault of that Jewish girl. This island would be peaceful if she didn't exist.'

The clever little Jewess waved a self-righteous finger and declared, 'We've been homeless for centuries and you people are to blame for it. As far as I am concerned, the Palestinian doesn't exist.'

A skinny Abyssinian, caught up in all the squabbling wailed, 'All I want is enough food to exist.'

A well-trained Chinese child chanted, 'Only the State has the right to exist.'

An insane-looking German with an unpronounceable name rushed in to announce, 'I have killed God. God no longer exists!'

A dictatorial Latin thundered, 'I don't know about God, but **I** exist.'

SOUTHFALIA

An Oriental transcendentalist who didn't look to be all there, bowed his head and asked, 'Do I really exist?'

A rotund Frenchman retorted, 'Life is absurd. Therefore you exist.'

The hapless Sybilla gazed at the romantic Aegean down below and wished that somebody would take notice that *she* existed.

She found their life tedious and lonely, for those young people were interested only in their own causes. There wasn't much to eat either. They were all too busy dreaming of changing the world, and nobody wanted to work.

Paul, who had listened attentively to the story, exclaimed, 'what a strange community! By comparison life in Southfalia is really not so bad.'

Sybilla proceeded with her story.

One day the transcendentalist, who was always mixing up new concoctions to attain ever-more rarefied trances, blew up his mind, literally, and proved his point. The explosion caught the attention of a ship passing on the horizon and Sybilla was thus able to leave the Community of Dreamers.

There followed many months of wandering in which the resourceful Princess undertook a variety of respectable jobs in Odessa, Baghdad, Constantinople and Cairo. Then in Alexandria luck turned her way again. She met the Sultan of Elshad in a respectable gambling house and he was so mesmerised by her beauty and voice that he asked her to be his favourite wife. This she naturally refused but agreed to give his children singing lessons instead.

'*Et enfin, me voici!*[11] That is how I come to be here,' she said, wiping a bead of tear from the corner of her eye.

To be sure, she didn't look any the worst for her ordeal. She still emitted the same radiance. Add to that a touch of mystery that experience bestows and you have that most desirable creature of all: the complete woman

The Sultan proved most unwilling to part with his children's singing teacher. But when Sybilla herself expressed a desire to go, in front of the visitors, he had to consent.

XLIII

Celebrations

On his return to Southfalia Manuel spoke about his journey with unconcealed enthusiasm, to a cheering crowd, 'I am delighted to report that we are far from alone in our desire for peace...All the leaders I visited agreed to initiate talks aimed at establishing a Peace Zone in our region...The way will not be easy, it has been made tortuous by decades of rivalry and suspicion...We must be patient, we must be determined...'

The speech was so well received that it caused Sir Matthew to comment privately, 'the young peasant's rhetoric has come a long way. Yes, it's a real pity he was not a Lemonist, my dear Sir Bart.'

Manuel's return to Southfalia coincided with the second anniversary of his election, and the people of the island were eager to celebrate. In the past such events were marked by military marches, speeches and jousts. Manuel did not care for any of that.

'Celebrate? I'm all for it,' he said, 'but let's have fun too. We've all worked well these last two years. We're entitled to it.'

They daubed the city in the gayest colours for three days of celebrations. Peasants flocked to the city, inns were packed, the streets noisy, the Gracchi Square was taken over by dancers, musicians and merrymakers, the B.A.D.S. ladies stayed indoors and Madam Magdalene did a roaring business.

It was a celebration of life and for the man who had made the changes possible. It was a gesture of gratitude towards the leader—a commoner like them—who gave them hope in that region of the restless 15th century world.

For three days the Big Dragon stayed open. People filed into the large courtyard of the castle to meet their Consul who, they thought, would be greeting them from a grand chair, looking dignified and condescending. Manuel, instead, threw himself fully into the spirit of the celebrations.

The old scaffold from which thousands of unfortunates had hung, was set up in the square and turned into a stage on which actors, musicians, poets and clowns entertained. On the last afternoon Lusty Simon Spurioschenko recited some of his torrid verse,

THE FIRST SIN

The Lotus flower lures me to
The forest of the lusty lutanist.
By day it hangs its sultry head,
At night it wells a million cells
With almond milk
To suck and drink
The pain of birth and joy of death.

I've roamed down the tree-less forest
Where the lutanist plays his song,
I've crossed the valley
Fanned the branches
Stroked the leaves
Laid me on the velvet reeds
Sank my head
Kissed
And died
Upon the Lotus flower bed.

So, when the lusty lutanist
Fills the forest with its subtle song
I'll scent the air
Taste the roses

SOUTHFALIA

Bite the apple
Drag me down the downy petal
Drink the sap
Rise
To fall
And end the Lotus flower's song.

Oh, let me live to lie, to die
Upon the Lotus flower bed.

Spurioschenko's intense, husky voice ceased, but its echo lingered over the breathless audience before applause reverberated from one end of the square to the other. The idol acknowledged the applause, accorded the ladies a flutter or two of his languid eyelids and strolled off the stage, with his two mistresses under each arm, amid sighs issuing from expensively perfumed bosoms.

Prominent among these was Princess Sybilla, whose reappearance in Southfalia had caused its own vibrations in the Patrician camp. Her recent experiences had changed her. No longer did she seek the company of stout, bejewelled gentlemen of refined habits. Now she started to be seen by the side of Paul the Red, dressed in peasant style, wearing neither jewellery nor cosmetics—except for a subtle smear of rouge, enough to suggest the peasant's rosy—cheeked look. In short, Paul's fiery temperament and the romantic one of Sybilla proved to be the perfect complement and the two had become inseparable. The Princess, who never did things by half, turned herself into a fully-fledged Prole and renamed herself Sybil.

Europe's most fashionable woman now wore faded old cassocks, peasant-style, with runs and tears in several places and became a fervent revolutionary. When she marched down the street with her fellow Proles she added a touch of Continental style when she chanted:

'*Liberté! Egalité! Fraternité!*'

History does not record—and she did not realize I am sure—that our Sybil was probably the unlikely initiator of that famous cry, some three centuries before the storming of the Bastille.

Now came the highlight of the afternoon: the long awaited eulogy specially composed for the occasion by Professor Thomas Equinus, in collaboration with other erudites from Ivory Tower, all subscribing to the belief that after Homer, Virgil, Dante and Spurioschenko, there were only imitators.

Thomas Equinus came forward and before commencing, gave proper acknowledgement to his colleagues, who had co-operated with him during twelve months of painstaking research and composition of the work, then cleared his throat and declaimed:

Heavenly Phoebus! Whose incandescent chariot
Diurnally leaps from Aurora's auburn bosom,
While tardy Zeus, confounded lingers yet
Aspiring to fathom fickle Hera, more restive
More obdurate than Persephone, captive
To brutish Pluto; thy aid I do invoke.
Enflame my sabled spirit, oh lustrous Deity
Erato's song to sing, of Manuel thy son
Southfalia's sun; his glory to be vaunted
His name to be emblazoned in eternal poesie.

When Cronus did assent to Gaea's bid
And flung mighty Uranus from his throne,
Vanquished, though immortal...

Mentor Thomas' cultured tongue delivered the mighty lines, but no one had expected quite so many. Soon they were completely lost in a labyrinth of gods and goddesses, Titans, Tritons, Cyclops, Muses and scores of other dwellers of Mount Olympus and Hades; bizarre creatures known only to Professor Thomas and his learned colleagues and dreamt by the uninitiated only in devilish nightmares. Overwhelmed by this poetic avalanche the audience did not know quite how to put a stop to it. Finally it was left to Manuel,

SOUTHFALIA

'Leave it there, Professor Equinus,' he said, 'let me have the full text and I will read it in an atmosphere that will do it more justice. Let's put on our masks and wear our costumes. It's time to join the people in the carnival.'

XLIV

A Night of Revelry

It looked as if all of Southfalia had gathered in the square, which had taken on the aspect of a Mardi Gras. Formerly masks or disguises of any kind had been illegal, as they were regarded both immoral and a security risk. Now the city had turned the final night into a riotous celebration.

It was a night for people to live out their strangest dreams. It was a night for mockery and self-mockery. The square fluttered with garments of kings, princes and paupers; grand-dames, devils and buffoons; tigers, mice and butterflies. Gay Ganymede wore Beatrice's heavenly veils, Gabby became Hercules, Professor Equinus: Socrates. Manuel too joined the happy revellers dressed up as Lycidas, the young Sicilian shepherd.

There were many performing groups in the square. Most colourful were John's people, come all the way from the desert for the occasion. They sported naked torsos decorated white, red and ochre. Over their shoulders they carried large totems depicting indigenous animals and reptiles.

Manuel could not have had a more pleasant anniversary gift. The two friends embraced; their bonding was of the kind that only the desert could bestow.

'Reports reaching us are encouraging,' Manuel said.

John's people had to overcome drought and famine, which frustrated their efforts and decimated their numbers. It was the price to be paid to re-enter the land of spirits. So they learned how to approach these spirits and appease them in the way that their ancestors had done.

'We been learnin' to dance again,' said John.

Now by the ghostly silhouette of Apollo, a God foreign to them, they danced of their spirits to Roman Southfalia.

The Snake-River dance told of an ill-led tribe which attempted to cross a sacred river without first invoking the assistance of the Water-Spirit. For punishment the Spirit infested the river with venomous snakes which decimated the tribe. Children, young women, old men who came to get water from the river were found dead along its bank. On each victim the snakes fed and multiplied.

On a gloomy night of full moon the tribe sat around their Elder, their desperate eyes seeking elucidation. Soon they would all be dead from snake-bite or thirst, said he, unless the Spirit could be appeased and the curse lifted. So the Elder beckoned them to join him in a propitiatory chant at the end of which a lean young man rose and announced that he would go next to fetch the water.

At dawn the young man went down to the river, tinted amber by the sun. Down crouched the youth to the water and broke its glazed surface. A snake slithered up to him and he speared it. Another charged up and suffered the same end, then more and more came and he speared each one, until the whole river was quivering with a thousand swishing, flailing, recoiling snakes. Boldly the young man pursued their quicksilver bodies toward midstream, turning the brackish water vermilion as he killed the snakes one by one.

In the end the river was clogged up with reeds of floating dead snakes. But when the young man attempted to make his way back he was caught in a tendril of dead snakes and was carried downstream. And so the river was cleared and the tribe saved.

The dance affected everyone profoundly, Manuel no less, then John invited the Consul to join him and his people in a happy dance.

And dance they did: the shepherd and the nomads, their movements finding complete harmony in the simple steps which trace the inevitable struggle between good and evil.

Other groups danced too, each their own dance. Because it was a night when the unhappy shrugged off their misery, the madman was judged sane and the virgin gave herself without remorse. It was a night of dare and defiance. Like the eagle man who mounted the Big Dragon and tried to soar above the crowd only to plummet down in a hump of broken bones.

To everyone's astonishment from under the wings peered the head of Filomena of Spudsville. Her blood-smeared face was triumphant.

'It was our Consul that gave me the idea,' she said.

It appears that, on a visit to Bartholomew House—where Filomena now lived—Manuel had found her seated on the doorstep, sobbing. She had just been for a walk in the garden, smelt all those flowers and surmised that the Good Lord provides us with eyes, to make us witness to the infinite variety of His works—He too being something of a ham for applause. Yet she was condemned never to see them, because she had ruined her eyes scanning potatoes.

Manuel had tried to comfort her, 'Eyes are a wonderful gift, that's true, but imagination can fly us to regions more wonderful than any eye can capture.'

Filomena had obviously taken Manuel's words too literally, for she started collecting feathers which, like Daedalus, she wove into a set of wings.

'You shouldn't have done it,' Manuel admonished her, 'it could have killed you.'

'I enjoyed the flight, Sir, I enjoyed making the wings.'

The whole square was a gigantic bird whose wings, spanning from the castle to the cathedral, flapped with patterns of flames and shadows.

XLV

Terra

Manuel too took his flight. In the early hours, as the square simmered through its final bubbles, he crossed the threshold at Madam Magdalene's.

She took his outstretched hands to her cheeks and wept.

'You've come back, at last. I had no doubt you would. But see here I've got old, and I won't hold you down to any promise either. I've got several new girls, just say which one...'

Manuel placed his index over her lips, 'It's for you that I have come.'

They made love, rediscovering the way it had been on their first encounter. Aware that this time they could be together for a few hours, they wanted to lie awake afterward to talk and to enjoy the closeness of their sated, freshly tamed bodies; instead they fell asleep at once.

Dawn lighted their bodies and they woke to a faint scraping at the door, like the paws of a young pup. Magdalene sat up nervously, as Manuel went to the door. A child of three or four scuttled in, ran to the bed emitting a chirpy laugh. She was not surprised to find a man in her mother's room. She clambered onto the bed and went to curl up against Magdalene's ample bosom. Manuel sat on the bed and studied the child intensely. She was a stringy child with expressive dark face, black eyes and a mass of frizzy hair. Manuel did not need to ask who she was. He ran his fingers through her hair.

'It's like wire, can't do a thing with it,' said Magdalene.

Manuel did not hear. His face was aglow with discovery. His was the face of Filippo Grassi, or Black John, or Magdalene herself, seeing their portraits for the first time.

'Why didn't you tell me, Maggie,' he whispered, and there was so much passion in his voice that it startled her.

'Would they have you as their Consul if they knew?' she said. 'She doesn't talk you know. She's mute.'

Manuel was not shocked and perhaps he did not think it relevant.

'What have you called her?' he asked.

Magdalene giggled.

'She was so pink and dark that the midwife says, 'Holy Santa Barbara! She's the colour of terra-cotta. You must've gotta' from one of them pot-makers!' So we called her Terra.'

'Terra! ' He exclaimed, jubilant, 'Teh-rrah! Terra! That's it, that's exactly her!'

He sat the child on his shoulder and hopped around the cluttered room, mimicking a horse.

'You're a great woman Maggie.'

His eyes looked delirious. They expressed humble joy and the gratitude of a man discovering that he too could father a child, like any ordinary man.

He would not hear of keeping Terra's identity a secret.

'I am prepared to place my trust in the people's good sense; besides, how can I expect sincerity from others if I show none?'

Nevertheless, the news gave Lady Virginia and her friends plenty to get outraged about and even Sir Lucas, who had never forgiven Manuel for spurning his anaemic daughter, added his weighty voice to the chorus of criticism.

'It's one thing to father an illegitimate child, that's life. But to show a total disdain for propriety...that's too much effrontery!'

The people refused to believe the rumour at first; then towards evening with the child by his side, Manuel started to take regular promenades in the square. Even then the people did not condemn.

'Look how patiently he converses with the dear little mute,' said one woman to another, 'have you ever seen a more fond father?'

And they readily forgave. Theirs was the forgiveness of the indulgent parent for the caprice of a brilliant son. Still, inherent in that forgiveness was the intransigence of an age-old moral code.

XLVI

Spudsville Revisited

One day Alfred Murphy—Spudsville's Grandee and proprietor of the Potato Complex—arrived at the castle in a huff.

'I go abroad on your advice and you let them turn the place upside down,' he complained.

'You agreed to let us make the changes,' Manuel reminded him, 'so long as profits improved.'

'Well...I must admit, profits have gone up by nearly three and a half per cent. Not a bad figure these days...but I'll be damned if I'm gonna let that lunatic run amok. Not on your life! No Siree!'

The 'lunatic' that Alfred was referring to was Auldjock, the eccentric Physician. Now, in Southfalia a physician looked up only to a judge in the professional pecking-order. He demanded equal respect and remuneration for his services, knowing full well that, in order to maintain the prestige of one's profession, there is no method more effective than a superior stance and a good income. Auldjock had brought his profession into disrepute because, unlike his colleagues, he treated clients like intelligent beings, prescribed little medicine and much common sense, preached prevention rather than cure, dressed in old baggy pants, travelled on an ancient cart and gave his services free to everyone except rich hypochondriacs.

'Och, money can only make a stingy auld Scott stingier!' he would say. As a result, he was disliked in equal measure by makers of pills and fellow-physicians, who regarded fancy clothes and a glossy carriage to be indispensable professional accessories.

Like the ordinary people, Manuel too was fond of the old physician and had expected him to bring unorthodox methods to Spudsville's politics, but wasn't quite prepared for the radical alterations he found.

The town, once a desolate rectangle, bisected by a very wide and dusty road, had re-invented itself into clusters of dwellings, clumped around a square, a park, a church, a theatre, a fountain, or some other 'centre'. Though the single units presented distinct designs, the whole appeared harmonious through the colours of the local materials used in the construction.

Though it was still early morning, there was an atmosphere of vibrancy in the town. Most people hurried about cheerfully purposeful, while others stood around gossiping. The noises intermingled.

The visitors spotted a curious little man who, with tape in hand, was intent on measuring various parts of a house under construction. Manuel approached, interested to know what the man was up to.

'Jesus!' exclaimed the other, jumping. I thought you was Bill, back already from the Complex. I wouldn't want that bugger to catch me out.'

'Trying to steal were you?' accused Alfred Murphy.

'Only his ideas, Sir, but what the hell, we all cheat. He copies me too.'

'That's wee Jeremy, Sir. He's oot to show 's all up with his new hoose,' said Auldjock, coming forward to welcome Manuel with a warm glow in his little blue eyes. The glow turned to glaze the moment he saw Alfred Murphy. AuldJock was a tall, red-faced man whose air of self-mockery contrasted with the assertiveness of his stature. He spoke with the kind of hesitancy typical of the man who attains success late in life.

'These houses here are too close together,' complained Alfred Murphy, 'Southfalians enjoy their privacy.'

'Four walls and a wee private garden facing the skae's all the privacy we want, Sir,' replied the physician.

There had been a time when Southfalian families lived close together, often several generations in the same household. With prosperity, families became smaller and individuals more introverted, suspicious.

SOUTHFALIA

Observing so many people in the square, the Grandee asked, 'Does anybody work around here anymore? I mean real work, for production and profit.'

'Oh that? Certainly, Sir, we all do,' replied Auldjock. Then as they walked around the town, he proceeded to explain the new set-up.

Briefly, what had developed in Spudsville was a system in which all able individuals were required to do a number of hours per week of communal work; enough to maintain all services. There was no payment for this work, but in return every person in the community had access to basic items of food, clothing, services, health-care and other 'essentials'.

'That's the philosophy of the Red Proles,' accused Alfred Murphy.

Auldjock assured him that no one was compelled to do a job to which he was averse. In the case of a particularly unpleasant or difficult job incentives were offered in the form of improved conditions or money. The rest of the time was a person's own. Most worked in their chosen profession, for which they were paid according to the law of supply and demand; and because the 'basic standards' allowed one to live quite comfortably, most people spent a good deal of time improving a skill, a special interest, their home.

Going past the school, they noticed some children working cheerfully with utensils in hand. Some weeded flower-beds, others swept the paths. The physician then explained that children were not exempt from communal work. This scheme, he maintained, had been particularly successful, as it gave the child a sense of participation in their community. As a result the children had come to value time and self-discipline, friendship and co-operation. They acquired a clearer perception of the world about them and a respect for people and objects. The teachers had noted that school results had improved, self-esteem among students had risen, boredom was less prevalent and vandalism decreased markedly.

No other part of the town was a more eloquent witness to its success than the Potato Complex. The main building had been expanded and opened out by way of large windows and skylights, so that it was no longer the dingy place it had once been. Gone were the rows of mechanical men and women. In their place were ingenious little machines to do the washing and sorting of potatoes. The Potato Workers' Guild had at first campaigned to keep the machines out 'to safeguard the jobs of guild members', but in the end, reason prevailed and the members were able to find more rewarding jobs in the community. However, Auldjock did mention the sad case of a former potato-washer who still sat at her kitchen sink each day and washed the same bag of potatoes for hours.

The high rate of production surprised Manuel and the Grandee even more. Auldjock put it down to the fact that, ' each worker brings enthusiasm to his job', whereas once the same worker employed all his wits to get the most out of the system with the least effort.

'It's a question of attitude,' said Auldjock.

Back in town, Auldjock invited both men to his house. Waiting at his surgery were two women friends of his, looking pale and drawn. He took a glance at their faces, and without attempting to examine them, enlisted their help as he cooked up a meal for his guests. Then they all sat down to enjoy a tasty lunch, a bottle of good wine and animated conversation, during which the dishes were duly complemented. When they left some hours later, both women looked a good deal healthier.

XLVII

Two Friends Re-united

'Vous-voilà!' Exclaimed Iscar welcoming the Consul back to the castle, then noticing his elation he added *'Qu'est-ce que vous est arrivé?*[12] You look as if you've climbed Mount Olympus.'

Manuel could see that the old philosopher was in low spirits.

'Not quite old man, somewhere closer and far better. I've been to Spudsville.'

'Et bien?'

'The whole town is prospering, not because of what they own, but for how much they are willing to share.'

'Share, Sir? Share? What nonsense! Once people begin to share, it means that they have lost the main thrust for success, their 'raison d'être', that is: competition, or if you like: the need to oppress one another.'

'I saw no sign of oppression, only progress.'

'Progress? Pish! Do you really believe in it Sir?'

'Of course.' Then, more pensively, 'you know Iscar, what we achieve ourselves in our lifetime may be less significant than what we inspire others to do, even after we are dead.'

'And what good is to us then? Enjoy your glory while it lasts Sir…and while you can. Look at me now: old and heavy, cursed with too much weight upon my legs and too little between them—surely the only place where I could do with some weight—*et alors!* What consolation is it to me to have a secure life now? What good is it to have life at all?'

'Your life is very important Iscar.'

'To whom? To the undertaker?'

'To me for instance. Your outlook provides me with a much-needed counterpoint. You are the other side of me, the one I have had to repress.'

But Iscar was not impressed.

'If you must know, Sir, I find this comfortable existence tiresome. Life can be a great bore when you don't have to run, cheat and deceive to survive.'

'I agree that striving is essential to our nature,' replied Manuel, 'but there are more constructive ways of striving than cheating, are there not?'

'Well Sir, I can't build bridges, convert the people or discover new worlds either. And what's the point of it all anyway? Take that demented little Genoese, *Signor Colombo*, I hear he has finally got his ships to sail forth. What's the point of it all? If he discovers new lands he will only bring them our troubles to pile upon their own. Then, after he has satisfied his vanity and the destructive urge of his crew, he will wish to sail off to somewhere else. Life is an endless struggle trying to get somewhere else. Nor does he have to prove to me that the world is round. I've seen enough of it to know that life is a circle, mainly of lows and occasionally a high. It does not pay to get excited about either, they never last. True, history has recorded some brief flashes of brilliance, breaking through ages of darkness; but just when men think they are scraping star-dust with their finger-tips, darkness swoops down again, and plunges the world into another millennium of ignorance. It always happens that way.'

'But the Spirit, Iscar, the Spirit advances just that much after each cycle.'

'Do you think so, Sir? I think the methods change, but stupidity and oppression remain. The struggle goes on. The Patricians are right after all: it's no use being wealthy if there are no poor people to look down upon, just as there can be no real feeling of happiness without knowledge of suffering. *'La condition humaine'*: such a mockery!'

Manuel could see that his old friend would not be easily rescued from his mood of depression. But sometimes in moments of despair, Nature finds a way of focusing our attention on something which completely restores our faith in goodness and beauty. And so it happened then. The beautiful object in this case was none other than Andrew Gay Ganymede, whom Iscar had not seen for a very long time: a fact which might have contributed to his mood. His entrance was like spring sunshine lighting the coldest dungeon.

'Andrew, my dear boy, how glad I am to see you!' cried Iscar, throwing his arms about his friend's golden curls.

Which goes to show that our Creator knew what he was doing, when he gave us that weak heel for life's arrow to prick, just when the intolerable burden of mortality numbs us from head to toe.

XLVIII

Abbé Stanislaus

Monsignor Macdomus, weary of his ecclesiastical burden and disillusioned by the fact that since the end of the Crusade, fewer and fewer distraught ladies came to his confessional, transferred himself to Paris, to pursue his pastoral work in that city of sin and gaiety. In his place arrived in Southfalia a certain Abbé Yerolamus Stanislaus.

Rumour had it that the Abbé had been confessor to Emperor Otto at one stage of his career. Whether true or not the Abbé was certainly a man of uncommon pedigree, judging by Iscar's description of him:

'He is a gaunt man, with a long bony face which is given to flushing at the smallest provocation. His eyes are small, very blue and fierce, and his long-fingered hands shake vigorously as he speaks in the peremptory tone of one accustomed to be listened to and obeyed. '

It was strange that such a man should have been chosen to replace Monsignor, for there could not have been two men more different. Unlike Monsignor, who might have been suspected of one or two vices, the Abbé was a strict ascetic who allowed himself no pleasures and claimed that he lived only to serve the Church, the Emperor and God, probably in that order.

He wore a poor monk's sash, a pair of rough wooden sandals and no rings on his fingers. But on his chest sparkled an enormous gold crucifix, a gift from the Emperor, it was said, reminding all and sundry that the Abbé had kept company with the high and the mighty, a man for whom poverty was a matter of choice.

His connection with the Emperor served him in good stead with the ladies, many of whom became converted to asceticism so as to be numbered among his followers.

As may be expected there were many things in Southfalia, which displeased the Abbé. In no time he ensconced himself on the cathedral pulpit and condemned the island's 'libertine trends'. His speeches were charged with so much vehemence that where they failed to convince by argument, they converted through fear.

'You have given yourselves to pleasure and sin. You make daily sacrifices to the Golden Calf and arouse the wrath of the Lord. Beware people of Southfalia for His curse, when it comes, will be swift and terrible! Yes, mark my words, swift and terrible!'

'Put him on the first boat and pack him back to the Emperor!' suggested Paul.

But Manuel, who was proud of the freedom enjoyed by Southfalians under his leadership said, 'I have too much faith in the good judgement of the people to let the Abbé worry me.'

Most people simply dismissed the Abbé as a fanatical doomsayer; while the Red Proles lampooned him to the point of sending him an invitation to Madam Magdalene's for a 'private party'.

Now, that was one thing that sent the Abbé into fits: that a house of sin should be so openly tolerated in a Christian country outraged him. If they existed in other parts of Christendom, they at least had the decency to tuck them well away, in dark alleys of remote slums. Nor was it a secret to the holy Abbé that mobile bordellos were always a colourful adjunct to the armies of Europe, but these were a necessary evil in the service of a good cause.

'To have one in the very centre of the city and at a stone's throw from the Cathedral! Never, never!' raved the Abbé, flashing murderous eyes in its direction.

The B.A.D.S. ladies did not fail to take the cue. One evening when the congregation met in the cathedral for vespers, the Abbé said, 'Daughters, you are God's chosen. It is your duty to save the island from damnation and the time to march is ripe. We will begin our crusade from the very place selected by Satan as his fortress of evil. Come, all of you!'

So the Abbé led the congregation to Madam Magdalene's, armed with chasuble, maniple, crucifix and holy water, in full battle array against Satan. Flanking the Abbé were Lady Virginia and Sir Marc, the latter armed with his scimitar.

When they arrived at the gaily-daubed door of the bordello, they began reciting 'Aves' to the Virgin Mary while the Abbé, with an expression of revulsion towards the house of sin, spoke to Sir Marc.

'Hence you go, and seek ye Satan and root him out of his den!'

That night the bordello was particularly lively—being a night of full moon—and not a girl could be spared to post outside, to advertise the wares of the establishment and keep out unwelcome intruders. Consequently when Sir Marc flung open the entrance door and gave out a roar similar to the one that had sent El Vampiro reeling off his horse, everyone was caught in the act, and that enchantment of refined pleasure was broken abruptly.

As candles were hurriedly put out, swoons turned to shrieks and love-promises to curses; sheets were torn, negligés went misplaced and underwear no longer fitted; tables and chairs were upturned, wine bottles and glasses shattered, and everyone ran for cover at the sight of Sir Marc's scimitar flashing in the dim light. Everyone that is, except Magdalene, who had no fear of swords.

'So it's you, is it?' she cried, raising her bountiful front in bold challenge to the sword. 'What do you mean coming to my parlour like this and upset my customers? Be off you fool, and take that silly sword with you before I break it over your back.'

Sir Marc was dumbfounded. It was left to his wife, who had been eavesdropping outside, to come to the rescue.

'You lewd woman, is there no limit to your effrontery? How dare you speak to a respected knight in that manner! You temptress of our men, you corruptor of our sons, do you show no repentance? And what about all the diseases spread by all your dirty companions...'

Madam Magdalene, who went to a good deal of trouble to provide a clean wholesome service for her customers, was furious.

'Dirty? Are you calling my girls dirty? Why, you shrivelled-up old hag...my girls are chosen from the best and cleanest in the profession: young, healthy girls that take pride in their work. Dirty indeed!

Why, my bordello is patronized by the cream of the land. None of your pith less little dandies, but men of spunk and breeding...'

'Hear that Sir Marc, she freely admits to running a house of sin,' interrupted Lady Virginia, 'if the Consul will not act, Sir Lucas, the Chief Justice, must.'

On hearing this, Madam Magdalene broke into shrill laughter which, coming as it did on the heels of her rage, added brilliance to her looks.

'Lucas? Did you say Sir Lucas?...Hey Luke where are you honey? Where did you get to? Light up these candles, I can't see a thing around here.'

As the first light shone on the further recesses of the boudoir, it revealed a sight that would have disconcerted a woman much less virtuous than Lady Virginia. All about the room, peering from under tables, chairs and sofas, behind curtains and closet doors, partially hidden by sheets and bedspreads were pairs of buttocks in a great variety of shapes, hues, sizes, and pelosity.

'Ah, there you are, Sir!' said she pointing.

All eyes followed Magdalene's over to where a white, large, round buttock—an aristocratic-looking buttock, in other words—was wriggling under a chair like a young, inexperienced rabbit trying to furrow through granite.

'Come out of there Luke,' called Magdalene impatiently, 'show us your face, not your arse!'

Thus exposed, the owner of the buttock was left no choice but to reveal his identity.

It was indeed Sir Lucas Pompous Curse. As he cupped one hand over his knightly parts, Lady Virginia's hand went over her eyes and she screamed. A scream which impelled many other virtuous ladies to overcome their modesty and come rushing into the bordello, flocking behind Sir Marc like hens to the cock. But really there wasn't much there to cluck over. Stripped of his judicial garments there was nothing formidable about Sir Lucas, definitely not his parts which, in any case, were adequately shadowed by his projecting belly.

'Sir Lucas, *you* here?' cried Sir Marc in disbelief.

Sir Lucas cleared his throat, raised his free hand to attain some sort of judicial composure and spoke as grandly as the circumstances allowed.

'May I ask you, Sir Marc, who gives you warranty to break into the premises of citizens conducting their normal business?' Sir Lucas paused, but his hard stare made it clear that his question was purely rhetorical and he would not tolerate a response. He continued, 'Now, I don't know about these others, but I happen to be here for treatment for a sore lumbago...yes indeed a most devilish lumbago...I trust, Sir, that your imagination does not get the better of you, for you are considering slandering my name in public, I shall have the full weight of the justice system come crushing upon you.'

Sir Marc was aware, of course, that the Chief Justice stands high enough in society to erase all shadow of suspicion, and he said something to that effect. But then one of the ladies let out a scream and fainted at Sir Marc's feet, for in the midst of all the buttocks she had spotted her husband's familiar one. Other ladies grew suspicious and started scrutinizing each buttock in detail, and soon the boudoir was strewn with fainted women, and echoed to the wails of men complaining of all kinds of ailments. The women had to be carried out. Meanwhile, outside the frightened congregation had stepped up its recitation of Pater Nosters, Aves and Credos.

And then, adding further confusion to the chaos, they heard the voices of a mob approaching up the street. It turned out to be—of all things—a group of drunken sailors about to visit Madam's girls to make up for months spent at sea.

The appearance of the fierce, glassy-eyed sailors sent the whole congregation scuttling, once again, behind the Abbé for protection. But the sailors, who for months had dreamt of the moment when they would be squeezing one of Madam's supple belles, found the virtuous matrons a most unappetizing alternative.

'Wot's this? A roost of ole 'ags! Ole Meg's done it this time, couldn't find a uglier bunch of 'arlots 'n the back streets of Cairo!'

'Goh, blimey! Lemme sail back t' sea!'

The Abbé perceived in the state of the sailors the spirit of the island's perdition and seized the opportunity to deliver a homily.

'Observe, women of Southfalia, how evil begets evil. Look at the state of these creatures. That's what sin breeds: men who are no longer men, but puny slaves to vice and the body's desire. Look ye and be warned!'

The sailors looked in each other's eyes (what they could see of them, anyway), for some light to their confusion. A preacher and his congregation outside a brothel door was something they had never heard of before, even in unseemly sailor tales.

Alcohol can spread havoc through a man's emotions and when a bunch of drunken sailors, who have not seen the inside of a church since the days of Sunday School, are confronted with the stark blackness of their conscience the result can be traumatic. Soon they were prey to a mix of guilt, self-pity, repentance and devotion so violent that many fell on their knees sobbing. Their leader, a big, hirsute character with a face like brown onion, confusing contrition with love, lumbered up to the holy Abbé and, clasping his rope-strong arms around his neck, sobbed profusely as he smothered the Abbé with so many kisses that it nearly took his breath away.

Abbé Stanislaus was neither prepared for, nor inclined to, such effusion. Their lack of respect piqued his saintly pride, not to speak of the sense of revulsion he experienced in having to whiff up all that bad air.

'Away from me!' he cried, 'your soul rots beyond repair! There's only one prospect open to the likes of you: the pit of hell. There you'll roast like boars on a spit; you demons!'

With their rare burst of devotion so abruptly rejected, the sailors soon lost interest in the Abbé and returned their attention to the original object of their visit, feeling, no doubt, that if they were doomed they might as well go down in pleasant company.

So they started to roar, to sing and to call out, determined more than ever to get what they came for. They banged on the door, threatening to bring it down. Their persistence finally brought Madam to the balcony.

'Come on! Open this door, Maggie darlin',' they yelled, 'come down 'n open the bloody thin'. I'm warnin'ya.'

But Madam would not be intimidated, 'Go away, sailor, we're closed for business tonight.'

Suddenly it occurred to them that the Abbé was the cause of all their frustration and they began to discuss it aloud, their voices rising ominously as they flashed angry eyes towards the congregation. This did not escape the women who, shaken enough by the incident, heeded the warning and shot through like sheep before the wolf, pursued by the protesting Abbé.

The Abbé gone, the door was opened to the sailors and Madam Magdalene's parlours swooned once again to soft lights, music, laughter and groans of pleasure.

'The first round in the Abbé's Crusade went, as always, to cunning old Satan,' writes Iscar.

XLIX

The Abbé Convicted

The next day a brood of tearful women took their woes to the Consul. As if he had the power to turn their husbands' infidelity to devotion...He listened to the pathetic pleadings of women, no longer young, victims of a blind faith in promises that would never be kept. He understood the unfairness of it and was saddened. He could see as well, the dilemma of men too proud to bow down to life's inexorable advance, too blind to the hurt they inflicted, too foolish to realize that they were chasing an illusion. Above all, he felt the full weight of people's expectations of him on matters over which he was powerless.

But a scorned woman does not wish to face life's realities. If she cannot have what she's lost, then she seeks fuel to enflame her bitterness. And no man could better provide that than the Abbé Stanislaus.

'There is an anti-Christ in our midst,' he warned daily, 'beware of him!'

To the puritans, the snobs and the greedy, who for different reasons began to support him, now joined the small minority of former slaves, who could not cope with freedom. These existed in a state of chronic lassitude, lacking both the initiative and the imagination for any kind of activity, even a dissolute kind. The Abbé relieved them of their burden of free thought.

He founded 'The Crusade For Light', whose aim it was 'to return to traditional moral standards'. From the pulpit his predictions became more portentous.

'I feel the curse of the Almighty approaching and nothing will save the unrepentant!'

On a calm Christmas Eve the people of Charlesville: a city in the far North, were preparing for the evening's victuals when the wind started to rise. Leaves rustled, tree branches shivered, women's skirts flapped as they stood on their threshold calling their children indoors. As evening approached the orange dust advanced from the desert spreading an early twilight over the sun.

The people sat crouched waiting, listening to the whining of the dogs as the wind started to tear and rip. Tiles were lifted off roofs, windows flung off hinges, trees were uprooted and the night was strewn with flying debris. Just as it seemed as if a whole mountain might be hurled into space, the wind subsided for a while, only to start up again with renewed fury.

Christmas light peered over the devastated city. The people emerged out of their shelters to see their houses vanished beneath mounds of rubble. Why? For the people of Charlesville the question may have been rhetorical, but in the capital the Abbé had no doubts at all.

'People of Southfalia, how blind can you be! You've let your cities rival Sodom and Gomorrah, your squares are defiled by images of nakedness and perdition, your homes are no better than whore-houses, and still you ask why? Why, don't you recognise God's curse?'

Driven by guilt and by their own moral righteousness, the Crusaders For Light followed the Abbé to the shrine of Saint Stephen, the martyr, for an expiating pilgrimage. On the way to the shrine they came across the remains of an old Moorish palace, at whose moat pilgrims stopped to refresh themselves and their horses. As ill-luck would have it, on that very day, art students sat by the moat, engrossed in painting a Venus of ethereal proportions, taking a bath naked, in the green-banked river—as gods are wont to do. And since women were not supposed to shed their clothes in those days, posing as Venus was none other than Gay Ganymede: all suppleness and blond curls, and languorous eyes.

SOUTHFALIA

The pilgrims followed the Abbé penitently, as he counted their sins one after the other like rosary beads, 'you made sacrifices to the false idols...you aroused the wrath of the Lord...The day of judgement is nigh!'

Artists are not known to be a particularly gutsy lot, and when they heard the coming of the Abbé who, as they well knew, regarded artists as heretics, they concluded pretty fast that their life was more important to them than art. So, for their life they ran, leaving everything behind, including the model.

Lovely Ganymede was not unduly perturbed. His looks had always had such a power to soften, that no man worth his meat had ever turned harshly on him.

Unfortunately, the Abbé had long buried all sense of beauty in a mountain of religious fanaticism and, confronted with that raw flesh, Stanislaus flung himself on Ganymede like the Archangel upon Lucifer. He seized the half-submerged youth by his golden crop and lifted him out of the water exposing to full view of the pilgrims a scandalous spectacle. Then he let go of him as if he were something putrid, proceeding instead to gather all the scattered canvasses of still-unborn Venuses, tore them up, trod on them and finally flung them on a pile to be burnt.

Meanwhile at the fountain the pilgrims had surrounded the terrified youth who, realizing the full seriousness of his predicament, tried in vain to wriggle himself free and make his escape. Many of them, unmoved by his child-like sobbing, jumped in and started beating him. Others joined in, and now the fountain was a mass of hysterical figures, splashing in the water as they kicked and punched their victim.

'Give it to the son of Satan. Beat away his sins!'

And beat him up they did, and judging by the victim's screams they must have cleansed him of all his venial sins—as well as many of the mortal ones—by the time he finally got to the Good Lord for judgement. The youth put up a frantic resistance, with his head immersed, for a long while, as if Satan himself was making a last stand within him, but in the end his body slowed down, his feet stopped kicking and there was no more Satan left in him—or anything else for that matter. A couple of hysterical women kept on beating him, just in case, but he was dead all right, as proof of which, a pair of shapely legs floated to the surface as a final proof that Sir Bart would have no one to leave all his money to.

The Abbé, who had kept himself busy lighting a fire, was angry with his congregation when he saw what they had done.

'You shouldn't have done it,' he admonished, 'burning is the proper way to execute heretics. Now let's proceed at once,' he concluded, 'you will need to ask forgiveness at the holy shrine of Saint Stephen, the Martyr.'

When Manuel learned of the lynching his fury was unstoppable.

'Who the devil does he think he is, the bible-bashing bastard!' he roared, with irreverent anger. In the years that he was a Consul, Manuel was never seen—nor would he again be seen—in a display of such temper.

The Voice chose to take its traditional objective stance in the affair.

'Unfortunate as the whole incident may have been, it points clearly to a new direction in people's attitudes, as they seek to return to more traditional moral values.'

Peter was astute enough to realize that *The Voice* had, in these matters, the first, and quite often the last, word.

'We can't risk a confrontation with the Abbé at this stage,' he said to the Consul, 'he is too big. The best course is to let the whole affair ride over until things cool down.'

Paul, on the other hand, would have throttled the Abbé without delay.

Rejecting both courses, Manuel had the Abbé committed for trial for having instigated the lynching, as a consequence of which, the holy man found himself in a prison cell.

L

New Riches

The headline in *The Voice* could not be more jubilant.

'From the desert rises a new Golden Dawn as the Queen of the South Sea uncovers new treasures to the world's eye.'

The 'treasures' were new mineral deposits discovered in staggering quantity and variety: coal, lead, iron, sulphur and more. The news had foreign capitals in a frenzy. Gunpowder had recently been introduced into warfare and military strategists were leaping with excitement.

'Just imagine,' they said, imagine if you had a dozen cannons firing on an advancing army! Why, you'd have them all wiped out without the loss of a single man!'

The new mineral finds gave the island almost unlimited potential for manufacturing artillery whose power—as with all new inventions—was greatly exaggerated. And exaggeration was hardly needed to stimulate the ambitions of proud fifteenth century Princes!

The Emperor would have given anything to re-equip his depleted army, while the Pope, jealous of the other's power, was prepared to exchange any number of blessings and indulgences for a share of Southfalia's riches.

It was left to Manuel to pour water over the flame of excitement.

'The Golden Age is already with us. It lies in the freedom enjoyed by our people...'

It was the kind of speech that did not inspire the likes of Sir Bart and his friend Sir Matthew.

'True, very true Sir,' agreed Sir Matthew with diplomatic optimism, 'and the new mineral finds can only but enhance that.'

'More likely they will demolish what we have built these last years, Sir Matthew; which is one of several good reasons why we must leave it all where it is.'

'You mean, not mine at all!' exclaimed Sir Bart, stumbling to find words to express his amazement.

'For the time being, anyway.'

'But that wasteland's worth a fortune!' Sir Bart insisted.

'To the Natives it means more than a fortune. It's their home,' said Manuel.

The Patricians did not think so, and in any case they could not have cared less. Already they had lain claim to the region, by virtue of the fact that it bordered their lands. The Natives 'after all' had no other use for it

'Anyway,' concluded Sir Bart, 'we'll pay them compensation if we have to. After that the Natives can buy the choicest lots of real estate right 'ere in the city and live like kings.'

'We're sittin' on a gold mine,' raved Sir Bart, who took Manuel's silence for acquiescence, 'better than a gold mine; take sulphur for instance, everyone's after it. We can practically ask our own price.'

'And that's another very good reason for leaving it where it is. We cannot claim to be striving for peace while exporting war material.'

Sir Bart was too upset to reply; besides, this needed Sir Matthew's debating flair.

'All Nations need weapons to make them feel secure,' he said.

'That's the kind of fallacy which has cost us dearly in the past.'

'Be that as it may, no nation is prepared to risk the alternative. They will get their weapons from somewhere.'

'But not from us, Sir Matthew; which leaves us free to pursue peace.'

Sir Matthew's lips formed one of his rare, superior smiles.

'The world is not ready for it,' he said, 'it's doubtful that it ever will be. Look around you, Sir, and you will notice that the very same nations who speak about peace the loudest are most eager to strengthen their armies.'

'Exactly! That's why we need to find ways to give nations reassurances, so that they don't have to pursue security by way of combat.'

'Hell,' exploded Sir Bart, 'we got a simple issue in front of us and we go and bury it under a heap of idealistic hogwash. It happens all the time. Why all this complication for Christ's sake! As I see it it's like this: here we have an opportunity to make a mint practically throwing itself at us, and what're we sayin'? 'No thank you, we don't want a bar of it!' Well that's the silliest notion I've ever come across.'

Sir Bart paused, but not long enough for Sir Matthew to contribute his own rejoinder.

'Wait a minute, Matt, I'm not done yet.'

Then turning an angry glance towards Manuel he added, 'Anyway, if I remember rightly it was you Sir, who promised no interference in business.'

'Is business not flourishing, Sir Bart?'

'How long for, but? The arms trade is virtually finished, and that's hurt the economy badly, if we turn our backs on a chance like this, we might as well all retire 'cause there's no hope for business.'

The Consul looked into Sir Bart's angry eyes before he started to speak calmly and deliberately.

'My responsibility as the elected Consul is to provide a safe and happy future for all the people of this island, including yourself. Now I believe that a lasting peace—and I don't mean merely lack of conflict—will give us a stronger guarantee for the future than any added wealth. I believe also, as many others do, that if we don't begin to act now we may not have anything to salvage in the future. We in our corner of the world have made a start: small, but it's something, and the human spirit can move with the speed of fire, if we allow it to burn. Once again I ask for faith. If I can't have faith, allow me a little more patience. If my course succeeds then one day Southfalians may be able to exploit their wealth in a way that will serve, not enslave them. If I am wrong, events will not take long to catch up with me.'

Sir Bart looked disarmed. It was a posture he abhorred. It seemed to him that Manuel's tactics were not altogether fair.

'What do you say, Sir Bart?' asked Manuel hopefully.

'Me? I got nothin' more to say.'

And turning on his heels, Sir Bart marched out of the hall.

The Consul now turned to the other knight.

'And you Sir Matthew, what do you say?'

'What can I say, Consul? Sir Bart is such an impulsive man, no diplomacy in him at all. One wonders how he manages to be such a successful merchant. Still, successful he certainly is, and so many of us on this island are aware that our prosperity depends a good deal on the continuing success of Sir Bart's affairs. Which means, in effect, that once he goes I have no more to say either.'

Left alone, Manuel called in Iscar.

'You, old man, what have you to say?'

Iscar was not surprised by the question, Manuel still consulted him regularly.

'Why, you know Master, the knights…you should have been one of them by now. So much is possible for a Prophet and a Statesman, it's true; but in this country a knight survives them both. And really…I don't know what your God is; mine—as you well know—is Survival.'

'God!' exclaimed Manuel pensively, ' God must be a paradox.'

LI

Return of a Prodigal Child

From then on the great knights no longer took part in the affairs of state. They retired instead to their country castles where they amused themselves as best they could, with lavish banquets, hunting parties and the like.

One major feast was held at Sir Bart's castle in honour of Monsignor, recently returned from Paris, after being wrongfully implicated in some scandal concerning the young niece of a leading Parisian gentlewoman.

On this particular day, some of the invited knights were on a hunting party in the green park of the castle and had been chasing an elusive fox for more than an hour when the tired dogs stopped suddenly, hesitated, sniffed incredulously, paused, sniffed again, then bolted wagging their tail with pleasure towards the high poplars by the bridge. The hunters followed. Just when everyone expected a fox to rush out, through the thicket appeared instead a beautiful amazon on a grey steed, galloping towards them in full flight.

Was it an angel? Was it Diana joining the chase in the woods? No, it was Princess Sybilla in full flight. All hearts paused for an eternal moment, reassuring themselves that it was neither dream nor miracle. Sybilla was returning to the fold.

Lesser mortals would have shown at least some resentment, but not those tender-hearted cavaliers. Sybilla in turn accepted their warmth with the graceful mien so natural to a beautiful woman.

They rushed to help her down, laid her on the soft, green clover and proceeded to comfort her. Sir Bart took off her rustic necklace of wood beads and replaced it with a pearl one he happened to have with him. This did a lot to revive the distressed lady's spirits. Sir Lucas read to her from 'Daphnis and Chloe', while Monsignor nursed one or two unkind scratches she had received on her leg during the ordeal.

Later, at the castle, when her wounds had been tended to, she spoke of her rupture with Paul the Red.

'I cannot deny, gentlemen, that my heart was lost to him. His voice was so strong, so proud, his fiery red hair tossed on the wind like flames, and I being a woman of romantic disposition…he captured my foolish heart.

'Nor can I deny that he's a man of fire, but after all the talking, marching and chanting of slogans, there was little time left for…other things. What can I say, gentlemen, it was simply too much.'

In short, the gentle Sybilla was fed up with the revolution.

'This morning I awoke and looked at my rags, at my hands so coarse, and the anguish surged inside me. 'Helas!' I cried, 'is it for this kind of life that I abandoned all my good friends? Me, who was married to a Consul! Who was regularly confessed by an Archbishop! Who was carried in the arms by an Emperor! Me, who was named the most fashionable woman in all of Europe, and the most beautiful navel in Alexandria!' Then, without hesitation I mounted a stallion and I have ridden back to you, my dear friends.'

Everyone felt inexplicably joyful, like they had not done for a long time. It was as if the return of the divine Sybilla to the fold was the happy presage everyone had been waiting for, that would lead to a Lemonist return to power.

All the knights lost their heart to Sybilla all over again, but none so completely as Sir Lucas, the Chief Judge who, however, was already married. As misfortune would have it, Lady Perpetua—Sir Lucas' graciously aged lady—died suddenly of unknown cause. Nothing seemed to console the Judge, who had been married to his lady for longer than he remembered. Nothing that is, except Sybilla: only she possessed the experience, understanding, the delicacy of emotions to soften the poignancy of his loss, and soothe his nerves.

Sir Lucas recovered with miraculous speed to ask—perhaps out of gratitude, perhaps on advice from his physician—for the hand of his rescuer. The Princess was so ecstatic that she accepted before someone had time to remind her that her dear Sir Pepin was still listed as missing. Now, that sort of thing may present an obstacle for ordinary couples wishing to be married, but not if the groom happens to be the Chief Judge. That delectable gentleman, simply declared Sir Pepin officially dead. The Church had no objections either. Monsignor commented wryly that anyone who could keep away from a lovely flower like Sybilla for so many years, was dead or as good as dead.

The wedding was an exclusive affair to which only the froth of the *crème* of Southfalian society were invited. At the head of the banquet table, sumptuously set was Sybilla: all glitter and charm; her cheeks faintly flushed in an otherwise serene aspect. On her left she was flanked by an enraptured Sir Lucas and on the other side Monsignor—celebrant of the happy union.

From afar, Sir Marc had been eyeing the bride with untypical fervour. Drink, they say, can bring out the romantic in a man. Sir Marc hardly qualifies as a romantic cavalier, but then, if there were such a figure below the Spartan, it had never had the occasion to be drawn out by the bouquet of wine. All his life, Sir Marc's mustachios had bristled only to the frothy bitterness of golden ale.

On this night, however, he too was lured to the sweet taste of Burgundy and soon he was indulging in that decadent libation with keen gusto. After the first glasses, Sir Marc found himself wondering why in all those years he had disdained the delicious manna. Unfortunately for him, he did not know of the danger that lurked within each glassful.

By the sixth glass his eyes focused on Princess Sybilla's round, white breasts quivering in irresistible titillation to her full-bosomed laugh. Another glass and before his veiled eyes appeared beautiful Helen and coarse Menelaus, while he, the gallant Paris, was sent by Venus to ravish the loveliest woman on earth. Already he saw himself dashing forth, seize her into his arms, sweep her off to a waiting barge and then, in full sail towards Ilion.

Sir Marc was ready for action. With a loud battle-cry he flew to Helen's side, and kneeling at her feet, he delivered one or two lines that would have caused old Homer turn in his grave:

Divinical Helen! Sh...Shelestical Helen!
Forshake that dandy dodo of your shpouse
And shail away the high osshen wi' me
To high-toored...high-terrash...'

Not a bad effort considering that Sir Marc was not a man of words, but of swords. Unfortunately for him this display got the attention of his wife, Lady Virginia, who strode up to him, raised her walking cane and dealt him a powerful blow across his back. The romantic prince then passed-out and the enchantment was broken. The incident proved that one should never count on a promise given by that mad-cap Bacchus.

The unfortunate interlude was soon forgotten, as Patricians have a penchant for sweeping aside whatever interferes with their enjoyment. The wine flowed, the dancing became less orderly, the conversation more animated.

One group which did not partake in the celebrations was that comprising of Sir Matthew MacKiavel together with Sir Bart and Lady Britt. All three seemed engrossed in some earnest conversation. None of the others took much notice; they were having too good a time, besides, those three were known to be devoid of all *'joie de vivre'.*

At the height of the festivities—as was customary on the island—the bride moved to the centre of the hall to give away her virginal garter to a single young man chosen by lot.

In the excited hush the fortunate winner was pushed forward by Sir Matthew. He was a tall, haughty young man with brown hair, rich yellow skin, refined features and a very Roman nose. Weak and spindly as he appeared, he was not exactly the one that Sybilla would have chosen. Still she proudly stretched out her long legendary and rested it invitingly on the cushioned stool. The hall went wild. The young man, who was indeed very timid, had to be helped to slip off the garter by the obliging Monsignor. There was a roar of approval and wolf-whistles. All the men returned to their places, except the youth who stood alone in the centre of the hall holding the garter. The people's merriment was cut short by the appearance of Lady Britt, flanked by Sir Matthew and Sir Bart, marching out to join the young man. Lady Britt held out her hand to him and he took it respectfully; then she faced the hushed crowd, superior and composed, scanning the tables with raised eyebrows. After a breathless interval, her clear, controlled voice finally broke the silence.

'Fellow Patricians, meet my dearest nephew: Octavius Mendacit Humble; like his immortal ancestor he was born in August and has decayed teeth. He has been carefully groomed to lead us to a Lemonist victory.'

Respectful cheers were followed by subdued whispers of approval; for indeed the youth was of purest Roman strain. The posture was right, the colour was right, the nose was right. And with a name like that!...Things were beginning to look up for the Patricians at last.

Octavius allowed them a humble smile; just enough to show them that his teeth were indeed rotted, then he cast a stern glance around the hall, held out the silken garter before them like a prosecutor waving a damning piece of evidence at the criminal, and said,

'Noble friends, don't you know that life was not meant to be sleazy?'

LII

The League of Peace

During the next year, Iscar's Journal loses its sketchy appearance and weaves tangles of political sub-plots, which we merely need to touch upon. In this period, the support of the Red Proles became more and more of a liability for the Consul as the people came to resent their extreme stridency. Ex-soldiers, unable to settle down to civilian life, joined the ranks of the Proles, and their comparative idleness made them dangerous. Contact with other societies free from governors, knights or grandees made these men resent the titled Patricians.

When landowners and merchants, who controlled all goods, decided to increase prices, the workers demanded more money. The others resisted, professing: 'much hardship due to poor crops, decline in production and widespread labour unrest.'

At the insistence of the Proles a tribunal was set up to arbitrate. The judges—all nephews and cousins of Sir Lucas—after considering all evidence, concluded that:

'In the present economic climate an increase in wages is unwarranted and recessive.'

The Voice thought the decision wise.

If the home sky looked patchy, the outlook in foreign policy could not have been clearer. After months of negotiations, the Southern Peace League was about to become a reality, thanks largely to Manuel's diplomatic efforts, to which he devoted great energies, sometimes—said his critics—to the neglect of internal affairs.

The Consul employed all licit means at his disposal to sway his overseas counterparts. He worked assiduously to build trust.

'Southfalia's mineral wealth gives us immense potential for growth. We are prepared to contribute fully to the development of the region, so long as we have the security safeguards that will come with the kind of League we are seeking.'

Iscar writes that the Consul was able to convince them—by the simple means of openness and fervour—that peace could be realized in defiance of history. Their initial, half-hearted interest grew into enthusiasm as the vision progressed towards a common commitment.

Many months had passed and now Southfalia City was preparing to welcome foreign Princes coming for the signing of the agreement that would bind all the states of the South Sea *'never to cross one another's frontiers. . . . to adopt a policy of dialogue and mutual consultation.'*

Southfalia decorated itself with banners and standards as *League Day* approached. Many were incredulous. Was it really possible that all these states, which has been battlegrounds for as far back as history could record, were finally going to be freed from the fear of wars?

Of course, there was no lack of opposition. A.L.E.R.T. saw the pact as suicidal: Sir Matthew was quiet; while Lady Britt feared hordes of foreigners coming into Southfalia and contaminating further its racial purity.

'Our children will see the chocolate-faced barbarian supplant the noble Roman strain on this island!' She warned. Political correctness was not that lady's forte.

To which the Consul retorted, 'Then we may more easily identify with the rest of humanity. Southfalian means first and foremost a citizen of the world.'

Lady Britt brooded.

From the Emperor had come frequent warnings for Southfalia to contain its diplomatic 'offensive'. The Emperor regarded the proposed League as a threat to his influence among the Southern States. Aware of this, Manuel had been careful to explain his motives and send regular messages of appeasement to Otto. The incarceration of the Abbé, however, had not pleased Otto. Even so, nobody had expected any trouble from him, besieged as he was by grave domestic problems of his own. Yet, at the end of winter, days before the signing of the Southern Peace League, came the shock news that an imperial fleet was heading towards the island for a punitive invasion.

PART FOUR

THE SOLDIER

LIII

Victory!

'It was to be expected, there are limits to the patience of Otto VIII. For those who have forgotten, we are still a state of the Holy Emperor of the West. It was foolish to cross him. The best that Southfalia can do at this stage is to raise the white flag. '

However, despite the accusatory tone of *The Voice*, the Consul's mood was anything but conciliatory.

'No effort must be spared in repulsing the invader. Whoever believes that what we have built is worth defending, come forward!'

They did not need to be told twice. Convoys of volunteers left their families and came to the city by the thousands to join the ranks of the regular units. They were farmers, miners, artisans, tradesmen, serfs and small merchants. The only dissent came from some knights and grandees, who attempted to dissuade their workers from enlisting. Paul was furious and called for the culprits to be executed on the spot.

'There is no time to waste, Paul,' said the Consul.

Aware that Southfalia City was too well fortified to be attacked from the sea, the Emperor decided to land his forces on the northern coast, from where he planned to march on the capital. If he had counted on the co-operation of the conservative Northerners—who had on many occasions opposed Manuel's liberalism—he was soon to be disappointed. Critical they may have been but, in the face of the Emperor's arrogance, they got fully behind their Consul. As a consequence the Emperor had to capture each town by force, at the cost of many men and the loss of time.

In the south, meanwhile, such was the confidence of Manuel's army that they decided to go north and give the Emperor open battle, something that no vassal state had ever dared before.

As they marched Manuel's mood was one of exuberance. Iscar, who was accompanying the army, writes:

'Loath he may have been to wear a soldier's armour, but it was not long before he proved himself the ablest of generals. All who knew him as an artist were muted at his Hector-like valour, all the more wondrous since he had always disdained arms and abhorred violence.'

Their aim was to preserve the freedom of their island and Manuel was determined to succeed, even if the means he had to employ conflicted with the principles extolled by the young idealist.

He followed rigid self-discipline and took meticulous planning, because he believed that bad luck was often the excuse of the negligent and the inept.

'Good luck has to be deserved,' he would say, 'when it comes unbeckoned, it's too often misused.'

His faith in people was unshakeable.

'If conditions are favourable, the seemingly mediocre will excel where men of talent would fail.'

They had hoped to cover the distance in four weeks. It took less than three. Thus, they had ample time to prepare for battle and surprise the Emperor with refreshed men.

Even so, persistent reports from the north spoke of a mighty army descending upon them.

'Let them come,' said Manuel defiantly, 'the more of them, the greater our victory.'

On the night before the battle, the General spoke to his troops,

'In the short span of two months we have moulded our units into a formidable army. What has spurred us on is, I believe, the value of what we are defending and the righteousness of our quest. There is no doubt that victory will be ours. We are unstoppable!'

The next morning on the battlefield his figure on horseback was everywhere: urging, stirring, directing, firing the men with belief in their own invincibility. Iscar, who was watching the action from a safe distance up the hill, comments:

'The gentle youth who had painted sensitive faces, who had helped the weak, and led the people dancing in the street, now led soldiers into battle with the fury of a lion: striking down man after man, unmoved by their pleading. His face—once so serene—was now re-struck with lines of experience and passions. He became another man, another spirit, brandishing Destiny's sword. His eye exulted with a murderous light. He struck down one man, unseated another from his horse, listened to reports, gave orders. He took decisions swiftly like a general, he killed with the indifference of fate...'

All around the battlefield were feats of courage and daring. One man in particular was decimating the enemy ranks. His armour, topped by a bronze gargoyle upon his helmet's peak, camouflaged his identity, but it seemed to Manuel that his stocky frame, those savage thrusts, exuded a chilling familiarity.

When a request for reinforcements came from Paul the Red's unit, which was under great pressure, Manuel himself rushed to Paul's side. The two of them fought like lions and carried the unit with them to a point where the left flank was no longer the weak front, but a strong wedge on the attack. Then Paul, who was valiantly fighting off two men, went down. Manuel flew to his side and executed his assailants.

Having spotted a cove, protected by a jutting stone, Manuel carried his companion to shelter, laid him back and stripped him of his helmet and beaver. Paul bled profusely from a gash that had opened on his forehead, but would not hear of being nursed,

'Return to your position. The soldiers need you there. Don't worry about me now,' then he yelled, 'look out!'

Manuel looked up to find a sabre raised above him, ready to come swishing upon his head. Then, miraculously, the arm which held the weapon went limp, the grip slackened and the sword, which for a frightful instant looked poised to take his life, fell from the assailant's hand, its force barely enough to put a slit in his gorget. Looking up Manuel noticed that his saviour was none other than the soldier with the gargoyled helmet. Who was that man? Once again

Manuel was struck by a sensation familiar and disquieting about the figure.

By mid-morning it became clear that the Imperial army had been dealt a blow. One after the other the enemy units crumbled before the thrust of Manuel's men. The Emperor was enraged, made rash decisions, blundered and finally had to flee to save himself.

LIV

Aftermath of a Battle

'The Emperor has fled!' announced a jubilant Peter as he came galloping up the rise. For the General, who had stood there directing the final phase of the battle, this was hardly news, yet his tall frame stiffened inside the armour. Astride his horse he looked inscrutable behind the black eyes, which narrowed as he watched the Imperial army retreat chaotically beyond the barren hills.

'Send out a pursuit party for Otto's capture,' he ordered, but a certain quaver in his voice belittled his peremptory tone. Peter hesitated as the Manuel turned away and surveyed the plain littered with vestiges of the battle: overturned carts, burning tents, dead horses, the glare of scattered armour, and everywhere dead or dying men.

Isolated puffs of cloud, which had threatened all day, thickened into patchy layers and presaged the first rains of summer. Manuel turned a sad gaze upon Peter and said.

'No, let him go. And the survivors too, let them escape back to their country.'

Again Peter was surprised by this decision, the camp-aides sat silently on their horses, keeping a respectful distance, waiting for new orders.

'Start the rescue operation. All the wounded must be taken to the camp before nightfall.'

As he spoke he looked around, searching for a pair of eyes in which to recognize his own features. Nothing. Their heads stayed bowed as they left one by one to execute his order. Only Filippo Grassi stayed with him, falling behind as the two of them headed down the hill, holding back their horses to a canter.

The rain had started, coming down in thick, sparse splotches. The rescue teams worked feverishly. The first cartfuls of wounded were taken to the camp: the mangled, blood-splattered remnants of men. Thick masses of clouds shut in the groans, the curses, the screams.

'Bravo, Sir! A truly magnificent victory!'

It was Iscar coming down from higher up the rise. His elation could not have sounded so incongruous, so obscene.

'Brilliant! Astounding!'

His face was flushed with admiration...

'*Per Bacco* Sir, how did you manage it? You must have fortune's arm on your side!'

Both men chose to ignore Iscar's enthusiastic prattle, or perhaps in all that inferno of wind and mud, and cries of men, any expression of joy sounded like a profanity. Finally Filippo said,

'*Madonna mia, che massacro!*[13] You don' 'ear de cries, Iscar?'

'Hey, what? The cries? Of course there are cries! How can you have a battle without bloodshed? We might have had worse bloodshed, had we lost. Frankly I would rather it be their blood,' said Iscar, tugging at the collar of his tunic; then seeing that Manuel had dismounted his horse and gone among the wounded, he added, 'he shouldn't do that, you know. It's bad for his image. A general cannot be seen to show compassion, or a bad conscience, or any such human weaknesses.'

Manuel's attention was drawn to a man slumped back against a jutting stone, staring ghost-like over the scene. His blood-drenched mouth opened like the beak of a starving nestling.

'Paul, Paul do you know me?'

Paul's mouth twisted to what seemed like a grotesque laugh, but no sound issued from it. After a while through a laborious wheezing came a whisper, 'I'm really no fighter, I know that...oh, but what a victory! At last we are going to crush the Lemonist traitors...get rid of the parasites...then the real revolution starts! '

His mop of red hair that once would have tossed, was caked with blood and dust.

'You've got the vision...and the dare. You shook us out of our torpor...now seize the momentum and show them how it can be done!'

His voice had once again attempted to rise to a revolutionary pitch, but tailed off instead to a whisper.

'Pity some of us won't be here to see.'

They were Paul's last words.

LV

An Old Acquaintance Reappears

As Manuel was getting ready to make a triumphant return to the capital, at the camp arrived, by special coach, none other than Madam Magdalene, her child and attendants. The soldiers, who believed that she was bringing them welcome rewards, were sorely disappointed to discover that she was the bearer of grim news: a well-orchestrated Patrician plot, had resulted in a Lemonist take-over of the capital, she announced.

'All your supporters thrown in prison,' she told Manuel, 'lucky I got whiff of it in time to save myself and my girls.'

Madam's luck was occasioned by a knight of high standing with a timely urge to do some lateral thinking over a pretty thing at the bordello, on the very night of the plot. After emptying his sacs, this volubly talkative Patrician spilled the beans, as he delivered lobe-kisses, on the ear of his paramour. After which Magdalene lost no time in saving the salvageable.

Manuel seemed unperturbed by the news.

'The Patricians have acted rashly and the people will not tolerate it. I have an army of valiant men here to uphold their rights. Tomorrow we will start our march south.'

Manuel was right about the people's feelings, but Lady Britt and her friends were no fools. Ever since Manuel had marched north, the prospect of his return to the city in triumph and, like Julius Caesar, becoming Consul for life, haunted the great knights.

Their coup was masterminded in a way that silenced the people, before their collective voice started to be heard. They infiltrated troops into the city through the western door and the next morning the city awoke to find all prominent Orangists either killed or imprisoned, the streets guarded by soldiers, and on the walls of the copies of an official proclamation given by the Governor himself:

His Excellency Sir Isaac Garrish Hippocritus, Governor, Grand Knight of the Silken Garter...

- a) *Aware of the people's disenchantment with the Orangist Consul.*
- b) *Disturbed by daily incidents of popular unrest.*
- c) *Concerned that our Fair Isle is sliding further and further into irresponsible hands.*
- d) *Alarmed at the deterioration of moral and religious standards.*
- e) *Distressed by the ailing economy due to gross mismanagement.*
- f) *Saddened by the rupture in the special relationship between this island and its Emperor and Protector.*
- g) *Determined to retain the predominantly Roman character of our country.*
- h) *Eager to regain our unique way of life.*
- i) *Moved, above all, by concern for all the people of Southfalia.*

Announces that he has accepted the advice of the land's foremost judges and by the power invested upon him as legitimate representative of Caesar, declares Manuel deposed and raises to the Consular seat, Sir Octavius Mendacit Humble; in the certainty that he will steer our Fair Isle back on the road of progress, while upholding those traditions inherited from Rome, and which every true Southfalian holds sacred.

After the official declaration came the announcement that, 'The Consul, Sir Octavius Mendacit Humble will speak to the people this morning.' The square did not take long to fill up with angry people, whose outrage rose as they felt safer with their increasing numbers.

'Manuel! Manuel! Long live our victorious General! Give us our Consul,' they chanted.

The bridge of the castle was drawn and the Big Dragon opened to allow a squadron of Law *and Order* guards into the square, led by Abbé Stanislaus.

SOUTHFALIA

The chanting died down as the Abbé sat erect on his horse looking fiercely down on the crowd, freezing them all into immobility. Then something curious happened: he began to remove his monastic garments. With the flourish of a magician came off the coif and then the habit, and behold, underneath the monk appeared Sir Herod Moronus Nero, in all his nightmarish blackness.

In the suppressed gasp which followed, trumpets blared and there appeared a lean-chested, haughty young man with mousy hair, rich yellow skin, refined features and a very Roman nose, enrobed in Consular attire (which Manuel had always disdained to wear) and riding a milk-white stallion. His hair was pomaded and curled under the Consular cap, adorned with yellow feathers. His tall figure stood erect, superior, unapproachable. Surrounding him was a glittering entourage of knights in their ceremonial best and next to them their equally resplendent ladies. Those born to rule had returned.

The Governor was brought forward on unsteady feet, supported by two attendants, and in a solemn voice he announced,

'People of Southfalia, your Consul: Sir Octavius Mendacit Humble.'

There were respectful cheers from the Lemonists and subdued whispers in the crowd.

Octavius allowed them a smile, then cast a stern glance across the square and proceeded to read out a very short speech.

'Since this heavy burden has been placed upon my humble shoulders, I shall require your support to undo the chaos that we find in our society. I, dear friends, am not given to making idle promises. But this I do promise you,' and here he paused for a moment, 'I promise to give you back the good old days, to give you back our unique way of life.'

How pleasant, thought Lady Britt, to hear once again that refined tongue, free of emotion, as only true breeding can attain.

It may be thought that a man elected by the people, and who had done much for them, could not have been so easily disposed of, without causing a popular uprise.

In effect, from all over the island the people did take to the streets in support of their hero, but in the Capital the people had to be more pragmatic. With the Lemonists back in power, the leading Orangists either killed or imprisoned and Sir Herod anxious for action after a long, dry spell, the people had to keep their heads down to save their skin.

Sir Matthew's plume worked feverishly to consolidate the Lemonist gains:

'*SIR OCTAVIUS PROMISES A RETURN TO FULL DEVELOPMENT!*
'*TALK OF REBELLION IN THE* ORANGIST CAMP! GROWING PANIC.'
'*OUR MINERAL WEALTH IS OUR STRENGTH, SAYS NEW CONSUL.* '

Even so, the response to the call for volunteers to join the Lemonist army was so poor, that Sir Herod had to intervene, with his infallible means, to persuade eligible men to enlist. As for the Patricians, who had lamented poverty when Manuel had asked for funds, they were now willing to pay out huge sums to equip the Lemonist army.

LVI

The Dream

Outside the Capital, on a plain surrounded by chestnut and olive groves, the Orangist and Lemonist forces faced one another. Bayonets flashed and flags flapped, as soldiers went about busily. The air was thick with expectation. Sir Marc would have loved it, except that domestic troubles had forced him to stay away from the battlefield once again.

On the morning before the planned assault on the Lemonist forces, Manuel rode up to his look-out point: a hill-side olive grove, from which he was able to study the Lemonist fortifications.

His horse trotted up the gravel track and came to a stop by a huge olive tree, overgrown around the base with reeds of wild olive.

Both camps looked strangely somnolent, as if dazed by the high sun. Beyond the Lemonist camp, the walls of the city rose white and solid, while the river, emerging from under the drawbridge, curled its way into the spreading countryside like the tortuous tail of a sleeping dragon.

A tumultuous fracas was staged over the hill-side, dominated by the tic-toc of the cicadas. On the branch directly above him a turtle-dove sat brooding with its head sunk over its pouch and cooed intermittently, like a subdued counterpoint, or a drowsy invitation to sleep. The entire hill-side called the spirit to sleep.

Manuel felt overcome by a desire to rest. He dismounted his horse, lay under the olive tree, his head cushioned by the wild suckers, and fell asleep.

He dreamt that he was on the battlefield, amid a great din of arms and men, and although his soldiers fought valiantly, the enemy was fast overpowering them. But just when all seemed lost, on a bare hill-top appeared Black John and his people, fresh from the desert, in full tribal dress, complete with totems towering on their shoulders, like moving mountains.

Stunned by the apparition the enemy fled, as the Romans at the sight of Hannibal's elephants, while Manuel's own gladness was strangely dampened by a sense of shame and guilt.

Now he was being carried triumphantly by his men all over the battlefield, but for him the only joy was the arrival of Black John. And then looking up toward the hill, he could no longer see his friend. He jumped on his horse and galloped to the peak. No sign of John. Now, Manuel found himself completely alone, with the battlefield below and behind him, a few respectful paces away, stood his aides awaiting orders.

All at once he felt trapped by his power, pressing around his head like an iron belt, shooting tiny needle points into his brain. Its force was unleashed over that sprawling canvas below, opaque with violet dust, coloured with men's blood. The intensity of all that colour confused him. His attendants: the executors of his power, closed in on him, watched him with eyes pleading for those orders that would free their own conscience to commit whatever monstrous killings he demanded of them. He knew their eyes. They expressed fear, respect, admiration, and gratitude...anything but love.

Again he turned to the plain below, scanning the battlefield with hopeful eyes. The full thrust of human passions could be found there, arranged in various and unique forms.

He was overcome by a craving for closeness, to touch and be touched. He wanted to come down from his horse, crawl out of his heavy armour, like a crab from its shell, and join his naked body with the body of every man on that field, especially the dying, in whom the fire of life glowed the brightest. There was nothing else to do but to set off in search of Black John.

He met a convoy of pilgrims, who directed him to the river where, they said, some natives were camped. By the river he found instead an old cottage with ivied walls and roses in the garden. Weeding the flower-beds was an old woman with white hair and a slight stoop.

Manuel let his horse roam and headed for the gate on foot. The old woman, who had turned several times as he approached the house, now ambled up the path to meet him.

'Watch your head under the trellis, Sir,' she called out, 'the roses have some awful thorns.'

Then with a child-like chuckle she added, 'it was made for small people like me.'

The voice, like her aspect, seemed familiar. Manuel bent low to pass under the rose-arch, trying at the same time to recall where he had seen the white-haired old woman before. As he emerged from under the arch he recognized old Mary: smaller, older; her hair, white as cloud-puffs, cast about her an aura of serene composure.

'It's me, Old Mary, don't you remember?' Manuel opened his arms to embrace her. But Old Mary did not move.

'No, I don't recall you Sir...my eyes are not so good any more,' she squinted, brought her palm over her brows to look up, 'a big, handsome young man. A soldier. No I am sure I know no soldier.'

'Old Mary!' cried Manuel suddenly, 'give me your blessings.'

The pleading tone sounded as awkward as a prayer in a heathen's mouth.

'Me Sir? I am too much a sinner to give blessings. Where is your mother?'

'I have no mother.'

'No mother! Oh, that's sad! Then I shall do it, may she forgive me for it.'

Manuel kneeled down before the venerable old woman, but did not hear her words, for a gust of wind rose from the valley and stirred the high poplars. Old Mary's whisper was lost in a murmur of leaves and a clanging of the chain that attached the scabbard to his flank.

By the time he left a cool afternoon breeze had set in. He headed upstream looking for a point at which to cross the river, but though he travelled for what seemed to be an interminable stretch, he was not able to find one; so he camped by the river-bank for the night.

He was awakened the next morning by the gallop of a horse. It was Iscar looking frightened.

'Where are you off to, Sir?' he yelled panting.

'To the desert, to visit John.'

'To the desert! You must return at once. Some of the soldiers have gone on a drunken rampage.'

Manuel started back downstream, galloping at full speed toward the camp.

When he got to Old Mary's cottage, he was confronted with the first startling evidence that Iscar's account had, if anything, understated the gravity of the situation. The cottage was in fact no more, in its place was a pile of ash and charcoal. The rose-garden lay totally devastated.

'No time to stop, Sir,' said Iscar, 'you'll find plenty more like it along the way.'

'Old Mary lived in there. What have they done to her?'

Manuel went looking for her. All around the burned-down remnants he could find no sign of life, but a freshly-furrowed trail through the stubble of grass in the direction of the river, led him to what was left of Old Mary: a mangled, naked body curled around itself. Old Mary was not quite dead.

'Get away from me!' she yelled, terrified, 'please! No more... please!'

Manuel did not have to ask what had happened. All the sickening details were there in her ravaged body, in those eyes blown huge by horror.

'It's me, Old Mary. I am Manuel, see?'

But Old Mary turned her mad eyes away and yelled, 'oh, why didn't I die a leper!'

Manuel carried her dead body down to the river and threw it in.

On the road, not far from the destroyed cottage, they were arrested by the sound of drunken voices. Manuel bade his companion to stop and then quietly crept up to a sheltered tract where four soldiers were sitting around a flask of wine, drinking and shouting. Their leader—the one who seemed to shout the most—held a strange spell over Manuel. All at once he was overcome by a distinct sensation of 'deja vu'. Then he noticed the gargoyle on the soldier's helmet. 'So that's the man who saved my life,' thought Manuel.

An awful realization began to take form inside his head. A name pounded his brain, but he dared not say it. Then the slender hope that he might be mistaken was dashed with the next question.

'You recken you gonna be doin' plenty more fightin', Brute?'

' 'Ope so. Not a bad life, when you think about 't. Plenty of excitement...a bit o' stray snatch every now and then...' Brutus Callous managed a drunken wink, then he went on, 'mind 'ja she was a scrawney ol' stick, wan't she? Still, she 'ad some yell in 'ar...They're the best sometimes, when they're past doin' it fer fun...they squeal like virgins! More grog?'

In his dream, at least, Manuel made sure that neither Brutus, nor his equally brutish cohorts, lived to savour another sip of wine.

LVII

A Challenge Refused

While Manuel dreamed under the olive tree, the following curt message from the Lemonist camp was delivered to his tent.

'*Sir,*

In the remote event of an Orangist victory, the prize will not be a city, but a mound of ashes!

Sir Octavius Mendacit Humble'

When Iscar went up to deliver the message to Manuel, he was amazed to find him crouched by the trunk of the olive tree, his back quivering as if he were in pain. On closer inspection he realized that the General was in fact, crying.

Heroes, of course, don't cry—nor do Prophets for that matter, unless they have to do it for effect. But our hero did cry, and did not pretend to be coughing when he was thus surprised by Iscar.

'Helas, Sir! What could possibly make you so despondent? Very soon you will wear the crown of leaves up Victory Road.'

Manuel kept on nodding as he read the message. A darker shadow fell over his sombre aspect.

'What should be more important, Iscar, a crown of laurels, or the lives of men?'

'I am a stoic, Sir, and indifferent to both. But one thing I will say: victory is often to be found on top of a mountain of dead, as you have discovered yourself.'

'All that suffering, is it worth it?'

'*Et bien!* We are born to suffer, are we not?'

'I don't believe that, Iscar, even now I refuse to believe it. We are born to love, to create...'

'You have played your cards well against the Emperor. Tomorrow it will be much easier. Think no more of the suffering.'

'It isn't possible.'

'Conscience is really bad news for a General. If you must believe in sin, then learn to live as a sinner. Many have sold their conscience to the devil, for much less.'

Manuel's face darkened further. He looked distant, unreceptive. Iscar realized that the next few moments would be crucial.

'Listen to me, Sir,' he began, I have watched you these last few years, grow in stature beyond dreams. I've seen the flame of greatness light up and shimmer in you. There is so much you can do Sir! Such heights to aspire to! True, the path of greatness and that of goodness don't always run parallel but...*Enfin!* What is wrong with sacrificing one's principles—all that useless morality—before the icon of our quest? Greatness itself is amoral. Don't let morality tie your hands.'

In reply Manuel told him about the nightmare from which he had just woken to.

' *Porco diavolo!*' Exclaimed Iscar, 'that is really too morbid! *Mais enfin*, it is only a dream, is it not?'

'Is it, Iscar? Look at my hands they were made to heal and comfort, now they have struck down an untold number of men. And now this,' he pointed to the tents of the two armies dotting the plain below, 'what you see down there is madness. It will yield more madness. I will not be a part of it.'

'But then...but then' began Iscar, his voice choking with unstoical emotion, will you abandon us?'

'Only to save your lives.'

Now Iscar's anger became rampant, we will call you a coward! We will curse you!

'At least you will be there to curse. Life must prevail.'

'But on whose terms? On whose terms, Sir? There lies the question! Survival is not enough. It is important that we dictate the terms of our survival.'

SOUTHFALIA

'I will not be a despot, Iscar. I have spoken all my words. Maybe I was too early, or too raw. Maybe I tried to be too many persons. Maybe...after all, it doesn't matter who does what: time marks its own progress.'

'There I would agree with you,' commented Iscar, suddenly reverting back to stoicism. *Ce que sera, sera. N'est-ce pas?*

'And yet,' continued Manuel, as if speaking to himself, 'even dead men can cause a revolution, just as the fall of a leaf could conceivably bring about a landslide. Perhaps the essence is in the timing...I've won glory, it's true, but I'm no longer in harmony. And in a choice between self-mastery and slavery to circumstance, I must return to the former, while it is still possible.'

'Will you surrender to them?'

'Well now, I must play into circumstance a little longer,' Manuel replied. Then more resolutely, 'go to the Lemonist camp and issue a man-to-man challenge to Octavius on my behalf.'

Iscar looked confused.

'Don't frown, Iscar. He won't accept. I am at least entitled to appease my supporters and flatter my vanity.'

When Iscar was gone Manuel returned to his tent and laid down his armour.

As he predicted, Sir Octavius had no intention of taking up the challenge, it's doubtful whether he had ever held a sword in his aristocratic hands. His ever-resourceful aunt, Lady Britt, knew the answer off by heart.

'Tell the vulgar ruffian, that a noble Roman knight has many other ways to die, than crossing swords with a Plebean.'

LVIII

A Jolly Supper

In the late afternoon, Manuel announced that there would not be an attack in the morning and that further orders would be issued later. If the men were baffled, his relaxed manner set them at rest.

Then he retired to his tent and made love to Magdalene. They took a bath together, and slept for some two hours. Magdalene awoke as he lay still stretched next to her and her senses abandoned themselves to that orgy of beauty.

Manuel was almost thirty now and his body had filled out just enough to round off the sharpness of youth and reach that perfect balance of muscle and flesh; between the eagerness of youth and the self-confidence of man. It was a body which conveyed at once aggressiveness and promise; a body at its peak, enough to make Madam Magdalene, indisputably a connoisseuse in such matters, experience a kind of dying agony as she took him.

In the evening he and Magdalene dined with his General Staff. Peter, who was in charge of victuals, revealed that they had run out of meat.

'We have plenty of wine, but no more meat,' he said.

'No matter,' Manuel said. He seemed in high spirits. 'Drink enough wine and you'll think this bread was the juiciest lamb. This wine will restore the depleted blood in your body.'

Soon a gossamer of joy enveloped the gathering. Manuel joked, laughed, exchanged glances with Magdalene, and even Peter—never a fun-loving soul—made a pass at her.

'About time you loosened up your belt, honey,' said she, 'I've been waiting long enough to get my hands into that sack of yours.'

'Oh dear me, Madam, that cockerel will be busy in the morning,' cried Manuel with a sonorous laugh which drew everyone into the merriment. Then he took both their hands and declaimed, 'Let me give it my blessing!' He piled his hand on top of theirs and stroked them absent-mindedly. He was serious now as he said, 'I love you, Peter. I love you, Magdalene. I love you all. I love life. Oh yes, Life, I do love...'

In the ensuing silence Iscar slipped into the tent, went to Manuel and whispered in his ear. Manuel's expression did not alter, as if he knew already the news that had been brought to him.

'And that's why I must do this absurd thing,' said he rising, 'friends, thank you all. I'm off to do some dreaming before the morning. I'm sorry to leave this pleasant...victual. '

LIX

The End of a Dilemma

The camp lay sleeping as the turbid violet of the first light lifted the crystalline film of darkness. The chestnut trees re-struck their shapes against the hillside. Horses cleared the dew from their nostrils, chains clanged, dogs barked defiantly, men groaned through the last dreams of the night.

In the General's tent, Manuel, wearing his peasant cassock, was farewelled by beady-eyed Magdalene. He took Terra in his arms and the child settled her head into his elbow's bend. The two sets of black eyes fused into one knowing stillness, which an observer (unable to penetrate the mystery within) might have misconstrued as indifference.

Magdalene cried a lot and whispered nonsense from one to the other, because the silence between father and daughter terrified her. For an instant she was glad that she would never have to face it again. He gave her back the child. She did not turn to look at her father again as he disappeared towards the valley through the grove of chestnuts, followed by Iscar.

News that Manuel had given himself up did not spread through the camp until later in the morning. The initial reaction was one of disbelief. Then it changed to anger and disgust; which better befit a soldier's temperament.

'Iscar!' they cried, 'that's who it was. That old Egyptian eunuch betrayed our General. Hunt the bastard down!'

But when it came to survival, Iscar's wits had no equals. Although they searched every barrack, they found no trace of him. Finally the hunt settled on two night-guards, who, unfortunately for them, were sleeping in their tent when the frenzied mob got to them. They were slain and their bodies dragged through the camp.

Meanwhile, on the Lemonist side, the victors were faced with the dilemma of what to do with Manuel.

'Crucify him!' shouted Sir Herod.

But Sir Matthew was not of the same mind.

'I don't think that's wise,' he said calmly, 'we must consider the people's reaction?'

This further incensed Sir Herod.

'The people, the people! What have the people got to do with it? Let me deal with him, I'll crucify 'm in the square. That'll teach all them Reds in the Orange League.'

Monsignor had something to say on the subject of crucifixion.

'I should want to know in what manner you intend to crucify him, Sir Herod. You see the position is vital here, since our Lord was crucified the right way up and Saint Peter upside down, it makes it rather difficult in the case of a heretic...'

'Well sideways will do then, and crucify all his Red conspirators too and keep 'm all in agony on peanuts and water,' concluded Sir Herod secretly congratulating himself for his sound business sense.

Sir Herod's methods offended Lady Britt's Roman sense of justice.

'Sir Herod, Sir, really sometimes I wonder how much of the Roman is in you. These are not the Dark Ages, but fourteenth century, sorry, fifteenth century Southfalia. Surely this barbaric savagery is unnecessary. If an example needs to be set, then let's do it in the civilized manner of our forbears, who were too noble to get their own hands stained with blood. Throw the creature to the lions and be done with it.'

In the end it was left to that ingenious Sir Matthew to come up with a solution.

'All the suggestions put forward so far smack of revenge, each with the inherent potential of turning the man into a martyr. Now, if there is one lesson that history has taught us, it is that martyrdom can bestow on any fool the worship-cult reserved for heroes and gods. If we want a return to normality in Southfalia, then we cannot afford to have a martyr on our hands,' Sir Matthew paused, enjoying everyone's attention, 'I hear that the Orange League has some very hungry lions in its midst, eager to sink their fangs into our man. I suggest we let them take care of things, we shall have our hands full trying to restore law and order in the streets.'

LX

The End

Iscar has spared us the details of Manuel's end. Obviously for a champion of stoicism it's irritating to dwell on all the mawkishness which inevitably accompanies the exit of the protagonist. He may have thought it superfluous, irrelevant even. For the sake of the incurable romantics, or pedants, who insist on some kind of end to a story, it is likely that the Orange League was only too happy to put Manuel on trial and crucify him. Inevitably with the help of those who had acclaimed him loudest. And then *The Voice* would have led the whole island on a mass hand-washing pilgrimage.

Some of Manuel's followers fell victim of his changed fortunes. Madam Magdalene disappeared. But no need to worry about that resourceful lady, she could take care of things in any situation.

No more was officially heard of Terra. But in 1506 a black-eyed young mute of foreign origin was reported to have been in Valladolid at the death-bed of a once illustrious, now destitute, old man: signor Colombo.

Peter, who had no qualms about recanting Manuel on at least three occasions, retained his influential position with the Guilds, and was highly respected by Lemonists and Orangists alike.

Because all the mineral deposits turned out to be in the desert, Black John's people had their land taken from them, and they were forced back into the city. John fought to stop the exodus without success.

In the end even he was forced to leave the desert as the mines began to devour it. He spent most of his time dragging his people off the streets so that they would not be derided by decent Southfalians, stung by the flies or beaten up by the Squad.

Iscar, you might suggest, hanged himself from a tree. That was one of the stories he himself circulated to confound his pursuers. But we know better. The beauty about emasculation is that it leaves a man with very few reasons for grand gestures, to flatter his ego. No, Iscar didn't suicide. He turned himself into a tramp and for a time lived with the natives.

Late one night Iscar found John at the fountain trying to revive one of his people. It was one of those balmy nights when perspiration may wash away a man's mask. Iscar had had more than his usual fill of drink. He looked away from John's anguished face. They knew that they were both thinking of Manuel,

'He was doomed,' said the old stoic as if speaking to himself, 'they just had to have him out because he dared to show them what they could have been. He was doomed because their ideals go no further than publicly-displayed virtues and privately-owned mansions. And so they crucified the visionary, and raised in his place men whose vision reaches no further than their nose. It's no more than they deserve...'

Black John looked at the drunk man slumped near his feet and said, 'My poor country.'

Soon after Iscar was able to stow away to England where he met the eminent Leonard Roguefort, gave up Stoicism in favour of Inverted Logic and became a highly successful University Don.

Peace and tranquillity returned to the Lucky Isle. The *Law and Order* saw to it. As for Sir Herod, having made such a success of his camouflage gave him the choice of becoming either a monk or regaining his former post as chief of the *Law and Order*. Aiming at the best of both worlds, Sir Herod joined a religious order and became an exorcist.

His apocalyptic sermons played such havoc with the conscience of the people that they rushed to him in droves for confession or gave themselves up for exorcism. He decreed that all public buildings remain dark after sunset, all non-religious paintings to be burnt, and sculptures destroyed. All non-religious writings were set alight. And so each day a huge fire burnt in the square and repentant faithfuls brought books, pictures and other offensive items.

SOUTHFALIA

All arts and crafts shops were shut down if not by force, because of lack of interest. The artists fled abroad, others were beaten up and forced to go underground at The Strip.

So then, how did this fabled island of sun, riches, and beautiful people disappear?

With the Lemonist advent to power expansion became the policy and this meant full exploitation of the island's mineral riches. And because there was an abundance of weapons wars became bigger and better, nations were prepared to pay any price for bellic material to subdue their rivals. Things could not have looked brighter for Sir Bart and friends, who owned all the mines. Their houses became more luxurious, their carriages bigger and shinier, their ladies more splendid.

Eventually Southfalia was an island of cities, mines and little else. Hills were stripped of forests, orchards were uprooted from the valleys (fruit could be imported more cheaply) and the valleys excavated, the precious ores scooped up and carted away.

Towns, white and new, sprang up overnight, survived in a frenzied state of activity while the ore lasted, then were abandoned as the people rushed elsewhere to start all over again. Lakes and rivers disappeared or became poisoned.

But now there was the problem of what to do with all that money. Any knight worth his armour knew that money is invested to make more money. And that was exactly the problem. In a country where towns were disappearing every other day, it was difficult to find a profitable investment. You did not have to be as shrewd as Sir Bart to realise that!

So, Sir Bart took his money to the great centres of Europe and began to buy big homes, castles, entire estates; and because a rich man's heart keeps close to his money, Sir Bart stayed away with increasing frequency until eventually he made his home there. The rest of his friends did not take long to follow. With the money went the various Matthews, Britts and Sybillas; governors, judges and grandees; wet nurses, prostitutes, gigolos, servants, lawyers, thieves, and the rest of the 'parasitalia', leaving behind only workers, natives and the mine quarries.

Few had scruples about leaving the island which had been their country and that of their ancestors. Most thought, like Lady Britt, that the island was a self-imposed exile from the real home. A return to the old country came to be regarded not only as desirable, but a patriotic duty, a sign of the true Roman.

Eventually, the only people left on the island were the natives who, had they wished to leave, had nowhere else to go, since no one would take them.

By this time the sea had moved in to reclaim the island, it flooded the mine holes first, moving from channel to channel, slowly attacking the slopes of the few hills that were left, and on which the natives grappled for safety. One consolation was that they spent the last years surrounded by the great luxury of abandoned Patrician homes. These had been built on the highest peaks of the city; hence they were the last to be engulfed by water.

In the beginning the marble floors made cold beds, but native ingenuity got around it easily enough. They lit fires (the Florentine chairs made excellent firewood) and slept by the flames, whose shadows wove ghostly patterns around the intricate textures of European architecture. In no time all that baroque richness became soot-ingrained and was finally lost. As for the floors, those richly ornate mosaics depicting nymphs and shepherds in idyllic Sylvan settings, they were soon covered with layers of accumulated ash that made them soft, warm beds for native backs. And so in the end the natives too acquired a taste for gracious living.

SOUTHFALIA

EPILOGUE

Black John left the city and alone re-crossed the desert before the ocean had reclaimed it. But John was disorientated. Familiar scents, which used to give him certainty of direction, had disappeared. The vegetation was gone, even the spinifex and the lowly salt-bush. The gorges, once havens of so much desert life, were dried out, filled in and silent. The desert was vanquished by silence.

The landscape was scarred with excavations, slag hills, rubble mounds, artificial lakes filled with dead slate water, poppet-heads, and everywhere, ghost towns.

Rats, mice and the occasional wild cat constituted John's diet now, and sometimes he had to be content with the cockroaches inhabiting the damp store-rooms of ghost towns. But then, he was able to survive on very little nowadays.

Finally, he reached his destination. The Big Rock had not escaped the influence of civilization. Rich mineral deposits discovered under it had ensured its methodical disembowelment. Now it stood jagged and defused, punctured by openings and surrounded by ugly mounts of rubble. Gone were the caves with ancient figures that spoke of spirits long gone. Progress was stronger than any spirits and tore up their shrine with ruthless efficiency.

Hollowed out in that manner, it was a miracle that the Rock continued to stand, its thin shell like the carcass of an extinct monster.

One summer morning as the waves of the sea crawled ominously up the folds of the rock, Black John-by now an old man-entered the rock through the gallery leading to its centre. A large opening let in a shaft of light, which fell on an abandoned hill of dust. The caves of the Big Rock were filled with the sights and stench of death. So much death to deaden even the echo of the wind raging through the tunnels.

Black John stopped and looked intent. A feeble whining reached his ears. He was now almost blind, but in all that deadness a man could not fail to sense the presence of life, especially a man whose sense of life had been sharpened by years of contact with death. He cocked his head to it, as he had done long ago in the desert gorge. He listened for the bleating of a goat over the cascading water, and a million other sounds, which had filled the gorge. Only the groan of the wind and the trickle of stagnant water filled the musty darkness. His legs creaked a little further up the slope and there, at the bottom of the path leading to the top of the hill, stretched the body of a furless, mud-splotched body of an animal, with ribs almost breaking through the hide. Black John guessed it to be a dog, a wild dog, but it could have been anything, a mythical monster perhaps. Its head looked huge and skeletal, studded with two enormous eyes, covered with cataracts. Its blindness was confirmed as the creature began to dangle its head from side to side, trying to place the direction of the human scent. Unable to do so, it bared its toothless fangs. It looked so ancient that it might have been sitting there for millennia. Man and beast faced each other—the last survivors of a civilization.

Black John felt grateful for the beast's presence, and a great, great pity for it. Pity enough to want to kill it. But then, how could one man bear the finality of the loneliness that would follow? From his jaw-bones hung the stretched skin of his hollow cheeks. An awful urgency overcame John to feed the animal and prolong its life a little while. But what to give him? All that was left was what Nature had given him. His limbs? He needed them to grapple to the top of the hill. There was something, of course…

With great effort he squatted down, raking in the dust with his bony fingers for a sharp stone; he found instead a metal blade, a rusty remnant of an ore scraper. Still squatting he felt for his testicles, which hung down into the dust by a withered stretch of skin: Rip! Rip! Thud!

The animal's head fell to it voraciously and Black John, skirting around the beast was able to make his slow way up the hill undisturbed, leaving a trail of blood-stains in the dust.

SOUTHFALIA

Having reached the peak, Black John sat astride it, settling his ancient bones comfortably in the dust. Through the opening above, the sky was turning stone white, as the sun's outer rim began to peer over the edge. The man could not see, but felt the warmth soak down into his dry bones; and he was filled with energy.

In the blazing sunlight intensified by the darkness below, rose a tribal chant. It issued from that skeletal figure, hoarse and discordant, like the whining of the wild dog on a night muted by frost. Then cautiously the earth below stirred between the rocks, and it creviced beneath the dust, opening itself deeper and deeper, exposing Archeozoic monoliths. He stopped to hear the cavernous echoes reaching in from a past buried in darkness.

As the noon sun hovered above Black John worked two sticks feverishly to make a light. When it came, it struck with a vengeful flare, set off a series of flashes that retrieved the skeletons of civilization from the dark.

His blood-splattered eyes gaped wide as they saw frothing rivers, green valleys, whole white deserts awake to the chant.

His bones crackled with joy.

The lament had risen to a song, unsung since the island's conception. Now it exploded in myriads of reverberations from Man to Dust, to Stone to Man, into a joyful symphony. Finally a flash struck the man, rushed down his spine and fused the light above with the magma below.

The sea let the earth sink to its viscera. The wind battered the water. Waves attacked waves, snapping at their flanks, tearing at the raging crests.

Rain cascaded down from the sky. Then everything settled to sleep.

In the morning it lay, drowsy and naked, lulled by the sun's caress: the beautiful Southern Sea.

FINIS

SOUTHFALIA

NOTES

[1] You're altogether lacking in modesty, Old Boy.
[2] Just look at that, what a strange thing this is.
[3] Can I forget who I was, not feel who I am, deprived of all honour, of all fame?
[4] There! At last I've come across the first genuine man in this land.
[5] Out of the question, young man
[6] Good luck, (literally 'in the mouth of the wolf').
[7] What villanous luck!
[8] Let's turn to the present problem, Countryman.
[9] Give us back our children, give us back our dignity.
[10] The flies? They are the Furies, the goddesses of remorse.
[11] And in the end, here I am.
[12] What's happened to you?
[13] My God, what a massacre!

About the Author

Antonio Casella was born in Sicily but has lived in Australia for most of his life. His works include two published novels and numerous short stories published in Australia and overseas. His latest novel titled, *An Olive Branch for Sante*, is near completion.

Made in the USA